A Guide To Broken Roads

Jaroslav Karosac

Published by

Eleusinian Press Ltd

www.eleusinianpress.co.uk

First Edition published 2014

© Jaroslav Kalac

Printed and bound in Great Britain by

Copytech (UK) Ltd

A catalogue record for this book

is available from The British Library

ISBN 978-1-909494-05-3

Author's Preface

The "Guide" was originally intended to be a collection of disparate short stories, unrelated and often tangential in direction, but this concept somehow felt a trifle hollow and scattered in terms of overall effect. It later occurred to me that I was not simply a spinner of fiction tales fueled by a specific world philosophy, but I was more importantly a vessel that contained factual histories bestowed upon me by both my own experiences and family anecdotes that, in terms of absurdity and emotional impact, transcended even the maverick spirit of fiction.

I dovetailed the tales of fact and fiction to blur the boundaries of narrative. The ratios of fact and fiction in aspects of the book are almost equal. The only minor deviation from this formula was to weave my favourite childhood story of Luck and Wisdom by Jan Werich into the mix, in order to introduce the man's beautiful, cynical yet ultimately kind philosophies to the Western audience.

This book is dedicated to Sarah Emma van Rooyen, my partner, my great gift and joy, who was there rejoicing in each new chapter as it materialized, reading it out loud to her family on rainy nights by the fire. She held my hand when the Road became blurred.

She died three months after the work was completed, a sprite full of joy, whisked away by cancer at 47. The first wish on her Bucket List was to see the book published. She was granted that wish.

Fly well, my bird.

Jaroslav Kalac

o   o   o

Chapter One

The Orchestra in Rehearsal

It was a game that we played, both delighting in the absurdity of the act. Father and son locked deep in the theatrics that we called home. He would lean towards me, narrow his eyes in a Bad Cowboy manner and raise his hand. I would stand there, a startled bunny all aquiver. An iron fist pushed towards my face, slowly. My response would always be a gulp and a backward step, for this was our special dance.

"My friend," he drawled, a satanic low growl, "what do you smell?" I took the usual exaggerated inhalation and timidly sniffed at the proffered fist. My thick glasses sliding down my nose, tickled by the hair on the knuckles that hovered before me.

The array of essences that emanated from his hand during these encounters would range wildly from the heating gas that came from his trade as a gas fitter, to the unholy alliance of foodstuffs that made up his proudly working class diet. Herring, dank cheese, beer often conspired truly to disturb my frail young nostrils during these performances. I would gaze at him with bug-eyed wonder and in a voice playfully trembling would whisper "I don't know, Father. What is that smell?"

"Jaroslav," his answer always had the same menacing formality, "that is the smell of the grave yard." I would make a cartoon gulp, pause and then we would break out into cackling laughter. Grinning, we would go our separate ways, grateful for the warm stab of star light in our otherwise dark sky of a relationship.

The irony is that he was destined to die of a heart attack that would liberate him from the life of a permanent refugee. Forever uncomfortable within his own skin. A fish that never found the right water in which to rest its fading fins. All those essences that I inhaled during our burlesque moments, were part of a tiny secret orchestra that at fifty five would suddenly launch into a final fateful song. Diet and the toxic compounds that were the almost archetypical Czech gas fitters daily life joined hands to create a lump within a heart that had already stopped working as a source of passion and joy.

Prophetic times for those prone to reading the writing on the wall. Entropy has many guises and to a young child playfully sniffing a father's fist, all that was important was that the moment of union would last for ever. Upon occasion, I raise my fist to my nose, and breathe in deeply, but that graveyard smell somehow still eludes me. Maybe it got buried with the man.

As Aunt Sabrina would preach, "Wisdom has roots in the soul, whilst luck, my dear, is as fickle as a young girl's glance." I always nodded sagely at that ornate admonition. It seemed to make sense in a cock eyed way, and as a young boy I felt mildly frustrated at not being able to grasp the power of her words, but the meaning remained as alien as a dog whistle pitch to the human ear. I was determined to swallow my pride and around my seventh birthday, took a faltering step into what seemed a torrential river of maturity and asked her to explain her obtuse idiom. It had a reek of brimstone around its neck, and walked on scaly rooster legs.

o   o   o

Chapter Two

Sabrina

During the war Sabrina came from the deepest forest region in Moravia to serve in the opulent house of the Master Glass-maker, my grandfather. She swept and polished and cooked cabbage whilst playing minder to my mother and her brother, Otto. My mother grew up calling her Aunt. She remained in the service of the family until the factory was seized under the post war Central European zeal of nationalization. Grandfather was allowed to work in the factory, no longer the director but in the new post as the porter and handyman. A useful font of knowledge to tap into by his replacement, a bloated and servile man. An emblem of Stalinist progress, where kings become jesters overnight and the world is suddenly run by nervous gentlemen who smile brightly whilst strangling a country.

One uncommonly hot summer, Grandfather was given the task of polishing a mountain of blue green ashtrays on a large tarpaulin. Well beyond retirement age, he rubbed and sweated and poured out his love into the molten glass, until it shone with a halo of lights. Hours later, he was found slumped over the hot glass, delirious with the heat.

Aunt Sabrina and two men carried him home. He was still clutching an ashtray in his rigid hands. Heat stroke and liver damage pinned him to a bed that became his trampoline out of this realm, leaving a family that spoke about his death in whispers.

Sabrina stayed on, happy on a meager wage, devoted to the children and to the widow. Fifteen years later, she met her husband, a man with a face as brown and gnarled as a walnut. A drinker and a carouser, notorious for his bosom hungry eyes. He managed to steal her heart and the family lost their companion. Sabrina and the walnut faced man moved into the country where they built a ramshackle farmhouse, soon to be overgrown with weeds and thick dank moss. The husband drank and raged and would disappear for days. Coming home to sleep with pig like snores, urinating on the bathroom floor. Unhappily drunk he would shout for Sabrina. She would kneel on the coarse floor with a bucket, on bony hands and knobby knees, scrubbing while the cabbage boiled over. He would beat her and then entreat her forgiveness, merely to repeat the cycle once again.

My mother heard the rumours of his boorish behaviour, and would travel by bus across the town to hold her calloused hand and to stroke her grey hair. They found him in a well, some kilometers away, one morning. Nutty face down, the water and moss embraced him like old lovers. Sabrina had him buried in the garden under her bedroom window. Every morning she would pour out her chamber pot over the grave, the only part of the garden that she tended. She seemed oblivious to the eyebrow raising smell, but as she received few visitors it served well to remind her that she was now blissfully safe and alone.

Then the roosters arrived. A kindly neighbour, concerned about the apparent chaos and fetid odor that was finding such fertile ground on the widow's farm, brought over a well intended gift. A storm had come and released a deluge that almost drowned out the sound of the insistent knock at the door. Peering out of the window Sabrina beheld the rare and welcome sight of the neighbour, shrouded in gloom and adrip with the rain. As she ran down the stairs, the sky poured forth another torrential release and silver lightning raced across the horizon. The thunder crack almost drowned out the clucking that emanated through the door. The gods laid on the portends of ill luck drawing near with an admirable desperation, but by then Sabrina had already opened the door. Sodden to the marrow, the neighbourly crone from the farm across the way, extended her hands towards my aunt, each one holding a sorry looking chicken. Feathers matted, with water dripping down their yellow beaks, Sabrina reached out and murmuring thanks, took the birds from the hunched old woman. These gifts should have been baked within moments of the Samaritan's departure. But Sabrina's heart opened to the wretched clucking birds and installed them in the barn. When they dried out, they flourished and mated loudly and prodigiously.

I used to visit the farm, packed for an overnight stay with a suitcase of mittens and toys, having been escorted onto a bus by Mama and met with cheer by Sabrina. She seemed to be permanently clad in a floral apron and scarf, a picture of the red nosed Babushkas from a Russian novel. The yard, silver with puddles and mud heavy, suddenly had three generations of chickens that squawked and scratched at the boggy soil, and generally ignored me. Sixteen fowls that gave Sabrina great pleasure. She even allowed them to dig for worms in the bare soil of the perfumed grave. The odd aspect of the breeding cycle of the original Mother Hen and Rooster was the predominance of roosters in the clutches of eggs that were hatched as the result of the feather ripping mating sessions. It amused me immensely. In total, only three of the chickens were hens, and these died soon after birth. The females disappeared one by one. The hawks that circled in the sky above the broken roof took two, and a fat tabby cat attempted to run away with another. I threw a stick at the gleeful feline and it dropped the dazed bird. Nursing it back into health it was soon crushed under the wheels of the grocers van that delivered on Thursdays. Mother Hen simply vanished one night, leaving a new clutch of eggs that were still warm when we found them one morning. None of these hatched, no doubt wary of the toothy waiting world beyond the shell. Sabrina was left with many roosters, and these formed a formidable gang that preened, glared and spat at me.

Sitting on fences, they were a vision of supercilious belligerence. Sabrina purchased another hen, but the poor animal was so savagely and almost ritualistically raped, that it ran away, leaving the roosters in an even deeper state of slow burning irritability that seemed to hang over the group as a shroud. They seemed to blame Sabrina for their invisible plight and would turn upon her with wild wing flaps their serpentine heads rolling with red eyes even when she stood amongst them, throwing handfuls of oats for their supper. I always imagined them to be loose hair strands of some Gorgon, the winged versions of adders that crept and lurked, forever devising new ways to freeze the blood of the innocent. And Sabrina was that eternally hopeful innocent, patiently awaiting the day when the roosters would declare peace.

The gardens were spectacular in their neglect, branches of trees meshing to create verdant tunnels through which sad sunlight would trickle to the leafy ground. The grass grew high and the fences sagged low, sodden and green with mold and moss. A perfect play pen for a young boy with a fertile imagination. There were forever sounds emanating from within this verdant labyrinth. I would squint into the rag tag entrails that were the creepers marrying deadwood, but could never see the origins of the disturbance. The entire canopy seemed to shake with a living pulse, a living organ through which the roosters would stalk in an almost aquatic way. They would fly off into the branches, scuttle into the tunnel depths and almost instantly pop out in incongruous parts of the woody maze. Individually, the birds were a boiled down version of the pack. Isolation from the brotherhood did not diminish each lone animal's ferocity. Sabrina and I were once chased into the house by a maddened brown-red rooster that resented our presence in his corner of the yard. We stood inside watching the bird mount screeching attacks on the window. Damp wings left traces on the glass. She never washed the windows, and the streaks remained there for years thereafter. I secretly hoped that she or some concerned relative would one day wring their communal neck, and end the quiet terror which ruled the farm so absolutely.

Yet Sabrina seemed devoted to the birds and would become angry when anyone suggested a purge on the flock. Walking in the garden, she would carry a stick, which did nothing to prevent the roosters from pecking at her head when she walked in a crouch, under the dense overhang of vegetation. The scars on her hands multiplied. I cannot recall visiting her during the rooster years, and not seeing a new bandage here, another scratch on a crinkled cheek there.

During fierce thunderstorms that heralded the approach of winter, a strange phenomenon would take place. The blackened skies would toss and roar like mad seas and the roosters would grow quiet and still. Normally, at night, the gang occupied the barn where they huddled together on the straw, clucking sleepily to each other. But on truly ferocious nights, a strange phenomenon would take place. The band would arrive one by one, and slowly congregate in the doorway of the house. They would stand there, a mass of proudly erect statues and gaze forlornly at the handle. I do not know at what point in her tormented relationship with her infernal beasts Sabrina had the beautifully perverse idea of actually opening the door to them, but one night she did and they strode officially into the house. Thunder pealing and with the lightning striking irregular time, the birds took up positions in the lounge, each one eying out Sabrina with a critical gaze.

I once sat there with her and the birds, in the flickering candle light that the wind cajoled. The silence in the room, broken only by the unfurling of wet feathers and the occasional sneeze of a congested rooster, became almost unbearable as Sabrina sat frozen in her rocking chair. The bird audience sat and scrutinized closely the object of their apparently united loathing. And one by one, their heads slowly tilted down onto their proud red chests, the roosters fell asleep. Sabrina rocked gently in her chair, knitting and smiling away my bewilderment. The storm ended, the door opened and the birds left quietly without a backward glance. Only to resume their siege upon her the next day.

Then on one such evening, I urged her to tell me about the story of Wisdom and Luck. The house creaked and shuddered under the onslaught of the storm. She poured out some chamomile tea, and took my hand. I noticed a fresh nip wound and sat close to her on the Ottoman that smelt like fire

Chapter Three

Wisdom and Luck

"There was a stream that ran between two mountains and the only crossing point was a bridge, so selfishly narrow that it allowed but one person safe passage across at a time. A man approached the bridge from one side and stopped suddenly. For what did he see standing on the other side? Another fellow about to set foot on this swaying bridge, with a determined look in the eye, not looking ready to stop. Both men walked across the bridge, towards each other. Impatient swines, they stood, nose to nose over the noisy river, both bristling with self importance. 'Let me pass, sir, I am on an urgent mission of mercy,' said the tall gangly one, pompously, 'my time is a precious commodity.'

'You, sir, need to step aside and allow me my passage,' sneered the jolly faced porky gentleman dressed in a most flamboyant manner, 'for there is a great need for me across this valley and beyond. I have people waiting for my arrival.'

"Rarely was there such a meeting of mulish types, both men completely in the throes of their huffy puffyness. Lessons in humility, young Jaro." I nodded wide eyed, keen for the story to unravel. From somewhere outside, a cackling rooster call added tension to the tale. Pausing only to select a hazelnut from a bowl, she cracked it in a scrawny fist, fed me a sweet tasting sliver, and continued. "The two fools growled and bleated their arguments as to which was of superior importance so as to be allowed passage across the bored river.

'Do you not know who I am?' asked the livid rake of a man, Adam's apple bulging with irritation. More time had been squandered in this rhetorical debate. 'I am of more use to people than the average doctor, and called upon as frequently as the local priest. I would be most grateful if you appreciated the pressing nature of my speedy passage across this damned bridge.'

'Truly, sir, you are the most bloated of toads that has crossed my path of late,' teased the chubby one, 'and pray, do tell, who are you that answers to the call of men so attentively?'

'Your ignorance is my hindrance,' hissed the picture of impatience, 'my name is Wisdom, and now, please make way.'

'Wisdom, you say,' snorted the amused obstacle, 'it is a privilege to meet you, sir. I am aware of your function in this world, but you steer a sorry sterile path that leaves a lot to be desired in terms of healing the poor saps that call your name. My name is Luck, and I'm sure that you've heard of my magical career that spans the world.' Luck ground his molars with frustration. Gazing across the valley, he saw a distant herd of goats in happy graze, bells a clanging, udders swaying pink and swelled. A young herder lay nearby on his back in the shade of an elder tree. Luck turned to Wisdom, and smiled. The way a gourmet smiles at the steaming lobster that has freshly appeared before his hungry eyes.

'Since, Sir Wisdom, you present yourself as a saviour for the lost and the needy, why don't we try what we may term a, ahem, social experiment. A friendly wager between two fellows meeting at a river crossing. When your busy schedule affords, why not step into the mind of the young herder, there yonder, and lets see what difference your presence can make to the boy. Surely there's more to life than the admittedly gentle art of goat management. Step in, shake that boy out his reveries. Make something out of the lad. Impress me, sir, and I will gladly concede that your services are superior to that of my own, vital as air to the world of men.' Luck's twinkling eyes were constellations of mirth and irreverence.

"The mortician-suited Wisdom stiffened his long frame, setting off a quiet fireworks sound of cracking bones. World weary he seemed, yet game for a challenge. 'Done, Sir, I look forward to introducing you to a new range of humility, and now do make way. Urgent is their plight,' he motioned with an elegant chin across the valley and beyond.

"Luck retreated to vacate the bridge, and Wisdom stalked past him, a secret smile playing on his usually reserved face. It made him look quite handsome for a moment." Aunt Sabrina stood up, lit the candle that stirred up the moths from their late afternoon slumbers and suggested, "Why don't you go and get some fresh air, and feed those roosters while I make you your favourite stew of cabbage and ham. And I may tell you what happened next after supper." Grudgingly, for I had become molded to the couch and to the warm sound of her voice, I went to feed those detestable birds.

Chapter Four

Otto

Polio was twisting bodies and devastating cells when he was born. My mother's only sibling. Dropped into the disease like a puppy down a well, he was more fortunate than others of his generation. His bladder took the brunt of the malaise. My mother was spared but Otto grew up with the dread of the coming of the night. Sleep would salve the aches of the world, yet for the young man limping into his teens, the evening bore little solace from his affliction. His frail bladder would betray him, and he often lurched awake, not from a nightmare but in order to feebly hold onto the little control he had over an organ as slippery as dank fish. The rubber sheeting upon which he lay may have spared him the shame of watching Sabrina washing his linen each day, but his pride was gnawed away by waking up in a haze of the odor of his unbridled body fluids. At school, he was a solitary boy, nervous and tongue tied. It was there that he was befriended by my father and the two would spend countless afternoons listening to the still legal sounds of American jazz and blues. It was through his friendship with Otto, that my father met my mother.

Otto left home at eighteen, an accomplished pianist and budding alcoholic. His musical talent was legendary in the small town and he soon became the central attraction of the local ragtime band. He had hands that crab danced across the keys, fingers that sighed and salted out those sweaty songs. Young women adored this sombre maverick at the piano, but he avoided intimacy like a plague, fearing the inevitable night with its lurid crescendo. Virginal and resentful, he roamed the bars and clubs with his entourage, roaring for more beer and possibly daring to fondle a curvaceous buttock or two, but remaining a whipped dog wary of falling asleep in someone's arms. Instead, he hid behind the veneer of the carefree spirit, stumbling home at sunrise, to sleep poorly and compose greatly. Until he met Marta.

Sitting in a theatrical pose, cute of beret and tight of sweater, she watched the band perform in one of the many tiny jazz clubs that were so popular in pre–crackdown Prague. Otto was performing with the Crazy Kings and the audience, cheeks shining with the remainders of their pork supper, was stomping their feet, raising their schooners of beer in appreciation. Marta's gaze did not falter when he caught her eye. One of the boys in the band knew her sketchily and steered Otto towards her table. The band watched in fascinated amusement as the shy young pianist appeared uncharacteristically to welcome the seduction with which Marta plied him that night. She was the cat that finger prowled the shadows of his inner thigh. Her dark Gitannes breath blew away the walls of his self control and scoured away at his fears. She liked the fact that he was so agonizingly virginal, and was entranced by his tales of the glass factory that still belonged to the family. Czech glass had a huge reputation for quality all over the world.

She carried him to bed, undressed him, and removed the diaper padding of the rubber underwear. The stale cigarette dead beer haze that enveloped them that night was a halo for a coupling that the hands of polio could not dislodge. She woke up next to him, lying in a pool of urine. He slept the sleep of a conquering warrior whilst she scoured herself in a shower that could not dislodge the disgust that she felt.

When he awoke, she had gone. He cursed himself for his weakness. And reapplied the diaper. Yet he scoured the audiences for her face. He made tentative inquiries to her identity, to her whereabouts. The stories that abounded around her seemed to resonate with a common malicious conspiracy. Marta was bad. Marta was manipulative. Marta was imperious, opportunistic. Her family had a criminal gene.

Otto was dismayed, yet tantalized, hoping for her return. Dreading her return.

She rang his doorbell four weeks after her disappearance. She had been away to her family in the country. She was pregnant and defiant in keeping the child conceived on the rubber sheet. She wanted money. She wanted to meet his parents. Otto was overjoyed. The family was not pleased. My mother and father, now lovers themselves attempted to talk sense into the boy. But love had come and struck him deaf and blissfully blind to the coils that tightened around his life. They were married, keeping separate bedrooms. The child was born and the family shed some of their repugnance at the union. A home was built, grandfather sighing as he signed the cheque. In the nightclubs, Otto played the piano like a man on fire, rushing home to sit with the child, a gentle blond boy that was the echo of his father's innocence.

Marta became a fervent shopper, the clothing rail creaked under the weight of the ever new fashions. Her new home became a shrine to Czech glass. The ashtrays filled up, and Sabrina dutifully cleaned them. She was called in to nurse the child and would often be seen pushing the pram with its snug bundle in the nearby park, even in the gloom of approaching winter. Bored, Marta ate, drank and mocked Otto. She scorned his advances, laughing at his ever more pitiful attempts to maintain an illusion of a happy family. She seethed with a poorly disguised vitriolic resentment for the culture and apparent easy wealth that surrounded Otto. A peasant forever frowning belligerently up at the castle on the hill, from which sounds of music and smells of fine foods emanate. Otto shared a bedroom with the child, gently playing soft lullabies on the piano, whilst the boy fitfully snoozed. Marta lazed about in the lounge, smoking and paging through magazines.

Fretting for his son and grandchild, Grandfather tried to reason with her, appealing to her sense of loyalty to the family that had taken her in and lavished her with material delights. Imploring her to reach out to her responsibilities. She exploded into a rage of condemnations, spat against the old man's words of comfort and veritably lashed herself into frenzy of brutish hysteria. Otto was the polio cripple that spent his last drop of masculinity siring a son that she did not want, in a gilded bear trap of a family nest that soured her blood. She stomped around the room bewailing her fate, her lost youth. Her expensive shoes scoured the carpet in her foul mood, pearl earrings waving with outrage. Grandfather stood by, and being the gentleman that he was, let the typhoon roar and rip around him without comment. He finally turned away, and passing him in the corridor, my mother saw the tears that ran silent and silver down his elegant face. Marta left the next day. Disappearing once again, for destinations unknown. The child cried out for her, but between Otto, Mother and Sabrina, soon regained his composure.

Weeks went by, splicing to become months. Otto spent sleepless nights, drinking and composing. Father would visit him, mother would bring him food, and Sabrina would bathe the child, heat the milk and sometimes, not quite out of earshot, sob a sound that was reminiscent of a sick hen. The alcohol began to pull at Otto's health and he would often collapse into the lonely bed fully clothed, the bladder taking its morning revenge. Months went by, turning into a year. Rumours had reached the family that Marta was seen in the far off town of Brno, laughing carefree on another man's arm. New furs kept her warm and she had grown quite fat. Otto smoked all day, racked with coughs, and would sit morosely in filthy bars, angrily shrugging a concerned hand.

One night, as the beer hall was closing, he lurched over in his sorry seat, and vomited a stream between his legs. Soft fingers raised his sweaty delirious head and a cool towel wiped his brow. A blurred smiling face blocked out the smoky light and he looked up blearily into two wide green eyes that shone kindness and care. She was the waitress, a woman in her early thirties, who had watched his fall from grace, night after pitiful night. A single mother, lined before her time, crawling out of the wreckage of a sordid marriage, she felt drawn towards the crumpled Otto.

"Life is shit", he mumbled as she held him.

"I know, but there is more" she said. They went to her dingy flat, up above the stairs and they made divine, clean and unbridled love. She bathed him in the morning and cooked for him. They became inseparable, walking with the toddler, ice skating on the frozen lake, dancing slowly in smoke heavy nightclubs. Holding on tightly to each other in a chaotic world that drew them together. He would wait for her to end her shift. Her's would be the wildest applause in the audience when the the Crazy Kings stirred up the town. The family was astonished, overjoyed. Grandfather held her like a daughter. Sabrina would bake great steaming cakes and deliver them to the lovers' nest. Happiness and tenderness filled their lives again. Until Marta came back.

o   o   o

Chapter Five

The Virtues Of Wisdom

"The young goat herder awoke with a start. The sun was still high in the sky, the goat bells chiming gaily as the horned ones nibbled, plucked and stank. Normally, the herder would sleep fitfully, well into the afternoon, the bread and cheese lunch a pleasant ballast for his repose. He sat up, yawned and rubbed his eyes. The goats, as one, raised their heads and frowned. The boy stood up and looked around. The sky was the usual pale blue, the valley a dreamy midday haze of green and gold. But something had, sweet Jaro, somehow changed."

Sabrina paused dramatically. Behind her, the grandfather clock hand crept across the number face. "Yes? What had changed? " Jaro the small picture of impatience, wanted to know.

"Everything. The valley felt like a bowl, the sky remorseless in its height. The goats stood chewing stupidly at their cud. He looked down at his broken shoes, his blackened big toe saluting him from its peep hole in the frayed leather. The distant farmhouse in the valley below was a sad sight that somehow no longer whispered a homely pull to his feet. No pride filled his chest as he spied the hunched figure of his father chopping wood for the evening fire. With a sigh that was unusually leaden for the generally buoyant and spirited boy, he summoned the goats and the hopping leaping tribe followed him home. His father looked up, and stared at the sun, confused by the premature return of the bleating menagerie.

'What brings you home so soon, my son? Are you feeling ill? Did you forget your hat, perchance? This sun can blister a young man's brain faster than love and will turn your senses to butter.'

"The young man sat his father down, poured him a glass of wine and explained that he was leaving to seek his fortune in the world beyond the goat gnarled hills. 'Surely there must be more to this life than the sound of those clanking bells, and the call of the goats. This pastoral life is pleasant enough, Father, yet it makes no sense to me to squander my youth on such a trivial pursuit, when there are surely opportunities to be had in the land yonder.'

"He nodded towards the north. Towards where the king of the entire country had his lavish castle perched above a bustling, big city. Both men stared silently at the mountain that formed the natural barrier between the peaceful valley and the world bristling with men and machines. The goat stared at the two men, their faces blank. The old man knew that what he was hearing what he had long expected to hear. He was often amazed that the boy seemed blissfully happy with his lot, that the smell of goats had so readily become his perfume. They stood in silence, with the sudden gust of a wind of change blowing cold in space between them. The father shivered, and yet smiled, embracing the youth. Withdrawing inside into the smoke lined farmhouse, he emerged with a small bag of food and his savings. They embraced once again, more like brothers than father and son. The goats gazed on, tongues a drip with saliva as the men waved a heartfelt goodbye to their pasts. The young man felt both lighter at the excitement whose name was change, and age heavy with the merciless burden of sudden wisdom. At the highest point of the mountain that overlooked the valley, he paused and waved to apparently no one at all. Somewhere, down there, an old man waved back to the speck on the summit."

o o o

Chapter Six

Otto's Luck

She was a woman that would not be ignored. Western stockings tight on lavish thighs, her eyes hot felines that tossed mice into the air. As she stood in the doorway of his flat, leering and insolent, he felt his entrails turn into a glacier slide. And he hated himself. And he hated her for her ruthless instinct. She had made inquiries. Purred into telephones and befriended people in the know. She had heard disconcerting tales about his new found happiness. The rumours of his joy were sand in her bed. She came back to redress the balance. A few hours previously, she had walked, imperious and bejeweled, into the wine bar where the tired but dreamy waitress worked. Ordering a Viennese coffee, Marta studied the opposition. She smiled with contempt as the veined worker hands removed her empty glass.

Marta looked up into the trusting face and said, in a voice resonant with false kindness. "I know who you are. And I know that you think that he might love you. And, perchance for a mad instant, the fool does, in the quiet sentimental squalor of your flat above the bar." She laughed up into the perplexed face. "But know one thing, my pretty blond. I need only but to snap my fingers and he will come running back to me. Tail tight between his polio stinking legs. He will throw away the photographs of you. He will deny having had any worthwhile memories of you. He will say that you were old and that he pitied you. And you will know, as you may suspect that you do even now, that you were never worthy of him. And he will, in his uniquely pathetic accommodating way, in the way that only the truly broken know, agree with me. You are nothing. Have always been nothing and the times that you shared with him, all those apparent happy park walks with Otto and the kid, amount to a charity from both of us. A nothing time. Candy floss that melts to leave a cheap cheated taste in the mouth. An icky stickiness that needs a good rinse. May time offer you that mouthwash. Say goodbye to your musician and his rubber underwear. I'm taking my husband back."

She stood up, pearls swinging heavily on her pink fat ears, and with jowls firmly set walked out, the bill unpaid. Otto took her back, believing in the powder streaked promises that poured out of her as she held him. He did not question her disappearance, choosing rather to blame himself for the defects of the marriage. He praised her for her commitment and loyalty to the family. She had, after all, come home. They went on a second honeymoon to Carlsbad, to the healing waters and for the mountain air full of fireflies and dancing pollen. She spent more time at the spa than with him. Upon their return, she grew tired of both his demands and of those of her mother starved child. She left again. Never to return.

My father cursed her. The family exuded nausea at the slightest reference to the Harpy. The waitress resigned her post, and made a tight lipped vow to herself to avoid any further contact with Otto. The father and the son were alone again. The last that the family heard of the waitress was that she was well on her way towards sainthood, working with the tubercular and the criminal, in some far flung village whose people embraced her warmly. Fortunately, Central Europe had a great deal of recipients for her skills, enough to siphon and staunch her tears on the nights when they poured out, thick and bottomless. Her Crazy King record collection grew dusty and bedraggled.

My father broke down his door. The smell of gas gnawing at his guts and spinning his head around. He dragged the crumpled body out of the slow hiss of the oven. Otto's eyes were huge and dilated to shiny chestnuts that would never see another Christmas. Otto left behind a crying sister, a child that floundered later in life and a best friend that sobbed a lake into the clammy chest that stank of gas. My father's fists took in the first smell of the graveyard.

o o o

Chapter 7

Wisdom Finds a Way

"The road to the town was clearly marked and as the young goat herder approached rows of outlying houses his pace increased. His rural clothing, traitor shoes that revealed his toes and his goat like smell attracted the attention of bored locals who regarded him with a great deal of mirth. Children ran behind and alongside him making braying sounds and pulling at his rough cloth. He quickened his pace which seemed to delight the throng further and the children darted in his path like swallows. Some unseen jester threw a gnarled and tattered sandal at his feet as he passed a doorway, mocking his poorly shod state.

"He passed a sorry looking wretch, hands and head trapped in the manacles of an auto da fe, with a poorly scrawled sign saying 'Thief 'draped around his neck. Our young man could but not help his compassion surge towards the sentenced, but children started to pelt him with food scraps and so he hurried along.

"A post indicating a nearby inn lifted his spirits and with his head held high he soldiered on towards the dignity of a safe haven with a potato peel hanging from his hair. As often happens with the brutish, the easily amused crowd as easily grew bored and melted into the past behind him. The kindly innkeeper provided him with a steaming bowl of cabbage stew and a hunk of bread and after hearing of how the young stranger had suffered such ignoble behaviour at the hands of the locals, he disappeared for a moment to return with shirts, trousers and a pair of strong boots. He removed the peel from the young man's hair. Overcome with gratitude, which was especially heartfelt after enduring the more malign aspect of human nature, the herder shook the benefactor's hand warmly. The two men embraced as friends, for the inn keeper had lost a son very reminiscent of our young man in one of the many wars that blighted the world in those days."

"The young man, washed and handsome, went to see the Kings Castle. It sat perched on a cliff above the town. There was a great market in the centre and the young man idly browsed through the wares, for he had little money to spend yet was happy to receive attention from the sellers. He studied their faces for signs of mirth or mockery, yet they all seemed genuinely convivial and of good cheer. He noticed that there appeared to be a lot of flies hovering around the displays of fruit and meat and he, mildly tongue tied lest he offend, inquired about this unseasonable phenomenon.

'Oh those flies are born on the backs and heads of the corpses hanging there yonder, from those staves that encircle the castle walls,' pointed out one beet farmer. The herder stood back and gaped up at the castle. It was true. Scrawny cadavers swung slowly above him in the distance. He shuddered.

'And why sire, do those bodies hang there so ripe and bloated?' asked our bewildered innocent.

'Those are, my fine young fellow, the corpses of the suitors. They came from far and wide, so as to meet the King's challenge. And they all failed, the poor buggers. Must be at least two dozen of them, swinging and stinking up the place.'

'Why would the King kill these people? I have heard only of the good reports about the man, and he doesn't strike me as being unjust nor barbarous, yet the sight of those bodies must surely disturb and offend foreign visitors and terrify the young?'

"The man laughed, 'You, sir, must have been recently hatched out of an egg, or have surely fallen from the very stars that turn their heads from this not so pretty sight. The King has given a great challenge to all who are either brave or foolish enough to take it upon themselves. His daughter has never been of a cheerful disposition, not even as a child, but since her twelfth birthday she's turned into a right miserable cow. She mopes around all day, doesn't speak a word besides to her ladies in waiting, eats alone in her room and avoids her father as though he has the Plague. The poor King tried to surround her with clowns, poets and dancers but she dismissed them all and went into a solitary slump. Pale as death and about as lively. At his wits end, the King has offered as a reward, half his kingdom and her hand in marriage to any man fit enough to return to her the zest for life and to rekindle warmth to a heart grown so utterly cold. Many came, but as the death count grew there now remain very few that would risk their lives in the pursuit of such an obviously futile endeavor. Succeed and all is yours, my gentle squire. Fail, and you'll provide us with a new crop of flies to swat and to chase.' The merry face watched the young man frown deeply. The coins in his pockets were but a few. The bodies swung in the breeze."

"Sabrina," I asked, perplexed at the moral contradictions that hung over the tale thus far: "Were the people in the town good or bad? They seemed perfectly normal, but they treated the stranger with such cruelty. Death seemed a joke to them. And then they went back to their normal lives as though nothing was amiss. I find that quite odd, I must admit." I said, emphatically bewildered. The world seemed a maze of contradictions. Drunken husbands, urinal urns upturned on graves and savage fowl movements in the night did not suggest a comfortable universe awaiting my tread. She laughed and squeezed me tightly. I could smell the chamomile in her hair. She used to make a poultice out of the flowers for rheumatism and would wash using soaps brittle with the leaves of the herb.

"They were what they are, little Jaro. Is a zebra a white horse with black stripes or a black one with white markings? You tell Old Sabrina, I'm dying to know," she teased me gently.

In that moment, I was too tired to answer the peculiar riddle, but I quietly pledged to corner that contradictory animal that seemed to challenge even wise old Sabrina's knowledge of the world. I retired into bed with the visions of castles and their silent princesses. The pillows creased into valleys and mountains, and I tried to imagine a goat herd gamboling in the furrows of linen. Somewhere far away, the bodies turned slowly in the wind and the ropes that held them aloft, creaked. Sleep descended upon me flavoured with the scent of chamomile and potato peel.

o o o

Chapter Eight

Christ the Frog

There was a lake near our house that glinted seductively through the parkland that led to its muddy waters. Broad as it was long, it trembled with secrets. My father told me that when he was young and war raged across the country, he once sat on its banks, fishing for carp. Carp is swampy muddy fish, a pop eyed and dull creature that breeds noisily in the shallows and is generally a wallflower at any fish party. Yet through blight and circumstance it had managed to become a firm favourite on the national menu. Even spawning a legend, whereby if at Christmas time a person would dutifully fast for the entirety of the holy day, he might be fortunate enough to see a specter of A Golden Carp, manifest for a graceful magical moment. It always struck me as poor substance for a myth and I had never heard of anyone that even attempted such an act of devotion.

My father sat there, on the grassy bank, staring at the float that cheerfully bobbed in the tender current. The sun was high and hot, and he was daydreaming hazily, when an object flew over his head and plopped into the water in front of him. He heard foreign voices and then faces peered over the embankment behind him As my father turned to greet them, an explosion from the water ripped through the calmness of the day and flung him back. A group of Russian soldiers, starving and bedraggled, heaved grenades into the lake. Carp bodies floated up, to be racked into a fish pile on the shore. My fathers rod pointed mutely at the still smoking water. A soldier smiled at the boy, and threw him a metal badge. The red star twinkled prettily in his hands and he waved his thanks to the khaki clad man, who disappeared into the trees with an army bag of fat and wheezing wallflower fish.

I was seven years old and the summer school holiday dragged on. Sweat dripped from my small body as I walked down to the lake. Dragonflies chased each other and the carp splashed their welcome in the weeping willow shaded water. I decided to walk around the lake, to the wooded hilly ridge, where a soft stream burbled and fed the sun dappled expanse of water. Mossy stones and leafy boughs cooled my heated day, and I walked in empty minded reverie towards the stream.

I suddenly became aware of movement ahead of me. A number of older youths could be seen through the maze of poplars, milling around something that I could not distinguish. I crept nearer, walking only on the spongy moss that softened the sound of my small feet. The teenage boys were laughing in a way that rasped at my ears, shrill sounds that spoke of a bad joke. One spotty blond boy turned towards me and for a moment he paused and then quickly urged me nearer in a friendly fashion. The others made way for my wide eyed passage to the centre of the group. Giggling and slightly hysterical, the lads were gazing up into the branches of a thin tree. I struggled to see the focus of their attention and shook my head in confusion. Frustrated at my apparent stupidity and keen to have an appreciative member in the audience, a big boy picked me up and raised me towards the source of their nervous mirth. The hands held me tight and high, and the pain of being brutishly hoisted was about to become intolerable, when I saw the dull green form. Suspended by wires attached to all four limbs, spread-eagled between two branches of the tree was the painfully scared figure of a frog. Pale bellied with big yellow eyes, its flippers hanging loose and useless in the wire knots, the frog stared down at me.

The boy released me, but I was too mesmerized to thank him. I kept on staring at the frog and the group, noting my fascination, fell around laughing a fresh round of bilious cacophony. One pushed me and I fell into a muddy puddle, but I stood up and could not draw my gaze away from the creature hanging there, mouth parting dry and yellow, the belly swelling and falling against the onslaught of air. Slowly the group thinned out and I was left there on my own. The boys went to find other new and novel ways with which to fill the long summer hours. I could see green skin starting to dry out.

I tried to climb up the tree, but it was too scrawny and slippery for a foothold and the poor animal was tied up high, well beyond my meagre reach. I found a long branch, and tentatively poked at the wire, coiled around the branches. The frog looked at me with profound resignation, which inspired me to run around the tree, trying to find a stone, a springboard, anything that would allow me to release the tormented animal. Panting with frustration, I could hear the slow and happy sound of the stream dutifully filling the lake, refreshing the carp.

When in doubt, appeal to the adult world, I reminded myself. Higher powers that wait for the frail call of the lost and the hopeless. Strong men and able women, that had survived the war years to live with wisdom and with wit. Glancing up, I waved a reluctant goodbye to the dim body, hanging in the summer air, I turned and ran frantically up the hill, through the trees to the house. Panting and stammering, dirty of face and feet, I confronted Father, who was glaring into the confines of the motorcycle engine that he had dismantled. Grease and irritability oozed from him, but I ignored his frown and rattled off my dry mouthed pleas. I told him about the boys, the pitiful state of the frog, stressed the urgent nature of the rescue. I even acted out the sad animal's expressions, the tearing of the air down a long parched throat. I paused, exhausted, quivering with emotion. He mumbled something about pistons, clogged vents and poor fuel flow, and went on digging in the bowels of the motor. I spat with youthful contempt and before he could chastise me for insolence, I bolted into the house in search of another adult that would listen.

Mother was sitting in the kitchen stuffing a chicken with garlic and mushrooms. I glanced around for Sabrina, but it was a Tuesday, and she was away at the market. In despair, with a tearful eye on the clock, I recounted my story, too exhausted to describe the depth and extent of my compulsion to save the frog. Partly, I suspected that I would be too late, returning with a rescue party that would stand witness to my defeat, cutting down a sun baked corpse and walking back home in silence.

My mother sighed and shook her head at the cruelty of boys and continued to stuff the bird. I never returned to that part of the lake. I knew that frog could still be hanging there, a husk wired to a tree, waiting for my return, mouth wide and belly still.

o o o

Chapter Nine

The King's Challenge

"It's not easy being a former goat herder, in a lively big city, and with but a few coins for company. Desperation followed his every stride." Sabrina's dress rustled like a porcupine as she rearranged herself on the sofa. I looked at the hunched figure, and at the endless yellowing photographs that adorned her walls. Lining the length and breadth of the tumble–down cottage. My face appeared amongst them, Otto and Momma were there. The walnut faced dead husband looked at us, rheumy eyed and bulbous nosed.

"Gentle and naïve, our adventurer was impatient to take up the King's Challenge. The innkeeper listened to the excited youth's plans with trepidation. He had grown very fond of the boy and dreaded the thought of seeing his corpse adorning the castle walls. He poured them both a large glass of blood red wine, and tried to gently coax the herder away from his foolish idea. To no avail, for the fire in the boy's eyes dried up his words of caution.

"In the morning he watched the young man walking feverishly down the road, pausing only to wave a last minute goodbye and thanks towards the concerned figure in the doorway of a highway inn. A crow perched on the branch of an ancient oak cackled ominously. The King was amazed to hear that a young man had presented himself and apparently seemed determined to follow in the footsteps of the dead men that hung so ripely outside the castle gate. He scrutinized his unblemished features for signs of dementia. It would be a pity to kill a simpleton with such grandiose aspirations, thought the King, whilst he smiled at the boy kindly.

"The skeletons through whose rib cages wind sang so sweetly belonged to men of breeding and substance who assumed that by their class and erudition they could thaw out an icy woman's heart. The young man before him appeared to be of a pleasant demeanour, adequately in charge of his faculties, albeit a little over confidant. A pity again. Papers were signed. Hands were shaken and luck was called upon. But there was little place for Luck to roost in the already crowded head that smiled as it made its way back to the inn.

"The princess gazed out of her morbid window. Saw the fine featured youth exit the castle, nonchalant and full of good spirits, pausing to pat a dog that skulked in the gutter beside him. The canine population grew around the poles from which the corpses swung. Hoping for a falling morsel, they congregated, only to be regularly chased away by soldiers on guard duty. She felt a surge of grief and an odd yearning to run in the fields with goats. And now, sleepy Jaro, you must drift and wonder about the wisdom of such an undertaking. Do goat herders make a suitable match for a princess, let alone as kings to countries?" She smiled me a smile of a thousand creases and of a multitude of suns in its warmth and mischief. Outside, the sky was freckled with stars and the wind murmured with a storm warning. The roosters, sheer bastions of weather change, all looked up at the sky.

○ ○ ○

Chapter Ten

The Heart's Quest

"He fortified himself with a glass of red wine, poured from a stone jug, felt its warmth rush through his veins and sparkle up his senses. The herder boy rose from the table, wiped his lips with a cloth, and with a lilt in his stride made his way to the castle. This time he was expected, and a bent white haired old man led him down long corridors, ornate with tapestries and murals of hunting scenes, until they came to a splendid door, carved in ebony, sprinkled with gold. The elderly guide turned out to be the princess' mentor, a man stooped by years of servitude and learning. Now, his role was akin to that of an executioner's apprentice. He whispered words of encouragement to the bright-eyed youth, for he too was tired of the murderous challenge that had claimed so many bright fresh lives. The mentor knocked a secret, almost silent knock and put a wrinkled ear close to the impressive door, to hear an affirmation from within. The young man's heart beat with the delirium of a humming bird's wing in springtime. With a final throaty rasp, the rheumy old fellow opened the door and ushered the boy into the chamber heady with a scent of talcum powder. The goat herder blinked his eyes against the challenge of the low light in which the room swam.

"At first he thought that the old man had fumblingly played a cruel jest upon him, stretching his already racked nerves to a new treble pitch by keeping him a tremble in a sumptuous waiting room, awaiting fate's slow tread. Then, he detected an almost imperceptible movement from the dimmed Ottoman that stood in a distant corner of the room.

She sat there, delicacy made flesh, dark rings around haunted eyes, wide as autumn skies. Almost furtively embroidering a kerchief, she kept her gaze upon her work. Another young man swept to his end by the siren's sad song, she felt the guilt of a woman far beyond her years. A few years back she had felt the sparkle of childhood extinguish, dewy stars that were replaced by the cold fog of early womanhood. She hankered for the days of simple magic, where she could dream of talking fish and dancing bears. Her father did not see her fall from her own previous grace, merely a depressed woman that shunned his demands and refused to be be a virgin bride on a pedestal that quickly became the gallows. The men that came to her side were mostly boastful barons, sons of fat judges or of wolfish predatory demeanor that reminded her of all the fierce things that lived in the forests outside her window. Their self conceited prattle or sweet words of fluff did nothing to melt her heart. Bored of their worldly trivia, she would dismiss them and father's butchers did the rest. It made her sad, but at least left her to her melancholic musings, in which she found solace. She turned away from this new suitor, not wishing to meet his gaze and thus stir up false hope in a heart so near its extinction. A call from her would mean peace and death."

The storm crumpling up the sky, the roosters filed in. Wet wind was screaming outside and Sabrina opened the door in mid story. I leant forward in the armchair, willing the last bird its entrance. They plodded in wet and serious. Proud feathers archly fluffed up. The door closed and the story continued.

"She did not call out. Needle in small hand, she stitched a pattern that was innocent. The corner of her eye was most active though. And whilst he stood, a quake in the coldly neutral desert of the floor, she studied his stance, the delicacy of his movement. The young man did not bombard her with questions. Neither did he speak too hastily. He knew that a torrent of words would drive her into hiding. He understood that she was a fawn hiding in the bushes. His years of herding gentle sensitive animals came to his rescue.

He ventured to sit on the edge of the Ottoman. The room was a menagerie of dolls. Black-eyed pandas caressed the backs of unicorns. Little foxes stared out of cupboards at boxes of peeling skin dolls that lived beneath the bed. Book shelves laden with fairies that winged tipped the covers. Our handsome herder saw her friends. He felt her frailty, knew her innocence. The hand that worked the needle was a wind that spoke to the pines on a summer night. He breathed a sigh of relief.

"She slowly turned her face towards him and seeing a warm, aquiline profile that nurtured her trust through its innocence, she smiled, a smile that hung between them like a sunny bridge between two dark worlds. She put aside her sewing and asked him who he was. He explained his humble background, told her of the goats that would wake him up in the early morning, their hot tongues on his bemused face, the sun a myth yet to be born in the heavens.. Of how the ravens followed the herd to their pasture, the cawing from their dark throats summoning the dawn with an secret passion. The streams that hopped with trout, that glowed with rainbows. The winter storms that roused up goats' bleats, lifted farm roofs and caused the fire place to shake and billow soot and dust into the house. Chestnuts as big as men's fists over which the braying foul flock would fight. Thunder which made the roosters rigid with secret excitement.

"She listened, hands wrung together like two swans mating. He left after an hour. Wisdom is the father of timing and they both drink from the teat of knowledge. She followed him to the door and held onto the handle long after he had left. The warmth of his trace flowered through the metal and into her heart. He glanced up at the castle from the road. The turrets loomed grey and foreboding above him. With a small silhouette in the far left window, behind which candles flickered their yellow tongues. As the distance grew the whole majestic power of the castle was reduced to a tumble of blocks with which a child could play."

Sabrina poured out tea, and sighed a heavy sigh in the direction of the photographs that lined the mantelpiece.

Faces that were milestones on her uneasy road through life. "Remind me to empty out my bed pan before I go to sleep, Jaroslav." She winked at me, the mistress of conspiracies. We both chuckled.

o o o

Chapter Eleven

The Second Liberation

We lay on rubber inflatable mattresses in the heated garden. The wasps were humming in the trees and the dachshund lay panting in the shadow of the old pear tree. Father, young and fit and self-assured returned from the kitchen with a pitcher of iced lemon tea. Tall, brown with cheeks boned to razor perfection and prone to vanity with his James Dean hair, in the little Czech garden in 1968 he was the epitome of west made east. The wasps hung in the air, the dog snored and the sound of an airplane grew louder. Circling above us, the distant speck of the plane was an irritant. Remorseless in its orbit it added an essence to the sun's heat that made the whole narcoleptic haze unbearable. My father placed down the the tea tray and stood over us, hand on forehead shielding those blue eyes that imprisoned my mother and watched me grow. The plane was at an altitude that rendered it anonymous. Pollen hung in the stillness and sweat left trails down backs. He shook his head with frustration. The sound of the engine, thousands of metres above our Sunday, grated the ears.

To break the monotony of the ceaseless vision of a noisy speck that came and rapidly withered, I grabbed a long stick that propped up a dying gooseberry bush. Gun-like I raised it to my skinny child shoulder and when the plane made its next pesky appearance, I pointed it at the heat blurred form and made machine gun sounds to drive it away. The slap sent my makeshift weapon flying into dry garden behind me, whilst I reeled from the blow to my head. My father loomed over me. Anger and fear twisting his features beyond makeshift Hollywood status. He looked scared and ugly.

"You idiot," he snarled, "how can the pilot see whether you are a kid with a stick or a soldier with a gun? We could have all been killed." He pushed me again, Mother remained mute. He was right. I was a simpleton. The wasps hung around, excited by the violence.

The plane above eventually broadened its circle above the country. We heard later that the pilot claimed engine trouble. A request to land at Prague airport, granted to our benefactor, red guard neighbour.

Troops poured out. Tanks revved up. The capital fell quickly, with minor retaliation from poorly armed students. The radio station was stormed. Strained voices delivering the last truthful news for decades to come. We all heard the barricaded door of the broadcast room, kicked down and the thousand speakers in so many living rooms across the country went dead. A silence like a little death followed.

A strident rendition of the national anthem introduced a silken foreign accented voice praising the return to order of a country that was turning maverick. Music loving and horny, we danced into disfavour with our overseers. The Eastern bloc wasn't supposed to be a fun place, no carousel for the liberated. Stalin called the Czechs the laughing hyena of Europe. His successor shared these sentiments and had delivered a solution to the apparent national merriment. Western jazz that grew increasingly popular before the crackdown stank of moral decay. Pollution imported from beyond our sacred borders.

Renegade and goat-like in the face of the factory owner, the nation was herded into a pen. The family sat in gloom. Obscure uncles and family friends, sharing bottles of plum brandy, listening to the clatter of medal clad newsreaders extolling the virtues of a return to order. The goat castrated. The orchestra dissolved. A car, somewhere outside in the freshly fallen freedom night, backfiring.

"No doubt, the sound of the government shooting itself." Remarked an obscure uncle, dryly. No one laughed.

Tanks drew up outside my aunt's apartment building on the first day of the Prague Spring. There were more inanely buzzing planes in the sky, but by now no one paid them any attention. The turrets turned, pointing their barrels idly at the building. A sight repeated across the country. Helmeted drivers smoking foul smelling cigarettes, waiting for the sun to fall. As it did. All the apartments burning with lights, the evening meal tasting sour in the mouths of the freshly re-occupied. The crews of the tanks were amazed. Each apartment was proudly lit with its own individual light. An upsetting and bewildering phenomenon for soldiers with a foot on the neck of a country that afforded its people such unheard of privileges. Back home, in the better parts of Moscow, apartment blocks had one shared bathroom per floor. With intermittent lighting. Frequent power failures, cold water and lifts that rusted, as still as a strangled kitten. Truly a time of barbarians at the gates.

I remembered my dad's story of the carp being blown up by the Russian hand grenades. Beefy faces sweating as they raked in the fish, stuffing them into makeshift tarpaulin bags. Now the whole country was bagged and gasping. Rumours spread of the conquering tank crews, how they would rob the locals of anything of value. Shoes seemed popular as booty, as did necklaces and wristwatches. A soldier would jump down from the turret and point at what he wanted; "Dawai. Dawai. Dwai Tjasi." (*Give. Give. Give watch*). He would grunt, indicating the watch on the poor local's wrist, and approach threateningly. The grumbling Czech would hand over the timepiece and stand miserably on the street whilst the tank cheerfully rumbled away, rattling windows, setting the dogs to bark stridently.

My father had heard about this phenomenon and strapped a cheap watch onto his ankle. He put on a long sleeved jersey and swaggered towards a parked tank, whose crew lay around on the grass verge beside it, having lunch. Stuffing bread and cheese into their mouths, they watched the arrogantly good looking local yokel, whistling some forbidden Western tune as he sauntered past. Unable to resist the rooster to rooster confrontation, one red faced soldier stood up, hands on his belt buckle, the chestnut brown leather holster that had a wink of gun metal. The Russian put his hand out, burped corrosively and spoke those legendary words, "Dawai Tchasi, Dawai."

My father frowned and rolled up his sleeve, to reveal a naked wrist. He then, with a conjurer's dramatic slow movement revealed his other wrist, a bare twin of the watch-less first. The soldier's face fell. Dad held up a finger. Lo, there was to be a revelation. The Russian's face lit up. Father raised his trouser leg like a stripper pulling at a crucial ribbon. There on his skinny ankle, ticked a merry timepiece. The soldier was livid, shaking his head, slapping his own wrist. He didn't want the ankle watch, it was a wristwatch that he demanded. Turning away in disdain from the poker-faced magician in front of him, the trooper returned to his comrades. They motioned father away, convinced that they had encountered the local village idiot who had wasted their time with this useless accessory.

o o o

Chapter Twelve

Lovers' Strings

"The King's messenger arrived the next day. Pale faces watched furtively from behind curtains as the familiar carriage clattered up the cobbled street, horses breathing silver in the early morning frost. The innkeeper peered through the window and instantly grew old and cold with dread. Death, he knew, had many faces. And for many young men in the recent history of the town, the sight of the royal carriage arriving whispered of the end of dreams and of the embrace of an early grave.

"The official rapping made him jump and he opened the door as timidly as a man resigned to the role of the Judas Goat. Brushing past him, the messenger demanded to have an audience with the young man. The one that was impudent enough to distract the princess from her duties around the King. Awakening to the clamour of a house disturbed our hero came downstairs eyes wide with longing and apprehension. The messenger ceremoniously handed him a gold edged envelope that bore the regal seal. A stag in mid leap over a craggly mountain. The hands that tore open the paper trembled, and all those assembled held their breath. A beehive in the garden grew still, the insects ceased their buzzing in this moment of gravity. A coin fell out of the torn envelope and rolled across the carpet. A moving emblem of the beloved king in gold. The coin lay there in the centre of the room, eying them all coldly.

"The young man read and then reread the simple note. A frown furrowed his silken brow and he silently passed on the missive to the ashen faced innkeeper. Who with a breath that faltered like a horse dragging a millstone laden cart up a hill loudly read out the ornately written contents.

"'His majesty the King sends great compliments and respect to the young gentleman whose privilege it has been to have a recent audience with the Princess. It has been decided to grant the Good Person a further engagement, to proceed this evening, at the same location and time. To ensure that the gentleman spends the day in Comfort a token of the appreciation has been enclosed.'

"There was a reverent sense of disbelief in the room. The hive resumed its flighty humming, whilst the innkeeper roared with the laughter of a prisoner freshly released. The young man sat down whilst the messenger, strangely unsettled, withdrew. The carriage clattered away and more curtains twitched silently. He was relieved to have been spared, for the time being, the dry kiss of the gallows yet he wondered about the fickleness of a royal heart.

But the memory of her deer-like splendor gave him some solace. The grace and serenity of her company made him smile. He steadied his nerves and welcomed the call of the night."

Chapter Thirteen

Gone to Where the Music Plays

Sabrina would sit with me in the grand rocking chair in the huge lounge in my grandmother's house and rock us wildly. Glass ornaments would shine with a polished brilliance everywhere, from dancing horses to abstract form vases, ashtrays for a cancerous army. These were the gleaming relics of the Old Days, where the factory would supply many fine shops in Prague with such delicacies. She would softly intone a little song into my ear, as we rode the rocking chair's highs and lows. It was always the same song, and she would repeat it, with almost merciless glee, as I nodded my head in time to the cruel and sad words,

"The little dog stole a sausage
And not a very large one at that
The butcher caught him in the yard
And killed him with a swipe of a stick
right between the eyes,
all the dogs howled and sobbed
as they dug the tiny grave
above which they placed a headstone
upon which the following words were carved
the little dog stole a sausage
And not a large one at that... "

And so the song would repeat and repeat, whilst I grew giddy with the movement and as the nausea crept through my bowels at the casual cruelty of the world. The tanks had disappeared back to wherever tanks go when their work is done. Wristwatches became once again visible but the time they measured was not a happy one. It was as though the entire country was turned into a strict school with new rules being written daily, with monitors that could be your friends and neighbours. Making notes behind closed doors of petty infringements. Detention suddenly had a less frivolous meaning.

There were many stories of the official midnight knock, of muffled voices and bags quickly packed for destinations unknown. Some came back, drawn and nervous, refusing to comment at what they experienced at the hands of their "re-educators". Conversations in public took the shape of a farce, where the script was carefully limited to mouthing opinions both inane and neutral, where everybody forgave each other for the emptiness of spirit.

In the face of the deepening miasma which heralded a new dark age for a bright and lively people, Father decided that we should leave. As many Others had left. Some had walked over mountains, crossed borders at night, swum moonlit rivers to freedom. We sat the dinner table when he made his announcement. Mother and I exchanged glances, and then she ran out, into the bedroom. I could hear her sobbing through the door. Sabrina's little song started up in my head again. But this time there were no warm hands holding me tightly, and the rocking chair felt like a ghost of a dream that I had long ago.

Chapter Fourteen

A Trail Of Feathers

I watched the roosters sitting on the decaying fence outside my bedroom window, fascinated by their determined unison. A random bird would change its position on the peeling perch and within seconds the whole group would follow suit, clucking and staring into the same invisible spot, somewhere in the distance. If one fierce eyed cockerel would suddenly decide to leap down from the fence and to seek out and torment Sabrina the gang would be seen walking in a feathered line, earnestly following the first bird. There appeared to be no distinction of hierarchy between the fowls, and the group would merely imitate the actions of any rooster that got an idea into its head. Linked by an almost tactile bond, they reminded me of red headed vertebrae that made up a snaky spine. When you saw one roguish bird the rest were surely somewhere nearby.

I asked Sabrina if the roosters ever got lonely and pined for a mate, the old boys club surely being a limited institute to its members. Apparently not, for according to her knowledge of the gang's past flirtation with the opposite sex, the birds were women haters. She told me of a time when a stray hen waddled up the grassy path that ran to the house. Fat, absentmindedly pecking at things that lived in amongst the verdant tufts, the speckled hen meandered towards the main farm building. Sitting on the porch, shelling peas, Sabrina watched as the bird clucked closer to the house. In a sudden fury a rooster flapped down next to hen, fluffed up to a condor like magnitude and with a frenzied beating of wings crowed a ghastly scream into her bewildered fowl face. The yard filled with the sound of winged violence as the rest of the brotherhood descended upon the cowering female, beaks red and gaping with screeching outrage. The poor beast was so mortified by the sudden appearance of the multi-headed, single minded rooster clan that she flapped up above cruel beaks and vicious eyes and flew straight up into Sabrina's hair. There, manic with fear, the hen became ensnared, little claws in the net of Sabrina's mane. With the flapping bird as a wild hat, Sabrina ran down the road towards the gate, pursued by the heated pack that howled their frustration at being deprived of their kill. Unable to separate the hen from her hair, Sabrina was saved by the arrival of the grocer's van into which she flung herself. The driver, terrified by the sudden appearance of this crone adorned with a shrill, ceaselessly clucking hen with wings flailing, made a hasty exit through the door. Only to be confronted by the feathered gargoyle army that swooped around the truck like vultures. Sabrina had by then managed to rip most of her hair out to be free from the hapless bird, and sat there holding the gulping hen, both woman and beast trembling and wide-eyed. The driver was equally petrified, he jumped in and the three made good their escape. The hen was released further down the road and Sabrina limped cautiously back home. The roosters sat up in the branches of the massive old oak, and looked down at her with contempt.

No hen ever came down the path again and the grocer would idle his van at the bottom of the road, hoot furtively and wait for Sabrina to walk down to make her purchases. Their bachelor kingdom preserved, the roosters strode around majestically. I often wondered if Sabrina was to them, in some perverse fowl way, the queen of their flock.

o o o

Chapter Fifteen

Lover's Knot

"The room seemed different, the goat herder thought, as he was quietly ushered in by the octogenarian tutor," began Sabrina. It was dark, the fire raged and we sat side by side on the couch watching flames lick the wood that hissed with steam. "The princess had positioned herself in the middle of the splendid parlour and wore a simple dress that revealed her delicate shoulder blades and swan neck. Her hair too, had been released from its former severe captivity and hung free as a waterfall over her soft features. The tutor raised his eyebrow quizzically at this obviously unusual sight of regal frivolity, and retired hastily, leaving our hero to stand rooted to the spot by the magnitude of this splendid vision. She beckoned him to sit by her, on the velvet skin of the Ottoman. The chandelier glowed inferno like above them as he gracefully seated himself. The princess watched his face carefully, discovering new colours in his eyes that she had not noticed during their previous encounter. Inwardly, she smiled.

"'Tell me more of your mountains and the valleys. And of your kindly father too. I had a dream that we both were walking in the tall grasses that you described so beautifully the last time that you were here. I woke up and wanted to sing. In fact, I did sing, but stopped when I was summoned to the King. I told him that I did not wish to see you hang. He seemed pleased and promised to call you back to tell me more of the stories. Of the goats and their mischief.'" She blushed as she spoke, gazing at her own dainty shoes. Her first blush after many a summer. A gentle hue that passed across her face like a graceful mist, pink with morning. He was astonished by the sight, and the very living breath in his lungs almost evaporated at the warmth of her voice. Slowly and with a tiny quiver that gradually receded, he told her of his father and how the lonely man had raised him. Mother had died in childbirth and the widower took no other woman to his bed, choosing rather to devote his entire attention to the healthy development of his child. They swam in the lake cold with winter thaw. Walked the ravines and slid on the ice of the glacier that dripped like a jewel in the sun. He told her of the hawks that circled in the eternal sky above newly born goats. He almost became lost in the memories that came a tumbling out of him, each one begetting a dozen others, much as a prism breaks white light into wild colour. She watched his face as he spoke, and held her knuckles tightly when his voice stopped. There was a moment's silence that hung in the air around them. Above their heads, the candles dripped like icicles, soft sounds of wax melting and falling. She stared into his eyes, and lo, from which tears did flow. His hand, a fallen dove in the softness of her own. She could feel his pulse through her skin and she closed her eyes. They sat like that for a long time. The herder sighed, and continued with his tales. The princess sighed with pleasure, eyes still closed when he described the warm bread and fresh goat cheese that he ate as the dawn broke a fiery arrow across the sky, the animals with their old man faces clambering to be released from their pen. He had given them all names, and would lead them up into the hills, the goats skipping across the dewy stones, nipping and butting at each other. He smiled as he remembered the orange firelight that danced from the barn windows on winter nights, the goats herded in against the growl of the snow, metal drums aching with an inferno load of coal lit by his thick-jacketed father. Demon beasts with curved horns watching the flames with beautifully passive expressions. He held the soft pale hand of the princess tightly. She squeezed back, silently urging on his dexterous flow of magic words and passionate visions.

"Princess and goat herder became two rivers that met to become a deep warm lake, brimming with light and a maze of currents that shimmered with the joy of living. Castles and dead suitors, broken shoes and empty pockets faded into the darkness around them. The night became a glove in which their hands met. The knock on the door was as soft as a faithful dog's nose. Yet it signified an end to the evening's coalescence of heart and mind. He rose with the weight of the world's lead in his feet. He held her hands in his and murmured shy thanks for her patience and time. The young woman moved closer and shy as the first cherry buds in spring, held up his palm to her lips. The kiss became a warm cloud upon which he sailed out of the room, down the passage and into the lap of the night.

Chapter Sixteen

In No Man's Land

There was tension in the land, but there was an even greater crisis at home. Mother held long and secret meetings with Father. The grandfather clock beat out the hours and we all walked around each other like frightened animals. Dinner times were petty disasters, with tension that was a razor wire between us. Mother did not want to leave the country of her birth, no matter how maligned it had become. I had my friends, Sabrina and the dachshund, the love of my grandparents and the lake that twinkled gaily and carefree through the park outside my window. Father seemed to be possessed by a foreign spirit. He made us sit and listen to his ideas of change, to his reasons why we should suddenly become refugees. Reasons why we should learn a new language, feel different winds on our faces. The country had become a cul-de-sac to growth, with every other person an immoral cog in the mean machine that had replaced the spirit of the nation. We would have no future, either as a family or as individuals in the new dispensation; where free thought was a social disease, one that that required removal for fear of infecting the whole body of the state. Western ideas, fashions and culture were the manifestations of a blight that required special attention from well versed gardeners that pruned the moral garden with loathsome skill. My father had a wardrobe that would have shamed James Dean. Sunglasses from Brando's biker phase and a music collection that sang our epitaph.

My own future, a son of a determinedly provocative father, linked with my glass factory owner grandfather legacy, would ensure me a minimal future in the Great Republic. A bricklayer, or a milk delivery man, I would be the figurehead of a new generation lost in tragedy. Our kind were not to be trusted, a rotten branch that would need to be trimmed for the sake of the tree.

I swallowed hard when I heard the dire prophesies that my father, inflamed by rebellious zeal, bestowed upon us during dinner. He began to make plans for our escape. Friends of the family came around, nervous yet concerned. Odd men would appear at even odder hours and Father entertained them with pork crackling and beer. A quiet conspiracy was hatched to uproot us. I watched mother, confused and helpless watching me in my confusion and helplessness. She stroked my hair whilst tightly embracing Sabrina. The two women held each other as though a storm was about to separate them. I saw their trembling sadness and looked away. The house felt like a fridge and Father felt like a butcher, working with unwilling flesh. The country had turned rancid. A desperation had grown like a dense yet invisible lichen throughout the house. I kept myself busy by playing with the rabbits that lived in the hutch at the bottom of the garden.

One cold Sunday afternoon Sabrina took my hand and we walked away from the home, slowly following the road until we came to the edge of the forest that creaked and sighed with the autumnal winds that nipped at my face. We would often enjoy these spontaneous excursions together, for she was by nature a country girl, used to the joy of the soil beneath her feet and the smell of the pines in her nostrils. I followed happily, relieved to leave the confusion of home and the sense of foreboding that haloed over the family. She strode with a bustling sense of purpose, whilst I ran ahead of her, kicking up the dank leaves that made up the forest floor. We sat down beside a stream that bubbled and spoke in sighs. After a moment's silence, during which the birdsong grew merry and strident, she edged towards me on the log and I could feel her warmth merging with my own.

"It's a strange time for you I know, my Jaro," she said, and her words suddenly fished out my hidden tears, as though a spoon of kindness had dredged up my inner silt. I blinked and looked away, pretending to find great fascination in a torn cobweb that hung between two branches above me.

"And a strange time for me too, a cruel season. I'm watching something that I cannot stop from unfolding, forming and growing around us, threatening to tear my own heart to bits. We need to be strong here, my dear, and embrace something that is as inescapable as a season, with joy and with hope. There have been many lessons on my old woman's road, but they all pale beside the greatest and ultimately the most comforting lesson of all. Written in tall and elegant letters as high as the sky." She paused dramatically. I looked up and there the sky was, pale and unsmiling through the tree tops.

"And that wondrous and viscous knowledge is that All Things Change. People come and go, armies clink and clank into cities and into countries. Empires come and go, I have seen a good few fall and vanish in my humble years of getting these proud wrinkles. Many people fear the test of change, and live in dread and fear of the next moment. Remember the old story of the monkey's paw in the bottle, where the greedy ape refuses to unclench its hairy fist on the nuts and free itself from the trap? It can't get the nuts because the paw is stuck but it will not release its grip. As long as it remains greedy, the ape will go hungry. We must be flexible and endeavour not to hold onto that which we love or desire so tightly that it makes us less. I love you so much, my boy and I know that you are scared of the changes that your father's threatening. But we have to trust change. You and I share something that is greater than time and distance, and is stronger than fear, my Jaro. It will survive, whatever is to come. Be glad of the time that we have and of the place that we share under this barren sky together. Appreciate all this, but beware of being trapped by fear. The monkey's greed is simply fear of not getting all the nuts and is his handicap. In his ape mind now is the only time that is important.

"Your father's father, fought in the First Great War. Oddly enough, we were on the sides of the Germans that later invaded us. All the young men of healthy body and mind were gathered in the village and the army was doing a thriving business enlisting the enthusiastic smiling boys into the service of the Emperor. They were marched to the railway station and with a brass band playing the cheerful polka, boarded the trains that took them to the far off training bases that would mold them into soldiers. His mother and father waved him farewell, as the young man smiled back at them from the window of the train. Your grandfather and many others were captured in battle, and sent of to Italy as prisoners of war. He and a friend managed to escape from their camp and walked deep into the mountains, near the border.

"A local shepherd gave them lodgings for the night but while they slept he summoned the local village policeman and they were arrested. Leaving the prisoners manacled to a post in the mountain hut, the policeman peddled away on his bicycle to rouse the garrison stationed in a nearby valley. During this time, your grandfather managed to break free from his shackles and kill their guard. The two soldiers made their escape into the night, with dogs a barking and villagers astir at the consternation. A sniper shot ended your grandfather's companions life and he, alone and frightened, ran until day break. He hid in a cave and continued his journey north, guided by the stars and an old compass.

"He walked back home, over rivers, across mountains, living off the generosity of poor people tired of war, whose hearts softened at the sight of the tall ragged stranger on his unerring path northwards. The one guiding star that kept him on his feet was the dream of coming home. By then the war had ended and there were many young men, in various states of physical and emotional distress, making their way home from far flung battlefields.

"During his long absence, his mother took ill and after a feverish week of delirium, died in her husband's arms. His father mourned her death for a few months and then promptly married a nurse. He was killed in an accident six weeks after the marriage. The new widow inherited the house. The nurse was a pretty thing, and within a year was married again. Your grandfather was spared the turbulence of home life and after many weeks of travel, he finally came home one night. He had passed through many villages and saw the euphoria of families reunited. Standing with his bag over a bony shoulder watching the mothers crying and sons hoisted up on the shoulders of fathers and beaming uncles. His stride would quicken and his heart would lighten.

"He knocked loudly on the door that he knew so well, and his mouth was dry with the excitement of his journey's end. The door opened and a strange woman stood there, illuminated by the lamplight behind her. An unfamiliar man came to join her and placed his warm palm comfortingly on her shoulder. The three stood in silence for many seconds as heavy as tombstones. The couple had lived in quiet dread of this very event and shared a secret unspoken hope that the war had washed away this sad speck from their vision of a loving future. They were newly weds, after all. And had planned a family to fill the home with happy children running freely from room to room. No place for a war weary veteran in his twenties, face etched with the lines of his ardors. They took him inside, gave him a warm meal, a bath and made a bed for him in the shed, amongst the poorly packed boxes of his belongings which had rotted and glistened with spider colonies. The nurse presented him with a suitcase containing photographs, memorabilia and a copy of his father's will. The money that was left to him would not make him a rich man, and was certainly insufficient for the purchase of a new home.

"Grandfather looked out of the dewy window of the shed and watched the couple in the house sitting around the table, talking earnestly. He lay down on the crumpled bedding and stared unblinkingly into the murk of the night that hung damply above him. He felt a thousand years old and wished that he been born in another time, in another place. The next day he sorted through his meagre belongings and bade the couple farewell, and once again set out into the world. He found a student's garret in the town and became an apprentice carpenter to a generous man who took pity upon this orphan. What other family he may have had, was scattered across the

Republic and these had little time for an odd appendage that by all rights, should have remained but an inscription on a war memorial, along with all the countless others that sank into foreign soils. His benefactor had a young daughter whom the veteran shyly courted. They grew very attached to each other and marriage was announced.

"The wise carpenter offered grandfather a choice of wedding gifts. He offered to build the couple a house, or preferably, would give the apprentice an equal share in the business. The young man, beset by his long travails and homelessness, chose the former. His father in law rebuffed him for being a fool with such near vision. The factory was humming with orders, the country was being rebuilt. Profits from the shares would have guaranteed twenty such homes and would have benefited them all. He suddenly saw that fear controlled the boy, despised him for his frantic desire for a home, scorned at the myopia that kept him stunted and small. A cur's need for shelter. The father in law thereafter shunned the young veteran, and spoke of him only with contempt. The house was built, the couple moved in. Your father was born there.

"Grandfather grew ever increasingly reclusive and eventually refused to leave the house at all. Grandmother clung feverishly to her religion and spent much of her free time on her knees on the stone floor of the church, coming home to cook and to clean the home in which the windows were never open. Their child, your father, became asthmatic in those airless rooms and coughed quietly, so as not to incur the wrath of the severe man that spent his days gazing out at the world through an eternally dusty window. The grandfather grew as wiry and as twisted as the frost blighted trees in winter.

"Hold on too tight, my Jaro, and your soul will cramp and spirit shrivel. The man stopped living in the world, his wife became a bride of Christ, with their coughing wheezing son a small pale thing in the corner of a dank room. Very little here on earth actually belongs to us. So letting something go should not be that difficult. There are plenty of dreams around the corner, especially when you are young. The country is becoming another version of that small dank space with little light and less warmth for those children locked up in there. I understand his needs and his fears. I'm happy with my lot, sweet boy, with the roosters and with my friend the gout in my bones. I know your spirit, have seen its colours dance in your eyes, and I want you to be free in a place where the people prosper and never mysteriously disappear from their homes, never to be heard of again." She stood up, exhausted by the story and the emotions that clawed their way into her voice. I trailed home after her, envying the grass and the trees and the forests their apparent nonchalant permanence.

o o o

Chapter Seventeen

Goat Milk and Honey

Sabrina and I sat on the broken couch in the garden, watching the swallows dive and dart high in the summer skies above us. A rooster ran out and pecked at a worm. "The young man made many a nocturnal visit to the chamber of the princess," she began, and I sat up, hungry for the words, "and the whole town was astonished by the herder's success. The bodies that turned in the fetid breeze outside of the castle were taken down and buried. The dogs that lurked around, awaiting a chance dropping of flesh, wandered off and continued their scavenging elsewhere. Each day a messenger would knock on the door of the inn, and present our hero with a new courteously worded summons to visit the princess, as well as a gold coin with which to ease the day's travails. Our hero avoided the pitfalls of pride. He was nervous of the praise that was bestowed upon him whenever he wandered through the town. Old men nodded encouragement to him from doorways, young men raised their glasses to him when he strolled past a drinking tavern. He avoided invitations and enjoyed the sanctuary of the hills that surrounded the city, walking briskly through the shadowy groves, taking delight in the sweet air that cleared his mind and stilled his heart.

"He felt like a man on an invisible tightrope treading a path between hope and desire, with the abyss of failure hungry for a misplaced step. He would arrive at the castle and be welcomed in by all that he encountered, yet he was wary of the rarefied atmosphere that could easily turn a young herder's head. Instead he remained humble yet strong in his resolution to nurture the princess with his simple tales of beauty and of nature. Her sweet laughter and bright, excited eyes were the grail of his true quest. And he was thus greatly rewarded, for she found her own wings in the tales that he told and her heart fluttered warmly at the very mention of his name.

"Like two violins pitched to the same note, their music was both seamless and graceful. There was however an unseen jarring note in the hidden orchestra that surrounded them. The Minister of the Interior was a man, serpentine of tongue, that had found great favour with the King. He had devoted many sleepless nights to insidious schemes that would poisonously propel him towards seizing greater power within the kingdom. He silently cursed any suitor that was presented before the princess, and rejoiced when the hangman was summoned to terminate the poor match. The Minister surrounded himself with spies that peered into every crevice of the kingdom, seeking out any information with which he could embellish his formidable reputation of being the King's eyes and ears. He was trusted completely and was never too far from the royal side, advising here and correcting there. Stealthy as a vine that encircles a great tree, his grip over the King's decisions grew stronger with each passing day.

"The aging Royal Highness was prone to bouts of laziness and was relieved to shed some of the responsibility of running the kingdom, allowing him to spend more time in leisurely pursuits. He loved card games and many joyous hours were devoted in the pursuit of this harmless pastime. Harmless to himself, perchance but not without a cost. The Minister was feared and revered both in the kingdom and beyond the borders. Very few men had the temerity to suggest that he was a manipulative schemer and those that did met with deeply unhappy consequences. He had tried his moribund charms upon the King's daughter but those served to merely entrench her introspection. His medals and reputation meant little to her, whose mind was full of bright rainbows and deep mountain pools. To her he was purely a bright-eyed gargoyle that wished to steal her playtime. Another tedious adult, locked into a linear world of power and soul bargaining. The man reeked of aspiration and slimed with insincerity, frog like in his exudate of unimpressive charm and shallow bluster. Another man steeped in sour self-celebration, she scorned his intrusions upon her life. The spies whispered their news to him.

"The goat herder was hypnotizing the vulnerable princess. Others maintained that they saw him pouring unscrupulous vials of mind altering substances into her tea while seducing her with a mixture of gibberish and peasant folklore. One saw him dressed as a goat, on all fours in her chamber. They all laughed at that story. A wolf in goat's clothing, that may have had bewitched the young girl's imagination. There were many in the King's court that keenly believed that the goat herder's success with the previously icy maiden was the result of dark alchemy and necromancer's skills. The Minister read and reread the shadowy reports from the ghostly men that spied upon the couple. He was perturbed by their vague and innocent content, and he frowned with frustration at the description of the pair as they sat, faces almost touching in the warm amber glow of her candlelit room, murmuring softly. The spies scrawled notes about the nocturnal walks through the royal gardens, where the herder and the princess ambled through the fragrant foliage, their laughter a mutual caress. There was even a rumour of a midnight kiss, but that was reported by a near blind and ancient butler and could not be substantiated. Troubling news for the Minister. The spies reports were but a paltry meal for his appetite for deceit and clandestine behaviour. He would not tolerate another schemer at the trough and decided to verify for himself the true extent of the insidious nature of the young man's charm upon the princess.

"The King in the meantime welcomed the changes that had become so visibly apparent in his daughter's demeanor, the spirited laughter at their dinner table, the blushes that flowered upon her skin when quizzed about her new companion. It was as though spring had entered her soul, and the girl had emerged from a cold cave to blink and smile at the sun. She held her father's hand during musical recitals, and wove him a crown of flowers for his birthday, parading him before the lords and ladies, as they gathered in applause. She had begun to groom herself in a manner that stirred the scrutiny of the spies that hovered as insipid as flies in the background. Her hair, previously a tightly wound mound of gold that lay hidden under severe covers, was now released across her bare shoulders and glittered as she danced around her father. The King was pleased. She gathered flowers by the armload and her rooms glowed with their colours. The King grumbled mildly about the bees that occasionally hummed in to rejoice in the perfumed glory, but quickly withdrew his censure lest she relapse into morose shades, and another body would have to be provided as a sacrifice to her fickle nature. She merely laughed away his fears and he then knew that her joy had roots deeper than those of her sorrows.

"The Minister decided to personally verify his misgivings. He had a natural tendency towards mistrust and suspicion, and thus was determined to observe the young couple at play, through his own eyes. One evening, he dismissed all the staff attendant to the princess, and the instant that the young herder was received into her delighted company he positioned himself at the keyhole of her chambers. Kneeling down on the hard polished floor of the hall, he peered, as unblinking as a snake through the tiny aperture. And there he knelt for hours, the couple upon occasion flitting into his limited view, followed by agonizing long moments of gazing at an unoccupied couch. The cruel wind blew through the keyhole torturing his lone stare with its cold breath. The Princess walked past his lurk hole and he became mesmerized by the curvature of her calf, savoring the sight of the ladder in her right stocking, he strained to hear their soft whispers and forced his ear close against the wood of the door. There followed a long period of silence from the room, and his knees began to shake under his frozen weight. At last, he caught a glimpse of the young man, deeply flushed and smiling, followed by the demure princess. The Minister was perplexed, for the ladder that flawed the right stocking, had miraculously moved to the left leg of the maiden.

Unconsciously he shook his greying head, "Why did the minx change her stockings?" he asked himself, forgetting that the world turns ever onwards and lovers grasp time by the lapels, lest it leaves them stranded and alone with regret.

"That is how it was and always will be, my gentle boy," murmured Sabrina, and I gulped and with a pink blush looked away, dimly aware of the veiled substance of her words. She squeezed my hand tightly, and continued.

"The door opened and the weary Minister quickly leapt behind the cover of a heavy curtain. He stood there listening to the soft yet unmistakable sound of lovers in a farewell kiss. He closed his eyes as the goat herder's footsteps approached the curtain and passed by. The princess closed her chamber door and the castle lay in silence, like a sullen ship moored in cold black sea. Beset by an almost nameless panic, the Minister of the Interior ran to the safety of his own bed. Staring up at the ceiling as he lay on the covers, he resolved to end the happy union that had so tainted his own joy.

"Ambition can carve out a man's heart, dear Jaro. Evil is sometimes the only friend of the friendless and as he lay there, our minister suddenly experienced a surge of calm. In the loft high above his chamber, a castle owl shifted uneasily on his perch, clicking its beak at the dank night air." Sabrina's face took on a cadaverous tinge in the dim light of the candle, and I shuddered with delightful dread at the outcome of this intrigue.

o o o

Chapter Eighteen

The First Invasion

It was 1938 and my father was a freckled seven year old. The nation gathered around their radios, bewildered as the almost apologetic voice of the announcer informed them that the government had successfully ceded a fraction of the disputed north west region to Nazi Germany. A small price to pay for peace in a time when war appeared unavoidable. The army stood by as frustrated as watch dogs locked in the cellar whilst the house is burgled. The German troops marched into the towns and villages, singing and saluting. The Swastika fluttered gaily outside government buildings, churches and schools, the bent cross of our protectors announcing the birth of a new faith.

A great parade was held in the central square of our small town to welcome the peace bringers. Children were scrubbed and mothers sewed pink and white flowers into the young girls' hair. Shoes were polished. Everyone was given a little flag to wave. People lined the streets and children red-cheeked with excitement held gaily coloured balloons. The mayor and his entourage doddered onto a hastily constructed platform and a brass band stood nervously by. The school master kept his lizard eyes focused on the boys and girls that formed the front rows flanking the dusty streets, the cobbles glowing dull in the sunlight. A clown on a unicycle juggled past the mayor but was soon apprehended by an unsmiling policeman. The parade was a serious matter, the celebration of two great nations working together in harmony. There was little place for a painted fool. The local priest preened in his purple embroidery, surrounded by the black garbed old women that formed the core of his parish.

Most of the crowd stood around. Politely silent, yet there was a leaden undercurrent of tension and the occasional laughter was pitched high with unease. The sombre sound stilled the crowd, and in the distance they could hear the roar of the engines and the whinnies of excited horses approaching the village square. The German troops had arrived, hard faced men with muddy goggles on motorcycles leading the body of the goose-stepping soldiers that marched around the corner, with cavalry flanking the formidable spectacle. The band launched into a frenetic version of a popular polka whilst the bell ringer tolled the bells as though the second coming was being heralded. The loudspeakers upon the telephone poles screeched into life and blurted out a cacophonous rendition of "Deutschland uber Alles", that swamped all the other sounds competing for the tender ears of the assembled. Babies cried and mothers glared. Chained dogs barked and howled out their frustrations. The crowd cheered, the mayor and the priest puffed out their chests and the children waved their flags frantically at the troops, and at each other.

There were those in the gathering that turned away in disgust. The police diligently noted the names of these unpatriotic individuals for future referencing. The flowers rained down on the proud soldiers who came to protect a small country from the dangers of the world. The clown man, now washed clean of his amusing persona stood in the shelter of an oak tree, a small colourful flag lay in the dust at his feet. The schoolmaster had given the children strict instructions regarding their behaviour during the parade. The girls were to wave and laugh and to throw flowers into the air. The boys would doff their caps and cheer quietly and with sincerity. Tomfoolery and overt displays of apathy would not be tolerated.

Father watched the steely-eyed soldiers with an almost mesmerized fascination. The dignity of their posture, allied with the sound of boots crashing in unison upon the stones, elevated him into a state of trembling euphoria. The roar of the motorcycles, the jangle of stirrups and snort of the cavalry horses became an avalanche of sound that he had not heard before. He stood there, a small town boy, transfixed and gaping. He was mindless of the hissed entreaties of those around him, urging him to remove his cap. All the other boys had obeyed the much emphasized instruction. Following an urgently whispered prompt, the school teacher pushed his way through the throng towards the errant child. He was too late. A motorcycle ground to an angry halt by the boy. The tall officer stepped briskly from the side-car, and with a crane like movement strode purposefully towards the child. Father looked up and he noticed the lightning bolt insignia on the man's lapel a second before the officer's fist struck him in the face. He fell over as though pole axed, and lay in the dirt bleeding from mouth and nose. The schoolmaster stopped in his tracks, fearful of helping the shocked crumpled boy, lying dazed in the dirt. Two adults stepped out from the sea of silent faces and carried him home. He lay there for a day, his mother crying and praying over him whilst his father dreaded the knock on the door.

The protectors failed in their promise of bringing peace to a small country. Six years later the town was bombed by day by American airplanes and by the British at night. Every night the family would enter the shelter, Father clutching a biscuit tin that contained his birth certificate, a block of gingerbread and a toy plane. Walking to the shelter one night with his mother urging him to hurry as the sirens howled out their guttural mad animal sounds, a bomb exploded some distance away.

Throughout the downpour of mud and splinters he huddled in a doorway, watched in horror as his mother lay on the ground, embracing a street lamp, her clothing being stripped off her body by the shock wave that raged around them. Her stockings and shoes flew off, blown away by an invisible heat wave into the night. Shaking the dust out of her matted hair, she grabbed his hand and they ran laughing wildly to the safety of the shelter. There she knelt and prayed all night, shivering under a rough blanket mumbling garbled words through a cracked smile. He sat next to her as she mouthed her incantations and it was as though she had shrunk to the size of a child.

The war had turned against the proud men that had once marched into the village. The Russian army arrived from the east, grimy men in brown uniforms with tired bearded faces that were flushed with the heat of fear and of victory. A German soldier ran, pursued by his enemies, frantically down Father's road, screaming his pleas, beating on doors that locked the instant that he touched them. White faces at the curtains watching him as he struggled with the door handles, fists hammering on the wood. He died, shot through the body, hanging onto an ornate door knocker a few houses from where Father and his family crowded around their windows, silent spectres at a young man's death.

The park across the road from where the family lived contained a small cemetery that had stood forlorn and mushroom-rich for decades. Old tombstones that were weathered to exhaustion, barely proclaimed their legends. The Germans used these to build a sturdy bunker and dug themselves in, determined to fight to the last man and the last bullet. The Soviet forces merely surrounded the torn park, and leisurely let a rain of cannon shells fall upon the dugout. The craters remained there for years thereafter, forming dwarf lakes during the rainy seasons in which frogs hopped and birds hunted.

The forests and fields were littered with discarded arms and munitions. During an especially dull science lesson, my father fell asleep at his desk and a few live rounds fell from his pockets. With a voice as tight as a bear trap, the master ordered all the boys to empty out their bags upon the floor. The boys reluctantly poured out the contents of their bags. Flares, bayonets and sundry death dealing devices lay heaped guiltily upon the polished wood. The ancient master, green with dread, sweated as he tenderly tied a piece of string around the fin of a mortar shell and the young faces glowed with subdued mirth as he gingerly crept out with the charge dangling gaily from his trembling grasp. Old yet brave, the teacher quietly deposited the device in the school yard and the army bomb disposal squad was alerted. Three drunken soldiers arrived and waved at the children who had by then been evacuated to the nearby football field. They all waved back. A vodka sodden bunch, they quickly removed the fuse and threw the empty shell towards the saucer eyed gathering, who ran away shrieking with laughter in all directions. The school master ground his teeth and cracked his knuckles with irritability. With a final pantomime courtesy the Russian soldiers staggered off, singing into the distance. Sad songs from home, maudlin yet beautiful, the notes floated across the village.

o   o   o

Chapter Nineteen

The Wisdom of Retreat

Father called us into the study. We all followed, in a funereal procession fashion, Mother leading the way, Sabrina huddling behind her, with myself following, the dachshund on my trail, claws clicking on the carpet. Hollow-eyed adults avoided looking at me as we sat waiting for the inevitable announcement. We had observed the coagulation of his resolve, listened to his angry words, felt his partisan spirit gnawing at his intestines. There were too many nights disturbed by the loud debates that, plum brandy fuelled, emanated from the kitchen where his friends gathered.

Mother occupied herself by helping me with my school work during these occasions, slamming doors to isolate ourselves from the cacophony born of men in dissent. Father spoke with deep gravity and for those moments, he became the epitome of pure yet tragic reason. He had managed, at no little expense and after much tribulation, to obtain permits from a very skittish governmental potentate, allowing the immediate family a five day visa, which would allow us to cross the border into Austria, and ostensibly to visit our distant cousins. A unique opportunity, he said, completely at odds with the times. The border was becoming a cage for the people, and we had been blessed with a temporary key to the outside world. Many others had tried to leave, by illegal and arduous means. Rumours of failed escapes were abundant. Tales of imprisonment, of nocturnal shooting of families crossing forests and frozen lakes to reach the legendary safety of the West were gleefully circulated by those that embraced the invasion, seeking to find favour with the new authorities.

Sabrina squeezed my leg under the table. I looked at her but she was staring, pale and hazy at the plate before her.

Mother sat there with her hands in her lap, her face a marble carving of pain. I had to promise to keep the news of our little holiday abroad a secret. I was not to mention anything about our plans to anybody.There were jealous people everywhere who would seek to sabotage our quest for freedom. Father stood over me like a gargoyle over an entrance. "Not a word, nor a bleat to your girlfriends. Act mute, be dumb. It will be over soon." I nodded, tears swirling up from some deep cold well inside me. He moved towards me. Placed his fist under my nose. "The graveyard," I said, before he had a chance to ask me, "I smell the grave." He turned away from me, disappointed that I had side stepped the old, favourite game.

"We leave in ten days," he said, "I've already sent word to Cousin Gerhard in Austria. He's expecting us, and will make us welcome for as long as we need to stay there."

He ruffled my hair and reading the dark page that was my mother's profile, he left the room. We listened to him playing his now illegal jazz records, and the dusk grew around us like a web spun by a frantic spider.

But of course, I told everybody about the plans. Excited Jaro whispered the news to his friends at school. The big blue eyed refugee to be, told all to the grocer who gave me marbles and candy so often that I considered him a true friend and confidant. I had a secret and I wanted to share it, lest it burnt a hole through my chest in its mad desire for air.

Chapter Twenty

The Retreat of Wisdom

"The world is wide, my Jaro," Sabrina sighed, as she knitted one of the many jerseys that I would never wear, her penchant for wide stripes unnerved me and I was forever teased by brutish boys for resembling a skinny bumble bee, "yet it is full of eyes that watch you. Some glint with envy, while others, if you are fortunate, shine with shy love." I huddled nearer, the knitting needles making the sound of a distant train on leaden tracks. "Those with love, my dear, stay at home and create more heat, and those with no love seek revenge, in the pubs, in the street," she sang melodically, and I suppressed a shudder that ran cold and frog like up from my stomach and into my heart.

I thought of her dead husband, daily christened with the contents of chamber pots, and of Otto, haloed in the cigarette smoke of a late night dive. I blinked and looked into an imaginary distance. The needles continued their debate in our silence.

"The Minister kept a nightly vigil at the keyhole, red eyes watering with the dusty draught that teased his ducts. The young goat herder no longer kept a reverent distance from the royal maiden. Upon his arrival she would embrace him, resting her delicate face in the warm crook of his neck, while his hands squeezed her hips. The couple would whisper away the hours, their words punctuated by soft kisses or they would on occasion, disappear from his fetid view as though sensing a foreign presence on the fringe of their love.

"These occasions grew more common with time, and the frustration of the Minister reached new heights, for what is a Minister of the Interior without information with which to scheme and plot? Akin to a spider that has lost his ability to spin a sticky web, our bleary eyed spy seethed with resentment. His imagination, severely limited to matters of political power, was myopic to the matters of the heart. He had to act quickly, before the lovers could find the courage of their convictions and announce their devotion to a public that already sweated with rumours concerning the frequent nocturnal liaisons between the herder and the angelic princess. He summoned his legions of spies and constructed a huge, venom dipped portfolio describing the malodorous activity that had ripened under the King's trusting nose.

"The royal one was happily engrossed in a game of canasta when the Minister's messenger delivered him the envelope, stamped with the seal of the Minister of the Interior. With a ring bedecked hand he whisked away the servant, for the game had recently turned in his favour. But the encounter had bewitched his fortune and he lost resoundingly soon thereafter. In a black mood, he had the Minister summoned to the royal court. The man entered in a lupine manner, which served merely to heighten the King's displeasure. He shifted his regal rump and snappishly commanded the Minister to begin his report. Veiled in a tone of deep concern for the safety of the princess, the litany of denunciations against the young herder froze the hearts of the assembly. For a moment the clock on the wall appeared to still its ticking. The King sat rigid in his chair, and then slumped into a shrunken version of himself.

"The Minister droned on tirelessly, excited by the effect that his words had upon the old man in the golden chair. He read from numerous documents provided by his vigilant invisible army. Reports of magical potions poured into the wine, tales of pagan exercises that the young man practised in the gullible safety of his room at the inn. The innkeeper had signed a statement indicating that our hero had boasted of having infernal powers that had helped him to capture the virgin heart of the princess. Infernal forces were at work within the sacred confines of the castle. A young necromancer reeking of goat had almost achieved that which foreign armies had failed to do over the millennia, roared the Minister, apparently inflamed by the gravity of his accusations. The odious seizure of power from the King through the shadowy entrapment of a young girl's heart. Perchance, whispered the Minister to his trembling audience, the herder had been trained in alchemy and trickery by the enemies of the state, by foreign powers that coveted the throne. The gathering was transfixed with the potency of these allegations, delivered with such gusto and sincerity by a trusted minister. A father's tear dropped from the King's eye and disappeared in the ermine that cloaked his tired frame. The crowd sighed out in sympathy. Already servants were disappearing through hidden doors to spread the news throughout the town.

"The King stood up. The Minister and the crowd grew silent. Up above them, in her chamber, the princess felt a stab that went through her heart. She looked into the mirror, at her reflection that drowned in a cold pool of glass. With the vulpine Minister hovering close at hand, the King struck his cane three times on the heartless floor. The assembly quivered, as tense as dogs on the track anticipating the appearance of the rabbit. In a tone that reminded the crowd of his warrior past, the King roared for the immediate arrest of the young man, who had dared to abuse the sacred trust that had been bestowed upon him. The Minister dutifully clapped his hands. Unsmiling minions slipped as deft as daggers out of the hall.

"The innkeeper heard the pounding of the fists upon the door and had hardly the time to croak out his displeasure at the sudden throng that heaved in through the sleepy afternoon haze and trampled up the staircase, to descend noisily moments later with their astonished prize wrestling in their grasp. No explanation was given as the sweaty and leering mob laughingly dragged our ashen-faced hero away. To be forced brutishly into the same royal carriage that had so seductively swayed with him to his lover's side, crushed between two burly captors, his blood ran cold with dread. The images of hanged men, faces grotesquely discoloured, slowly turning on the end of ropes paraded through his imagination.

The coachman lashed at the foaming horses with an unholy zeal. Outside the cab, the throng of yokels stamped their feet and flushed with savage excitement, guzzling deeply from a bottle of brandy that was doing the rounds.

"It is a sad thing to see goodwill evaporate so easily, my Jaro. And it occurred to our beloved goat man, that he was doomed. The greatest dread that coiled so coldly through his innards, came from a growing realization that he had misjudged the human spirit. That delicacy and discretion could be so readily be rewarded by derision and brutality. The animal's hooves spat sparks upon the cobbles and the townsfolk crossed themselves as the carriage swayed towards the cloud cloaked castle that overshadowed them all."

Sabrina threw a log onto the fire. It lay there, hissing like a snake, steam crawling from its pores. I felt a surge of nausea and oddly, for the first time since the story began, felt a desperate need to seek the warmth and comfort of my bed. I resisted the temptation to voice my desires, for I could see that Aunt Sabrina needed to continue the tale. And continue she did.

Chapter Twenty-one

The Fall

In the days that followed the one man conference, there grew a morass of tension between my parents. I fell asleep to the sound of their voices merging into a sea of mutual recrimination, waves that broke with poisonous regularity through the thin walls that separated our bedrooms. Mother was fighting for a family, for the prospect of a future surrounded by kin of all ages, gatherings at Christmas, carp armies feeding the smiling lineage. Father preached freedom from domination, a new beginning that opened up the soul and freed the spirit. A place where severe men did not beat small children into the ground for daring to forget the doffing of a cap. The adult voices droned on into the night. I slipped into deep slumber, heavy with the dread of growing up.

The next day began with a tight lipped breakfast, daytime banalities exchanged between the night time adversaries, the air thick with stubborn glances. I picked at my toast as the table was evacuated around me, savoring the blessed silence that lay on an ocean of fear. The grandfather clock chimed mockingly. Father disappeared to seal our fate further, through last moment meetings in the village with the beery faced types that made up his advisers. Mother set about making alphabet soup for lunch.

I went to play with Kamosh, my teddy bear pillow. With the craftily designed pocket on his belly, and an endearing doggy face, Kamosh was both my headrest at night and confidant throughout the day. He would gently absorb the tears of childish rage and my dimmed whispers, listen to my magic prayers for toys and chocolates that I sighed into his scruffy ear. Buttons for eyes in which I loomed, round faced Jaro holding a cloth animal to his cheek, warm closeness against the oddities of the world that shook a silent fist at our lives.

The soup was ready and Mother and I sat side by side, the huge tureen steaming merrily before us, the kitchen filled with the aroma of the boiled alphabet. The kitchen table was nestled beside the open window, through which the summer sun streamed onto the gaily coloured tablecloth. We waited for Father to come home for lunch and soon he appeared, passing by the window which was at chest level to the floor. We waved at him merrily, impatient to dine. He entered with a scowl, face like murder. Mother stood up and he steered her harshly into the privacy of the lounge. Enraged he growled and stomped around the room, quite wild and buffalo like in his movements. I heard chairs being knocked over in his passion and Mother's voice rising, a lament for peace.

My name kept on reappearing in the rant that came through the walls. I could barely make out what was being said, and nervously ladled out a soothing lake of soup onto my plate, but was too agitated to eat it. Mother was begging him to forgive me, to remember that I was merely a six year old child, living in a crazy place. Apparently, someone in the village had asked him about the impending escape. The secret cat let out of the family bag by the idiot son who now sat staring at mad writing in his soup. A condemned man on death row waiting for the sounds of feet to stop outside my fatal door. I shuddered, silently cursing my wild tongue that had unleashed this avalanche of anger upon us. I looked outside. A sparrow was idly pecking at a straw. A sleepy dachshund lay in the shadow of the work shed, pink belly flecked with white. The heat shimmered off the metal of my push bike. Little evidence of craziness inside. The plate steamed pleasantly up to my nostrils.

The door flew open and Father stormed out, forehead bulging with veins. Mother followed him, imploring him to be reasonable. And me, attempting nonchalance whilst my heart toad hopped in my throat. He did not look at me as he strode out, and I let the air sigh out of my curdled lungs. Grateful for this narrow and almost miraculous escape from his pitch black wrath. He slammed the door as he stormed outside and I ducked my head nervously as he passed the window. He paused for a microsecond and reached out, grabbed my hair and pushed my face into the broth that has sat steaming so innocently before me. The painfull oily heat of the soup and the shock of his violence seared my senses, and he quickly released me as I gasped and Mother screamed. I looked up, hot soup running from my nose and hair. Alien words forming from the jumbled alphabet that clung to my cheeks and chin. He was gone. Mother scrubbed my hair under a jet of hot water. Washed and dried, I spent the afternoon lying next to her on a blanket in the garden, Kamosh soothing my pale face. I whispered my apologies and she held me, her breathing a song in which all kind words were born. There was little to say. The garden hummed and hissed its summer freedom.

Time passed painfully. He came home late that night. The scrawny sound of the gate. The lurching footsteps in the corridor for us all to pretend to ignore. Father the dubious chauffeur at the wheel of our lives. We were crossing the Styx with a blind oarsman at the helm. The clock ticked with a malaised tock. Kamosh is an archaic word for friend. And God knows that I needed one of those at that time. The dachshund at my feet in the bed, faithful toy at my side, the house see-sawed me to sleep that night. I never ate alphabet soup thereafter. The oddly distributed vowels and consonants conspired to unnerve me. It's funny how small things can grow up to become monsters. Sabrina often said that in a perfect world, that phenomenon would be constantly inverted.

o o o

Chapter Twenty-two

A Meeting of Gentlemen

"The musty carriage rolled on, the wood moaning alongside the sounds of the wild gallop of the mad eyed horses. Towards the castle that no longer seemed to hold the city within its cradle, but rather stood sentinel over youthful joy. With a final whip crack, the prison on wheels sparked to a halt outside the looming gates. The rattling of keys, the strident calls of the sentries heralded the end of the road for the young man, whose goat herding days now seemed a lifespan away. The carriage doors were flung open. Rough hands reached in and our hero was heaved out, to stand staring at the grinning servants, some holding burning lanterns, who mock saluted him, bowing down in the regal fashion. Dirty hands dragged him along the corridors to the hall, golden in the candlelight, yet dank with hateful eyes.

"The King sat as though carved out of a very heavy stone, white knuckles gleaming with rings that glowed like hot coals. As did his eyes. Pushed forward into the half moon circle of bodies that formed around the throne, our hero desperately searched the mass of faces for a glimpse of the princess. There was no trace of her on such a cruel night for lovers. She was not far from him, but sat, forsaken and listless, locked in her room with a menacing matron that stood guard in the corridor outside. Her toys and pillows, etched with images of fables, no longer called to her imagination. Love shouted in her breast and she feared for his safety with a dull ache that threatened her sanity. Strange sounds and coarse crowd noises emanated dully from halls beneath her feet. She paced the floor, to and fro. The movement did little to still her fears. She ached to smell his hair, to drown in the aroma of the goat that persistently clung to him. No matter how many times they had bathed together."

I let out a sigh like the meow of a tiny cat buried in a blanket. Sabrina laughed out, a kindly and gnarled sound. She put the end of her finger to my nose and pushed it gently. I grinned, blushing my young man's shame.

"Yes, and soaped each other with exotic oil from the East, my nervous Jaro." I scowled at her satire, but she merely chuckled and continued, stroking the nape of my neck.

"The King raised himself up from the throne, with a creak of bones and clink of metal. The audience moved back as a wave retreats from the pebbly shore in winter. The Minister of the Interior drank in the moment. 'According to evidence from reliable sources, you have, young sir, apparently both deceived me as a father and and as your king, and bewitched my gentle daughter. I have heard countless tales of your devious practices whereby through the application of some foul and foreign necromancy you have managed to ensnare the gullible heart of such a sweet maiden. I have hung men who failed to bring forth her warmth and laughter, and yet I am now faced with a serpent that hatches plans to usurp me from the throne. My minister suspects that you have been sent here by my enemies. Little is known of you. You lack noble lineage and there are doubts as to the quality of your origins. And verily, I have not seen a girl of noble standing to be so smitten by the charms of a yokel. I grieve that her happiness was so unscrupulously obtained. I am thus left with a sad decision. And have deliberated this at length with my most trusted of Ministers. Your execution will remove all doubt as to your intentions, the nation will breathe a sigh of relief that the threat to the peaceful glory of this land has been removed. Better safe than sorry, as they say. God will forgive me if I am wrong, for it is for the people of this land that I make such a sacrifice. The young noblemen that adorned the castle tenements with their bodies were at least trusted members of this community, whose families were made noteworthy by their allegiance to the King and to the Throne. You, sir, have proven to be a risk and I have no evidence before me, apart from the blind love of a naïve girl, that speaks of your innocence in the face of these accusations. For the good of the land, you will be publicly executed tomorrow at dawn. By beheading. A scarlet message to all those that seek to plot against us. Take him away. I need to grieve for my daughter's anguish in this sorry hour, a cruel joke played upon the most fragile of souls. I had hoped for a happy ending.'

"There was a hushed silence and many of those assembled exchanged worried glances. They were not aware of any threat to their kingdom. The last war ended an almost a century ago, and the neighbouring countries bore them little malice. Trade was brisk and foreigners were welcome. Deep frowns deepened as the young man was dragged away to a cobweb lined dungeon far beneath the carpeted floors of the hall.

"The King brushed away his retinue and walked away, solemn and alone, head bowed with the crushing magnitude of breaking the news to his daughter. Behind him, the Minister held his breath like a child opening a grand gift at Christmas. The princess shrank in her chair. Her father was astonished to see her crumple so completely. She put her head into her hands that were blue with veins, old woman's hands. He stood over her in silence. She hunched over in her seat and did not move. The dust hung dead in the candlelight. The very marrow of life was sucked from the room and for a cold moment the King imagined that his was the only heart that beat within the room. He no longer felt noble. Nor wise. Nor did he feel proud of his lineage. Doubts smouldered in his mind. He was frozen helpless in the winter of her pain.

She slowly removed her hands, but kept her head bowed and he was shocked to see her wide mouth stuck in a scream from which no release was possible. Strands of saliva quietly dropped onto her knees as she attempted to make a sound, her face pink with anguish. Horrified, he reeled backwards, turning away from this vision of utter grief. He felt cursed by the gods, his mind an icy mist. All that was real, in amongst all the previously mighty proclamations and poisonous rumours, was the picture of a young girl that sat like a broken doll in the oversized chair, her lips ashen white, withholding a thousand suppressed screams. Hopeless. Wifeless. The King quietly retreated from the room, calling for the royal doctor. A powerful tranquillizer would surely defang the wolves that threatened to devour the princess from within.

"A knock at the door made him start. The Minister peered in, mumbling words of consolation, cautioning against the weakness of vacillation. An example must be made of the young upstart, he warned. The people needed a king that dealt with threats in a firm and unyielding fashion, a ruler resolute and consistent in his decrees. Cruel duty bound every father, he whispered. The King, pale with rage, threw a chamber pot at him, bellowing for him to leave his sight. The Minister smiled politely and left the old man to dance with his demons."

Sabrina paused and pushed a bowl of radishes towards me. I held one up to the flickering candlelight, noticing the rooster peck marks that scoured into the pink red skin. Biting into the seemingly innocent offering, I winced at the blue and white heat that suddenly turned my young mouth into a quiet furnace. Not many radishes survived the ceaseless gluttony of the birds that even fought over mice carcasses long dried out by the sun. I tended to avoid eating this vegetable when visiting Sabrina. The biggest and wildly radishes sprouted proudly around the edges of her husband's grave. Enjoying a robust diet from below the soil, allied with the daily irrigation courtesy of Sabrina's gleefully full chamber pot, they glowed with an almost unnatural heat. As though the mischievous widow was being punished for her disrespect to the dead by the abundance of this malicious crop. Determined to triumph upon this culinary revenge from beyond earthly realms, Sabrina used whatever radish survived the beaks of the roosters, in a huge array of inventive dishes. Their rampant heat that sang from the depths of salads and hid under the innocent surfaces of stews always surprised me with its ferocity. The foul vegetable would appear within the most simple of snacks, but I was too polite to refuse such offerings, for fear of isolating her in the apparent feud between the living and the dead. I manfully swallowed mouthfuls of the infernal morsel and quietly prayed for an insect infestation or other blights that would decimate the angry legions sent to torment us. Sadly, while the plums fell fat and blue with mildew to the garden floor, and the pears hummed with hungry wasps, the radishes shone with an almost violent health.

"Our hero sat within the depths of the castle dungeon," she continued, watching my brave attempts to hide my fiery discomfort. "Confused and frightened. He had barely heard of the Minister of The Interior, and racked his exhausted brains for any causes that may have led him to this sorry fate. The love that he felt for the princess must have surely clouded his senses in terms of court etiquette, he surmised. The joyful times that he had shared with the beautiful Princess now seemed to conspire to his downfall. His tales of the wild prankster goats surely contained little threat to such a mighty kingdom with its spires and spies. The heartland that the two young people built up together and shared was not a foreign army at the castle gates. It was not even a pebble thrown at a palace window, for in its purity it was lighter than air; a balm of a song that old men reminisced sweetly about, when the fires crackled low. The herder frowned, his soul heavy with dread and dismay. None of the events of the day made any sense. The King's sudden wrath hung over him like a curse. Upstairs the old man paced, tearing at his beard. A father slowly boiled in the waters of doubt. He glanced at the Bible, a small monolith of leather and gold, lying dusty on a distant table. He looked away quickly. He was beyond the solace of ancient wisdom, and feared the words that destined to conspire against his fragile sanity. Truth seemed a slippery thing that night. And peace had left the town. He felt truly alone and damned. His legendary wisdom for which he was universally admired, was a withered husk in the light of his grief.

"Elsewhere in the castle, the burly executioner spat on the whetstone and began the sharpening of the silver blade. Outside the tormented castle walls there slept a town that had seen its fill of death. The Innkeeper knelt and prayed to all the Saints who fought on the side of lovers and to those Angels that lifted up their wings at the sound of the smallest kiss."

o   o   o

Chapter Twenty-three

A Home That Shrank

We stood in the living room, each of us with a large suitcase. Behind us, the grandmothers watched the proceedings grimly. Grandfather could be heard, rasping out a grimy cough, through the walls that separated our worlds from his. Sabrina had the pallor of crematorium ash, her eyes as dark as coal. It was a dilemma. Confronted by room after room of objects, each rich with memories, what to pack into a single container that would accompany the departed into the next world. I had shared a sworn secret with the outside world and as Father so rightly growled, who knew who was watching us now? For me, holding Kamosh under my scrawny arm, the town had overnight, metamorphosed into a creature of a thousand eyes and countless ears. I trembled lightly as I selected the hard wearing trousers, the practical shirts. I packed them tightly as possible, all adults nodding solemn approval.

Mother and father had bigger cases and I envied them their greater freedom of selection. I tried to smuggle in a wooden toy or two but was almost immediately shouted at by all. I had read that on some stars, the density of the matter was so huge, that a matchbox would weigh as much as truck. I was never quite sure if that was a good or a bad thing. It certainly seemed like an uncomfortable place for small people. My suitcase weighed as much as a few matchboxes from the heavy star, but contained nothing more magical than sensible cloth and wise shoes. The excitement of the adventure was rapidly wearing thin, replaced by a menacing realization that life was being condensed into a very small space, star dust dense with history.

The dachshund lay on the Ottoman watching us fumble with our choices. Usually, the animal would be forbidden such a regal perch, but sensing our distraction and being almost obsessively opportunistic, it had wormed its elongated way up onto the soft cushions. It sat there like a sleek Sphinx, willing us to look away, opting for inertia as a cloak of invisibility, the beast deserved applause. And we, finding the moment an oasis of absurdity in a desert of tension, applauded the beast raucously. The sound of our mirth challenged the animal to an even greater attempt at rigour mortis and it stopped breathing for a delicious moment or two, as though the smallest sign of life would render it suddenly visible to our outrage.

"You can almost see it turning blue under its facial hair!" Father roared out, and we fell about laughing wildly and for a few minutes we were free of the gloom of that room.

The beast uncurled its supine length and with the slow stealth of a chameleon stalking a fly, inched down from the couch into a more dignified position beneath the table. All eyes turned to Father. He stood staring at the dachshund for a while and finally sighed "Maybe we can take it with us. The dog's pretty portable and the Austrians love the dachshund. A couple of hours on the train and we're across, and the boy has something to distract him from the toys that he left behind." I hopped around him with joy, hugging him and dancing around with the startled dog wriggling in my embrace like a frisky eel. "Fortunately there are few quarantine laws between the Republic and Austria," added Father for the benefit of the other adults. "The Austrians would always visit us with a dog or two in tow, every summer before the troubles."

I remembered the bovine distant family emerging from their modern vehicles, laughing and embracing us, shiny shopping bags bursting with exotic chocolates, cheeses and aromatic smoked meats. They would spend a week with us, and depart, still smiling fatly, pleased with the crystal glass ornaments that Grandmother pressed into their hands. I never knew how we were related to these large loud people that spoke oddly accented Czech through mouthfuls of garlic salami and gulps of foam beer. They would be waiting for us on the other side of the train journey. I imagined a land where everyone had a triple chin, including the animals, fish and birds. I shuddered at the thought. A Gulliver among the gluttons, I vowed to keep a single chin.

○ ○ ○

Chapter Twenty-four

The Execution of Hope

Sabrina and I stood in the damp cellar, listening to the rain and storm battering the crooked house above us. Serenaded by the lively creaks and the cracks of ancient wood, we fed the fire beneath the great brass still that sat fat and proud, the gleaming heart of the home. Sabrina had a penchant for plum brandy, and I would help her drag baskets of the purple red fruit down the forlorn steps that never saw the sun nor felt the comfort of a scrubbing brush. It was the part of the house that I normally avoided. The fermenting plums released a gas that made my nose run and my head spin. A thick sweet cloud that made me feel as trapped as a fly in heavy jam, drowned in a sugar death pool. Rats, bats and feral cats leapt through my imagination whenever I chanced to peer through the dusty air from my timid position at the top of the stairs. I never ventured in on my own, and would follow Sabrina like a lamb, holding onto the plum basket handle with both hands as we hoisted the fruit into the cauldron cellar.

The fire spat and crackled, the still hissed and throbbed with Pan's own breath, and somewhere in the metal pipes that looped across the floor, a fiery distillate was being born. A soft sneeze above us made me jump up, wide eyed and anxious. Standing in a dripping cluster were the roosters that had somehow found an open window or perhaps a door left ajar, and now stood shivering and peering down into our warmth. I took a step back, fearing their descent. The fluffed up army of birds merely perched on the first three steps and seemed to relish both the heat that wafted up towards them as well as my obvious discomfort. Sabrina threw them a few plums soft with decay and the roosters pecked at these, clucking gratefully yet keeping one communal eye upon us, eternally vigilant. She placed a thick rug near the fire and poured herself a glass of clear white plum spirit, from a supply of bottles that gleamed in the fire light.

The roosters settled sleepy eyed on the cold stairs, small wet bundles whose heads sank into their chests only to jolt awake and glare at us. The rain drummed on the roof, the still hissed and gurgled and Sabrina sipped her brandy most noisily. I felt at peace with the world, and wanted to drown in that moment's bliss.

"The town gathered in the grand courtyard inside the castle. Stern men at arms stood in a wide circle around a make-shift podium. The executioner sat on the heavy stump that had known so much blood, a dark hooded sentinel to the pale rising sun. The crown was quiet and waited morbidly for the royal entourage to appear. The Minister of the Interior combed his wig whilst a man servant sprayed him with a fine mist of eau de cologne.

"'Angel's Tears,' muttered the Minister, reading the ornamental label on the bottle, 'how appropriate.'"

"The ashen faced princess had aged a decade in the throes of one infernal night. Her unnatural tranquility would shatter into jagged sobs that lacerated the hearts of those in attendance. Further medication was called for, and she returned to the passive land of the near dead. They dressed her in black lace, powdered her face into a joyous pink. She looked like a broken string puppet that limped into view of the large mirror that stood cold as a lake, brittle and silent before her. The ladies in waiting stood behind her fearfully, as she gazed into the infinite sadness of her reflection. She slowly pushed a manicured finger nail of her right hand slowly into the softness of her left wrist and gouged a crimson wound into her flesh. The stillness of the room grew ever deeper as she raised her delicate finger to her mouth and blood smeared her pale lips. Behind her a frail maid swooned softly to the floor. They covered the Princess with a blanket and she sat shivering in the pink radiance that announced the rise of the cursed sun.

"The King dressed as though for his own funeral. A man torn between his duty and the clamouring of his heart, he no longer considered himself a man at all. He prayed for a sign that would allow his doubts some solace, for some vision that could dignify his decision. Only the sound of the rats, their tiny claws at work in the hollows of the walls, accompanied his thoughts that day. The noise seemed to emanate from the confines of his head and he found a strange solace in its insistence. An old man distracted from his pain by a small sound in a wall. The kingdom had lost its leader, and a father had lost his heart."

Sabrina paused and we both looked up at the rooster huddle at the top of the stairs. All the birds had lowered their heads in comfortable unison and as though singing for a communal songbook behind their hooded eyes, they clucked and snored in perfect harmony.
Plum brandy drunk the wet feathered army seemed to dream a common dream.

"The King dressed in sombre grey. The Minister stood in attendance outside the royal chamber, face stony with insincere gravity. Inside him a circus of celebration was in full swing. The King emerged and a slow procession began, the group growing as others joined the retinue. He stopped heavily outside the bedroom of the Princess. He nodded sternly and the Captain of the guard knocked on the door. Three gloved, muffled raps and she emerged, eyes as hollow as burnt out houses. The King took a step back with horror at the sight of her sorry countenance and those in the retinue that still clung to their god, crossed themselves hastily. She joined them, a ghost amongst the frightened living and the procession moved silently towards the entrance to the arena where the town folk shivered in the early morning air. He maintained his regal bearing and gracefully greeted his people with a slow bow of his silver head. The crowd sighed as one but there was no applause, for the paleness of the Princess stilled all voices and chilled many hearts of those assembled. On the makeshift stage erected in the centre of the vast arena, the executioner sank to one knee in humble prostration before his sovereign."

Sabrina paused and picked up a lump of coal, tossing it lightly at the nearest drunken rooster, who awoke from his slumber with a splutter. I almost smiled at his consternation. As a stone creates concentric ripples around itself in the stillness of a pond, so too did the roosters rear up, one after the other. They sat up glaring at the old woman that crowed with mirth, craned and cackled like a large bird herself. I was mildly irritated at the Sabrina's prank, for I longed for the appearance of the hero of the story. I realized that Sabrina was gently tweaking all our noses and beaks in the brass golden glow of the cellar that night, so I nudged her with my knee for her to continue. Taking another generous swig of the aromatic spirit she cleared her throat and this time her voice was strong and energized with intent.

"The young man was led into the centre of the arena. His dungeon dull eyes blinked at the spectacle of the townsfolk, gathered in such an unsmiling multitude. The first beam of soft sun sliced through the heavens and struck the golden locks that peeked out from underneath the severe veil with which the Princess had crowned herself that fateful morning. The halo of gold stopped the goat herder in his tracks, and for a moment he thought that he was awaking from a sad dream to hear the comforting clank of the goat bells as the horned beasts grazed around his sleeping form, in the sweet meadows of his youth, that hummed with bees and peace. A rough hand on his shoulder drove him towards the awaiting executioner, who rose to his feet and stood as immovable as the sky, a human bridge between heaven and earth.

Next to him a sword lay upon a table to deliver the mortal blow that would set a reluctant soul free to roam the world. Our hero faltered but his brutish tormentors pushed him onwards, to at last arrive at the callous platform upon which his destiny awaited. Mounting the steps that creaked dismally, he chanced to see the ruddy face of the innkeeper gazing up at him forlornly. Our hero nodded a greeting and the innkeeper turned away, cheeks streaming with tears.

"The Minister of the Interior adjusted his cravat and sighed with pleasure at the tragedy unfolding before him. At a sign from the King, an ermine enrobed judge read out a laborious proclamation, denouncing the youth, appealing to the assembled mass to praise the King for the wisdom that he had shown by removing a viper from the bosom of the kingdom. The goat herder was not given a chance to speak. The King nodded his agreement, head as heavy as a mountain of crosses.

"The Princess sat down and stared deep into the sky, as the young man was pushed to his knees, and the executioner lumbered forward. The boy's head was placed onto the wooden block and held in place by knotted rope attached to metal rungs in the floor. The royal executioner picked up the heavy axe with both hands, raising it above his head in salute to the King. The Minister craned his head eagerly forward, as did the countless others that crowded into the arena on that day. Strengthening his grip upon the weapon, he placed the blade delicately above the young man's neck and drew in a breath in preparation for the swipe.

"Suddenly, the frozen air was torn asunder by a cackle of laughter. A sound that lived somewhere between the braying of a mule and a strident cockerel crow. All eyes turned to behold a merry figure sitting next to a gargoyle on a parapet high above the crowd.
The portly gentleman was garishly attired in a rag tag mixture of colourful cloths and waistcoats, with shoes as curved as Ali Baba's. A magenta scarf mocked the gravity of the events below. He stood up and shouted down at the astonished goat herder, who could barely move his head to view the jester-like creature that leered down at them all.

"So is this how far you have taken this unfortunate fellow, dear Mr. Wisdom," the rotund prankster bayed, "Impressive, yet ultimately sad. Surely an innocent such as our herder deserves a fate slightly more worthy than that of a public chopping block. Methinks it is high time time that you vacated this humble fellow lest even greater misfortunes befall the poor lad. I say, make way for Luck." he mock curtsied gracefully, startling a few pigeons that gazed at him, high on the parapets.

The bemused audience stood, mouths gaping at the sheer lunacy of the apparition that vanished as suddenly as he had appeared. The herder's body arched against his bonds as an anorexic gentleman materialized before the crowd, grinning apologetically to the executioner who grimaced even as he raised the mighty axe quickly and purposefully. The King gripped his cane with white knuckles and the Princess let out a low moan. The sound of the axe handle snapping under the weight of the double blade silenced all sighs. The cruel metal, now free of a lifelong attachment to the wood, spun in a crazy arc through the morning air. To plunge down, deep and true into the head of the Minister of the Interior, slicing him neatly in two angry halves. The crowd paled as the body cleft open and the Minister of the Interior was no more.

"The Princess wailed and sped down from the regal stage, rushed to embrace the supine boy. The former Minister's spies came one by one to stand at the foot of the King and with trembling lips denounced their former master. The evidence against the young man was forged, they admitted, their voices shaking with fear of the King's wrath. With the murderous minister lying in bloody twain, they now felt free to seek absolution from the King. The old man stood, eyes streaming and lower lip a tremble with the overwhelming emotion that, long suppressed, had threatened to explode his heart. His body creaked with hollow bones as he descended from the royal staircase and made his way painfully towards the executioner's podium. He stood over the two young lovers and with the tenderness of a loving father, removed his fur lined cloak and carefully placed it over their bodies shivering in the cruel dew of dawn.

The wild-eyed Luck threw his hat into the air with joy and the entire assembly followed in noisy suit.

"The King was applauded so loudly that even in the far distance the goat herder's father, who was about to start his lonely milking of the frisky beasts, looked up, expecting to see unseasonable thunderclouds gathering on the horizon. Only the twinkle of a fast fading evening star met his rheumy gaze. He smiled to himself, suddenly possessed by a desire to dance in the face of such beauty."

"And the goat herder, what happened to the lovers, Sabrina? Was there a wedding? Did the King share his kingdom with the young man?" I pleaded in the orange glow of the fire. "And whatever happened to Wisdom?" I added.

Sabrina sat staring silently into the fire for a while. The cellar was alive with dancing shadows as the flames flickered under the burnished still. "Wisdom, my young Jaro," she chuckled, "does not do well in public places. He tends to be shunned by and is easily lost in a crowd. He prefers the company of solitary men or small gatherings of thoughtful folk. A glass of red wine may bring him knocking on the door, yet he quickly disappears after an entire bottle has been finished. He's often overlooked when times are bad and shuns the places when men speak loudly. He is most often absent from the podiums of leaders. Luck, on the other hand is less of a fickle friend, he'll embrace the fool with as much gusto as he will dance with an evil doer. He is as comfortable sitting on a dung heap as he is on the throne. Who knows on which door he will knock on next, and why. And as for the happy Princess embracing the fortunate goat herder while the old King looks on, well maybe the story stops there, or it may appear later in another disguise." She stood up and the roosters let out a communal cluck of dismay. They seemed to have found both comfort and peace in the warm orange twilight of the cellar, away from the storm and the wet earth that waited outside.

o o o

Chapter Twenty-five

A Bridge that Divides the Heart

Silver bleak street lights with deathly auras illuminated the dirty snow. The sad little convoy of cars splashed through the mud, glassy with ice crystals. Father had chosen a rural train station for us to embark on our journey into freedom. To avoid the predatory eyes of the city, he morbidly added, when he announced the details of our departure. The convoy stopped and we huddled together in the entrance of the station. Soft snow was melting on our necks and noses. And flecked the red cheeks of Sabrina as she held onto me as though an invisible whirlwind would take me away. And it did.

In his thick shapeless coat Father looked like a grey polar bear as he stood in the pale light, suitcases at his side already slick with cold melt water. I hung onto the dachshund that was wrapped in a tartan blanket, Kamosh under my arm, my woolly red hat pulled firmly over my ears. I wanted to stand in that position for ever, or at least until the adult madness ended. Whichever came first.

A family friend slipped some chocolate into my pocket. Another took off his watch and strapped it onto my thin wrist. A warm squeeze and a hand ruffled my hat kindly. I smiled back but wanted to cry. Father was unpeeling reams of notes from the fat wads of money that stretched his pockets. Currency that was worthless across the border. Sabrina was given a veritable armload of the cash and the grandmothers shyly accepted their share. Sabrina leant forward and whispered in my ear, "I will write you stories, sweet Jaro.

We will not lose our time together. Be strong my pearl of a boy, my lucky lucky charm. I love you like a mother, like a bird loves the nest, or as a frog delights in the pond." She smelt of coal and of cloves and mildly of roosters. I felt something tear inside me, as though a jagged razor slowly turned in my stomach, slicing up into the walls of my heart. Behind us we heard the sound of the train stopping.

"Please," wailed my grandmother beside herself with grief, "go if you must, but can't you leave the child with me?" My Father reared up, and in a haughty tone replied "Mother, it is for the child's sake that we are leaving." He embraced her tightly, turned on his heel, and started that fateful walk towards the train. We followed him as though asleep.

Mother pale and proud, her gait slow and resigned. A bark from the dachshund in my arms raised a few frozen smiles that quickly bled from the faces. Snow fell through the steam rising from the train engine. A porter helped Father to load the meagre baggage on board. The dim red star emblazoned upon the side of the carriage was a cheerless pentangle that scorned our gaze. We stood at the window of the train, the windows streaked with our breath.

Our little group huddled in the glare of the overhanging lights, strange shadows making them look like freshly exhumed corpses that waved dead hands as the train started to move and squeal on the tracks. Staring numbly at my reflection in the window, at the boy in heavy clothing holding a bundle of a dog, I suddenly knew the meaning of the word "surrender". The compartment was stuffy with second-hand air and we sat down quietly. I rested in the space between them. The night engulfed our train and I fell asleep, rocking to the rhythm of change.

I awoke in a darkened room. The warm shape of a coiled dachshund at my feet, a thick blanket as snug as a tea cosy over my pale body. Pale moonlight drifted in through hazy curtains. Odd smells and unfamiliar furniture made me blink and sit up. The dog stirred and yawned. I was alone but could hear muted voices percolating into the room from somewhere deep inside the home. How I got there, and who carried my tired frame into the strange bed I will never know. I rose and timidly pushed open the bedroom door, blinking at the yellow light that assaulted my senses. Naked feet on soft unfamiliar carpets, I walked down the passage to stand small and frail at the top of a staircase. Seated in comfortable splendor on groaning couches in the lounge beneath the stairs, were my parents and the fat uncles. They all stood up and cheered me on as I shuffled down towards them. Oiled faces a glow with bonhomie. I clutched at Kamosh tightly as I sat down amongst them.

My father winked encouragement to me as the aunts filled the room, carrying large plates of steaming sausages, shiny cheeses and cases of beer. I was given a glass of egg liquor and a toast was raised to the family, so sleepily reunited. The room was well lit and noisy. The Austrian's were red faced and formally dressed. The dachshund happily swallowed another morsel fed by yet another cooing aunt. Our family sat together on a couch, as though on a fun park ride. Dog on lap, warm liquor in belly, the recent train ride and sense of tragedy vanished lightly into the ether. Pictures of round faced men holding cheeses decorated the walls of the sitting room. The uncles ran a prestigious cheese factory and were men of importance in the small town.

A moment's gloom passed quickly as a gramophone was cranked up and a scratchy polka made the adults mince and sway heavily. I sat back and watched, yawning and sneezing as cigarette smoke filled the air. Stretching out on the couch, I fell into my second sleep that night. I longed for the touch of Sabrina's hand on my brow. The music played, the floor creaked under slipper shod feet and the dog snored, its breath heavy and deep. I did not feel the hands that raised me up, and did not feel the cold air around me as I was carried back to my new room. I did not hear the door close slowly, nor did I hear the footsteps walking away from me. I was in a dark well into which dreams of train wheels rumbled.

The following weeks blurred into a mirage of noisy dinners, red faced Uncles and endless walks with the rapidly widening dachshund, who became a favourite amongst the boisterous Austrians. They rewarded his even most banal act with shouts of mirth and offerings from the cheeseboard. My father was distant, troubled and silent. Until the day when he pushed a crumpled envelope across the dinner table towards me. The action stilled the usual exhausting uproar that accompanied our meal times.

"The Pony Express brought it this morning," he said, drily. Embarrassed by this sudden launch into the social spotlight, I raised it to my eyes, already brim with newly born tears. The family exchanged pitiful glances.

"A little love letter from a broken hearted nymph?" quipped an idiotic relative, but not many laughed.

"I'll read it later." I mumbled, cramming the crumpled envelope into my pocket.

Mother and Father looked at each other and sighed in unison and at that moment I wanted turn to dust, carried away through the walls by a friendly wind. Instead, I picked at the pork on the plate before me. After supper I announced my desire to walk the dog, with grey gloom outside already whispering of the night to come. I dragged the poor animal through the snow and the slush of late winter with me, trying to get away from the bombardment of heavily accented frivolity that had become a daily chore for me to endure. The dog cast morose and lingering glances back at the home which had become the centre of his new gluttony. I dragged him mercilessly through the murk, determined to find respite in the cold silence of the tiny forest that bordered otherwise bland suburbia. My gloves became damp and I took them off, and put them into the pockets of the one and only coat that I possessed. I reached within the depths of cloth and my fingers grazed the outline of a thin envelope. I recognized the elegant script immediately, and sat down on a log to gently open the seal, fingers moist with mud and trembling with long buried emotion. Cursing the cruel lack of light that blurred the page, the writing became obscured by the sudden misty tears that stole up from my heart, I returned the letter to its sacred envelope. Time and desire are often at each others throats and I vowed to find a more favourable environment in which to savor the words from Sabrina. I ran home, the wheezing animal trotting sluggishly in my wake, short legs struggling against the deep grey slush.

o o o

Chapter Twenty-six

Sabrina's First Letter

Grimy fingers tearing at the envelope, I withdrew the thin sheets of paper that turned my breath into a dandelion wisp. The loft smelt of mold and dust. Downstairs, somewhere in the house, a fat uncle laughed, the sound a warm wave that rose up through the floorboards of my hiding place. With great delicacy, I savored the shapes and curls, the sensuous twirl of the writing, without any pressing desire to know the meaning of their beautiful patterns. After a few minutes, I settled down on a pile of old cushions and read those first words of so many to come.

"Dear Jaroslav, you are surely reading this in some strange and wondrous new place, far from my creaky old home and my wrinkled goat face." I laughed quietly, for there I lay, in a wind blown loft, imagining her with pointy pink ears, "and I pray that all is well with the family. Try to avoid the cheese eating marathons that the Austrians are so renowned for, it will only give you bad dreams and dank breath. The roosters are lively and have discovered that they can tunnel under the house, clawing their way into the cellar with their viscious claws. I went down there in order to haul up some firewood, and suddenly found myself surrounded by that brutish swarm of poultry, reeking of plum brandy and coal dust. Fortunately I managed to swing a bucket around to ward them of, keen as they were to flap up into my old shoulders. I am sure that they have developed a taste for those ripe purple plums. Why I endure them I have no idea, but they do protect the house with their foul presence, women and children are scared to come wandering up the path, and grown men cross themselves when they encounter the feathered army.

"I often dream of you, my sweet boy, and wonder if you are safe and strong. I know that Mama and Papa are there to hold you, but you are such a delicate thing that I do worry a little. Distance is a strange obstacle to love, but I always think back to that story about the Goose Lovers and that makes me smile and then mountains, borders and men with guns no longer seem so formidable as obstacles to joy.

"A healthy goose in her prime flew over a little village in rural Yugoslavia, where your distant Uncle Dragan comes from, but he's mad and we don't often see him. He apparently lives with otters in a forest near a lake. A bored yokel shot her out of the sky with an arrow, and she fell into a clearing. The arrow had pierced her wing and she lay there in the grass flapping wildly and crying for help. A group of children on a school outing heard her sounds of distress and their teacher bundled her up in his sweater. They followed him as he carried the anxious goose to the local animal doctor, who removed the arrow. The bird sat quietly on the table as he washed her feathers with antiseptic ointment, the children staring wide-eyed through the window. The goose was badly hurt and would never be able to fly again, the doctor announced sadly.

"The teacher took the goose home with him, and she grew strong and happy again, but was forever flightless. He named her Anja, after his favourite dance hall singer, whom he would watch once a week, love struck wretch as he was, at the local bistro where she performed.

"He was a shy man, and he was quite tongue tied when it came to the matters of the heart, and like the goose, he seemed to be condemned to watch life as a spectator from the sidelines. He and the goose would sit side by side on the creaky verandah on golden autumnal nights and watch the flocks of geese flying above the house, heading southbound for warmer climes. Later, when the chill wind started to nip, the man with the broken bird at his side would rise and return to the house. The fire chuckling in the hearth and with the goose settled into her basket, they both would gaze up at the ceiling every now and then, listening to the distant sounds of the flocks serenading the night, somewhere far above them."

I heard the unmistakable heavy tread of an uncle, slowly climbing the stairs, towards my sanctuary. I quickly replaced the letter into the envelope, and assumed a position on an old couch, my eyes closed as if in an imitation of a deep childlike sleep. The door opened slowly and I could feel by the chilly wind on my face that an adult stood watching me in my mock slumbers. I yawned and slowly opened my eyes to behold the inevitable, well meaning ruddy face of an uncle, muttering in accented Czech something about supper time. I closed my eyes again and tried to imagine a flock of geese, beating their wings high away above this portly suburban house, somewhere in the boring depths of Austria, calling me to fly up and to soar away with them. Little did I know that my wish was about to be granted.

o o o

Chapter Twenty-seven

A Dinner Of Heads

I recognized the look on Father's face immediately. I wondered precisely how many times would my heart endure the same cold sinking sensation that I had known so many times in the past year, and still bob up to meet the sun of a new day.

"Ahem," he cleared his throat, and we all sat in silence at the dinner table, carp bones glinting on our plates, "after much thought, and long discussions with Mother and the family," at this I frowned, for I was obviously excluded from that definition, being allowed to play forlornly in dim corners of the house while the dice of fate were again being cast, "it has become clear that our next destination must be further south."

He got up from the table and dramatically lifted an ornamental globe of the world from a spotless mantelpiece.

"Europe is no place for us refugees from Communism," he announced with gravity, "for who knows how far the plague will spread. Austria has offered us an open door, and has graced us with refugee status, but, and no offense is intended to our hosts here, it is far too close to the Iron Curtain for my comfort. England is glad to have us, but it's full of homosexuals."

Ignoring the multitude of raised eyebrows all around him and a goose hiss from Mother, he continued unabashedly.

"America is full of Gangsters, and is no place for a child. Read the news and watch their television shows, it's obviously a nation in decline."

The irony that his own world view was completely coloured by decades of exposure to the eastern block variation on reality, had obviously escaped him. Again I frowned deeply, convinced by the America that I envisaged, teeming with slick talking cowboys and moustachioed tramps in bowler hats.

"Australia is full of snakes and Switzerland hates people." Everyone at the table nodded with sage agreement. I felt that I had woken up in a lunatic asylum. I looked at Mother, but she was distracted by her fork.

"So where can we go, where will there be safety, a healthy climate and is a place where a man can come home to his family in the evening and know that all is well. I think that there is a place such as that, and after our numerous discussions," again the general slow wise nodding from the adults seated encouraged him, "I think that place is Africa."

I sat stunned and amazed at this news. None of us had ever heard much of the continent so beatifically described by my dubious orator. Had he mentioned resettling on Pluto I would have been less astonished.

"It is warm, with plenty of wide open space, and is a land where a white man is welcomed and rewarded for his European ingenuity and skills. A place where opportunity awaits for those with clear-eyed vision and fearlessness. Mother has studied English and has a gift for language. I am a plumber, a common position here, but quite appreciated in the developing countries. Africa needs plumbing. Jaro is bright, sociable and the sun will do him good after this spell in Austria."

He took to his chair again, nodding and grinning at us. I eyed the uncles, with their poodle belly pink pallor, jowls that spoke of cream and cheese. They all nodded. I sighed. Perhaps the idea of Africa, with its beaches, blue skies and rivers of jumping fish was not such a preposterous whim after all. I imagined running splashing in blue tropical lagoons in my loincloth, leaping in the salty foam whilst the palms nearby dropped a coconut softly into the talcum powder sands. I retired early, keen to return to the story of the Broken Goose.

"The lame bird followed the man to school every day, waddling after him with unblinking eyes and intermittent squawks of frustration at its earth bound state. The children in the yard would rush towards the ungainly couple and stroke the goose's tender feathers.

"The goose had a special place in the sun under a large oak tree, and there she would sit and wait until the teacher appeared during break times to feed her seed and delicious bread crumbs. One early spring day, the teacher awoke to the unmistakable sounds of another bird, calling and flapping outside.

"Peering through a window he spied a fine gander, golden in the light of the rising sun, perched high in a tree that overshadowed the house. The man opened the door and watched as the bird flapped his wings once and softly descended into the garden. The goose pushed past him and made a guttural sound that seemed to slide from its belly right up its long neck. The gander raised his head back and opened up his wings which seemed to span the modest garden. The teacher turned and went back inside to make himself a lonely cup of of tea and the two geese frolicked and nuzzled all day.

"The next morning, when the teacher set out for school, he had two geese following him. The man named the gander Micha and many children came to admire the couple on Sundays after church. The two were inseparable and lived in the barn, bright white birds that played and courted amongst the golden hay. Anja laid her first clutch of eggs and soon there were six chicks that ran around her calloused feet, following her with gay tiny cheeps from soft downy beaks.

"The autumn winds came, rattling through the barn, and the metal weather cock above them all spun wild and free. By then, the chicks had grown strong and fat. It was time to fly south to a warmer climate. A cold hand grasped at the teachers heart each time that he saw the little family together, for he knew that the severance of their special bond was imminent. Birds must fly south in Autumn, my Jaro, and so it was to be with these gentle geese.

"Early one day, the fowls were unusually clamourous and upon emerging from his sleep, the teacher saw the flock rise up as one, leaving Anja running around, stricken with grief, in the little garden below. Calling out to the beating wings in the heavens, she hopped up onto the chair on the porch and onto the table waddling from side to side, attempting to find higher ground. Micha and the six small geese hovered above the house for a few moments and with great noise slowly faded from sight.

"The man held the goose to his chest as the autumn winds sliced cruelly through both of them. Life, dear boy, is not always kind nor fair, but magic is still in the air, even though it's not always apparent. The goose walked around the house, making little hopeful sounds, peering under a table here and around a corner there. The teacher felt old, sad and tired, watching her anxiety turn slowly to silent acceptance. That night she lay in her basket by the fire, staring at him almost unblinkingly, orange lights from the flames casting goose shadows on the wall behind her. The months passed, with icy mornings turning into dull grey days, but at last the spring thaw came and pale children huddled together in the pale sun of the school yard.

"The teacher and the goose sat together, blinking up at the watery orb in the sky, when a familiar honk made them both rise to their feet. Proud and chesty, Micha circled in the sky above them. Alone yet magnificent, he had returned from the south, leaving six strong children to become noble geese in their own right. With their own families, joys and sorrows. Faithful and kind, he had not abandoned his love. And so the cycle continued, with the lame goose laying one clutch of eggs per season and watching the new family disappear into the autumnal haze. Micha would appear within the same week of each early spring and love flourished with his arrival.

"Years went by, and the man's hair turned grey, but his heart was full. It gives the good folk joy to see bliss in others, my gentle boy, and only the bitter of heart take pleasure from another's tears.

Stay pure and joyful, and if you listen closely, you will hear the wings of my love on the breeze above your head. Your mad Aunt Sabrina."

I put down the letter, my eyes were weary yet my heart a warm pond of memories. I lay down to sleep and dreamt of geese, roosters and goats.

o o o

Chapter Twenty-eight

New Horizons, Blue Skies

Within a month we received our refugee status visas and with much handshaking and back rubs from the red faced Austrians, we were driven to Vienna airport. The dachshund hid beneath the bed as we packed our small suitcases, his rat like nose pointing defiantly from its lair. A number of months on a steady cheese and biscuit diet, fuelled by long winter days and nights of staring inertly into the glow of the ever lit fireplace, had reduced our family pet and fellow escapee from Communism into a canine slug. The Austrians promised to look after the animal as one of their own. Gazing up at the moon faces resting upon their lumpen bodies in the photographs of past relatives that lined the lounge walls, I suppressed an inner shudder of pity for the dachshund. With rotund belly and sagging jowls, the once perky beast had become quite a figure of mirth amongst visitors to the home. I avoided looking into mirrors lest I saw that a similar fate had unwittingly fallen upon my own head.

Mother and I stood around the airport departure lounge looking forlorn. The men had retired to the bar to raise toasts to our new life. I clutched a toy car that someone had thoughtfully bought for me at the airport toy shop. The last purchase in the northern hemisphere. It felt heavy and cumbersome in my small hand. Crowds, announcements and goodbyes blurred into a feeling of emptiness. I hoped that the letters would keep coming. They did.

o o o

Chapter Twenty-nine

Africa

The plane was full of Czech refugees going south. I slept through the card games, the bottles of plum brandy shared and drained. I somehow managed to to avoid the lolling head of the reeking man that fell asleep in the seat next to me, the cigarette still smoldering at his lips. Mother glared around wildly, while she held me tightly. Father had won another round of drinks, the cards singing in his hand. The night flight circus with hope as its destination. Most of the passengers were single men, happy to escape a drab Central Europe for the land of opportunity down South.

"Where a white man can be a king," I dimly overheard my Father shout amongst the stable noises that filled the plane.

The morning sun burnt away the clamour as we landed. All sat in silence. The heat blurring the shapes of the airport buildings. The door opened and air rolled in, dusty yet floral. Communal sweat broke out in plum brandy and nicotine torrents. I clutched the toy car and rose to follow the crumpled backs of my parents.

Our rag-tag group was escorted by smiling blue uniformed airport security men, every one of them sporting a huge cavalier mustache and short pants that revealed bronzed knees. The immigration clerk paled when the voluminous, sartorially challenged mob arrived at his counter. My father was still reeling mildly from the night before and suddenly decided that his first gesture in a new country should be to dramatically remove his passport from his pocket, raise it up above the assembled mass and to proceed to tear out the main pages from this valuable document before cramming them into his mouth to shout through mouthfuls of paper.

"I am never going back" he announced in the most profoundly broken English ever to grace a tongue.

Everyone clapped and cheered and stamped upon their passports. I held the toy tightly, fearing a general descent into chaos where nothing sacred would survive. Fortunately, the bewildered officer ushered us into a private office and after half an hour of stamping of documents and much mute nodding from my Father, with Mother translating bureaucratic minutiae, we were released to join the throng outside. The officials winked at each other as they handed out plastic bottles of sweet fruit juice to all.

White Africa had just received another boost to its ranks. Buses came and took the group, now pink faced from the minimal exposure to the new harsh sun, away to the special hotel, reserved for noisy foreigners. There we would be wined and dined and housed and served until suitable work was found.

Happy Slavs presided over by fez wearing black waiters in white attire. Father squeezed my arm and whispered "What did I tell you, are we not in paradise now?" He gestured to the greenery, and to the huge turquoise sky above that went on forever.

I looked at him and smiled. He had a piece of passport in his teeth.

o o o

Chapter Thirty

Dear Sabrina

"Dear Sabrina, it feels like a long time since we sat together. I look at the photograph of you and touch those perfect wrinkles of yours that are starting to merge with the creases on the surface. Thank you for the letter and the sad story of the crippled goose, it made me think of your house. Are you and the roosters well? It must be winter there now, and I can almost see you sitting by the fire, sipping plum brandy and being pecked by the birds that have invaded the home again, with the snow on their beaks as they shuffle their way inside.

"Here it is sweaty hot, with fat lizards that lie around on the stony ground outside, like dead fish with unblinking eyes. We have moved out of the refugee hotel and into a cottage close to where Father works. His English is earth shatteringly bad and when I come home from school I try to teach him a new word or a phrase that I had learnt that day. He has a van and two black men to help him with the plumbing work. People call him everyday with their stories of leaky toilets and burst pipes. Yes, Africa does need plumbing. Sometimes he doesn't understand the thick accented English of the locals, and he gets savage when he can't find the address of the customer. The black men wear open shirts and shorts and sandals and laugh at his frustration with the language. Mother merely sighs and looks the other way when he comes home, shirt crackling with dried sweat, moaning about the laziness of his helpers. She spends her hours translating documents at the Foreign Department, because people are arriving here from home all the time, families and single folk, all with documents and certificates in Czech.

"We have been given three suitcases full of clothing from the local charity and the women from the neighborhood often knock on the door bearing hampers of food and kitchen utensils. Father hates the charity that comes our way, but has to accept it. As Mother reminded him the other day of the fact that beggars certainly cannot be choosers. He raged at that, and went out drinking with some other frustrated Czechs, all in their charity clothes and shoes.

"I have made some friends, with the boys that live next door. We often go down to the yellow and green river that glints through the trees on the bottom of the hill. The water smells like chicken soup and the mosquito buzz in hazy gangs above you when you swim through the pungent waters. Across the river on the far bank is an African village where smoke rises above the corrugated iron roofs and children in rags wave and call out to us, to swim out to them. They sometimes dance comically on the distant sand bank and drop their clothes and wiggle their bums at us, forever laughing and chattering.

"We never attempt to cross the river, making excuses about the current and about the poisonous fish that live in its sickly coloured depths. I've become quite brown because I walk everywhere, following my friends who have bicycles, and are not always kind enough to let me ride on the back when we go swimming. The river sometimes floods, and becomes a growling snarling thing, where tree trunks and clumps of vegetation swirl around in the foam, like instant islands that are born only to be quickly lost to the downstream roar. It had been raining constantly for the past few days and our little group of friends had grown listless in the endless games of monopoly and tin soldiers that helped us while away the hours after school. We were lazing around the bedroom of Hannes, when a ray of sun nervously entered the room from a gap in the curtains. A sure sign that spelt the end to our boredom, we who were so used to the joys of the open air and excitement that the African space can give a young boy.

"'To the river!' we yelled and trooped out into the fresh sunlight, the garden smelling of damp grass.

"The bicycles splashed in the puddles ahead of me, while I muddy footed, followed the path down to the river. The exciting sound of the water up ahead made me break out into a trot. The group watched the yellow mud streaked waves of the swelled river the uprooted tree trunks, spinning in the current, roots and broken branches clawing at the air uselessly. An incongruous yellow open umbrella sailed into view and we threw sticks at it to make it sink.

Hector, the little Jack Russell that follows us around, barked frantically and chased its own tail. The sun began to bake down cruelly and we took our tops off and sat under a tree watching the current for interesting objects that the river might have stolen from the land upstream. The black kids called us from across the water, but their voices were lost in the din of the frothy mayhem. We ignored them, as usual. Someone produced a stolen cigarette, and we passed it around, puffing and grinning nervously.

"Don't worry sweet Sabrina, I am not turning into a bad apple, down here in the swamps. It was a silly thing to do but quite fun, too. An hour went by, when suddenly sturdy blond Klaas stood up and pointed at something in the river bobbing up and down in the shallows of the nearby river bend.

"'What the hell is that?' he bellowed manfully.

"His father is the Chief of Police in the District and the boy is both loud and much mistrusted by the natives, who tend to shy away from him when he struts around the town. A born bully, he proudly walks in his father's shadow. Now he pointed to a dim shape that rocked gently from side to side in shade of a weeping willow, in a gentle bay away from the growling of the main water. We stood up as one, frowning into the gloom, silent as statues. The rumble of water became almost too loud to bear.

"'Is it a hippo?' asked someone.

"No one answered. The shape bobbed up and down quietly. A soft breeze blew hair into my eyes. We ran down the slope, laughing and shoving each other out of the way, slipping on grass, kicking up mud, Hector biting at any ankle within reach. Klaas got there first.

"'It's a pig,' he announced officially, 'a huge bloody dead pig.' And a pig it was, Sabrina. Muddy, bruised and dead. And very swollen. The belly had grown inflated with water or gas and the entire animal was a meaty, tight skinned bulge, half submerged in the shallows of the flooded river. A swarm of flies crawled and hopped over the pig mountain. The skin of the face had stretched and dried, pulling back the lips. A madly grinning pig, bloated and glassy-eyed. The stench was a haze of sweet melon and rancid butter. Some of us gagged and I could taste the cigarette in my bile. I remember you taking me to a farm feast after the slaughter, when I was a truly young thing, Sabrina. There was a trough behind the kitchen into which I nearly fell chasing a chicken. It was full of bits of stomach and greasy white fat that glinted up at me. This waterlogged pig smelt just as bad as that trough with the dank mud adding another layer to the cloud that glued up my nostrils.

"'What are we going to do with it?' I asked naively.

"'Whut aru ve goink two do vit tit?', Klaas mocked my broken English, 've aaar goink to pop de fat pig.' The group laughed and I blushed.

"'How about setting it alight?' offered another in the group, 'it would be like lighting a big fart!'

"'Yes!' We all shouted and clapped our hands and the dog went mad again.

"'Klaas can stab a hole in the belly with his hunting knife and Jaro can light the gas as it comes out,' some genius shouted and all eyes turned to me. Klaas swaggered forth happy that his pride and joy, a disturbing large hunting knife with which he sharpened sticks and which he threw into tree stumps, would finally have a carnal use. I gritted my teeth, smiled and nodded. A box of matches was pushed in to my hand. Hushed, we descended on the fly specked pig.

"Sweet Aunt, I have to pause now. Mother's knocking on the door and I have to help clean the house. Father is bringing his boss home for dinner. And we can't afford a maid yet. Mother never lets us forget that everyone here has maids. Kisses to you and the wild eyed roosters. More of the pig tale tomorrow."

o o o

Chapter Thirty-one

A Dinner Of Fools

Dinner was baking merrily in the oven and I was scrubbing feverishly behind my ears, soap suds slowly falling to the floor like snowflakes. The boss was coming to eat with us. The head plumber, chief of plumbers, Number One of the Dripping Tap Department was going to join our table. Embarrassed at our poverty, we rarely entertained the locals in our home. Anxiety hovered in the air, whilst the clock sounded out the dwindling moments of security.

The lack of money combined with a heightened sense of our otherness kept our family quietly secreted away from the outside world.

My father's English remained as broken as a tea pot and I was slowly developing a mild stammer, and the ear on Kamosh had frayed from my absent minded chewing.

Mother remained steadfast and tight-lipped as she fussed around the tiny kitchen. A photo glued to the fridge showed an obese dachshund sleepily staring out of large lap. Austria was far away, but I still shuddered on occasion when walking past that picture. There was a rabbit roasting in the oven, and the potatoes were on the boil when Father sniffed the air suspiciously and with a voice like a bear trap asked,

"What are we having tonight, Mother?" The tender woman stiffened whilst laying the table and looked up.

"Rabbit, of course. Why do you ask?"

Father sighed and launched into a monologue about the family failing to integrate with the locals, and how he was growing rapidly tired of being the brunt of his workmates low humour. I looked at him in his suspenders holding up his baggy trousers, at his feet cosy in socks and sandals and struggled hard to suppress a mad urge to whinny with laughter.

"The rabbit, whilst undoubtedly a central European delicacy, which would honour the palate of any honest worker after a hard day's toil, has a very poor reputation here down south. A poor man's food, akin to eating vermin. A black man's food. We might as well be serving our important guest freshly caught rats and crusts of bread. These people are used to a mild cuisine. Chicken or beef, but never rabbit," he announced severely.

We stared at him with disbelief. A week previously he had sung with delight whilst eating rabbit pie, slapping Mother's behind and banging on the table with fists happily glistening with joy.

"Well, we are not having chicken or beef tonight, Father. Perhaps you could call the important gentleman and postpone the dinner to another occasion? It will give me a chance to go out and buy some carrots and a scrawny bird I could boil the life out in the name of integration?" she hissed tartly. He scowled darkly at her.

"Funny thing," I interjected naively "I learnt today that there is a remarkable resemblance between the English verb "to integrate" and "to ingratiate". Should I explain the difference between these two verbs?"

"This boy is starting to become a 'smart ass'," grunted Father, using the English version of the word. In the oven, the rabbit sizzled with confrontational mischief.

"All those bloody books he reads. Making him disrespectful" he added, "and not at all bloody funny." I shrugged. "Yet another Rebel Without a Cause. You don't want to end up like Mr. Bloody James Dean, my son. Swaggering around heaven, no doubt. Crushing out dirty cigarette ends on the celestial lawns and scoffing at the Serafin." I barked with laughter at that, but the mirth did not spread to the group. For there was a knock on the door. An uncommon sound in our home, barring the odd African beggar that would on occasion stand humbly outside, risking misery at the hands of the eternally roaming police vans that served to keep the suburbs safe from undesirables. We exchanged startled looks. Mother bolted to the kitchen, to nurse the vermin.

Father cleared his throat, grabbed a newspaper and began reading avidly. "Well, come on," he nodded to me, with an official rustle of newsprint "do show the guest in." I mumbled my displeasure and shuffled resentfully to open the door to the large shadow that was imprinted on the glass.

A red faced colossus entered, uncomfortable in short pants, socks and boots with checked shirt that barely held in a beer belly. "Henk," he announced, "Henk De Villiers." He shook my hand, and I led him to the lounge where the odd couple awaited.

Father sprang up, and the paper fell to the floor. Mother curtsied from the kitchen doorway, and all three adults sat in the lounge, drinking sherry while I watched the rabbit browning in the oven.

"I see that you have no maid," I heard the chief plumber ask, "ya, I wish that we could do without our Bettina. Nothing but trouble and always takes the sugar and the teabags home with her. You have the right idea, save yourself a lot of grief and money." I heard Mother cough and there was a pregnant silence in the lounge, which I decided to break with a loud exclamation that the chicken was ready to be served. Mother quickly joined me in the kitchen and pulled at my nose playfully.

"You provocative jester you," she whispered, laughing as she sliced up the meat. All eyes were on the silver dome of the serving dish, which was raised to a symphony of sighs to reveal the bunny in a potato bed.

"Please feast your eyes on this splendid chicken, Henk, done in the Czech way with a recipe as old as Adam," shouted my Father amicably at our guest, winking wildly in my direction.

Fortunately the animal's legs were neatly arranged on the side of the dish, and did oddly enough resemble four slightly overdeveloped chicken thighs. Henk launched himself at this prize meal and within half an hour had managed to consume most of the bunny, a bucket of potatoes and a bottle of red wine. He began to expound on the ever popular topic of the "lazy black man", waving a half gnarled hind quarter with my Father who nodded his head in emphatic, slavish agreement.

Looking around the table, Dather appeared to notice me for the for the first time. "Jaro, come here, my son, " he exclaimed in English, for the benefit of our jug eared guest, "tell me what you smell, my son?" I dutifully approached his side of the table. He pushed the clenched fist to my nose. The old graveyard joke hanging in the air between us, I looked at the gnarled, scarred fist and then at the remains of the rabbit on his plate.

"Umm, plumbing?" I ventured, innocently. Henk howled with laughter, oblivious to the history of the joke. Father scowled and glared at Mother who rolled her eyes with exasperation. He turned to Henk and the men raised a glass to the future of plumbing. Mother and I retired politely to locations more demure.

The men remained, and hardly noticed our absence, goading each other in extolling the virtues of European prowess in the Dark Continent. Outside, somewhere in the night dank with sweat, the crickets sang their prayers. I returned to my letter writing, wondering where my father's ability to attract the idiotic elements truly came from. I shuddered at the prospect of involuntarily inheriting the same legacy.

o o o

Chapter Thirty-two

The Pig Jumped over the Moon, Sabrina

"The box of matches fell from my mud cracked hand that trembled as the boys pushed me towards the bloated porker. I gagged at the morbid cocktail of smells that hung over the distended body with its yellow death grin. Klaas was making stabbing gestures at the ominous cloud of flies that brimmed the air, his knife flashing silver in the brothy air.

"'Stab the swine, Klaas.' shouted a young voice from the back of the excited crowd of boys.

"'Lance him like a boil, Klaas!' shouted another.

I was jostled forward, through the sweaty bodies bottle necking together at the muddy waters edge. The jack russell ran around wildly in a delirium, nipping at my ankles. I kicked him away, furious at the apparent completeness of my isolation. Not even the bloody dog would allow me some air, peace or choice in that moment. The sun baked down as for a moment I closed my eyes, wishing to be far away, possibly buried underneath piles of soft silent snow. An elbow in my ribs made me start, and already Klaas was jabbing at the swelled flesh, laughing wildly as the distended beast rocked like a barge in the grimy shallows.

"'Come, Jaro, get over here with those matches. I'm going to make a hole,' he shouted at me.

His face was almost old as he concentrated on his stabs. I edged nearer and the crowd behind me fell silent. I could hear the dog panting and drinking from the bog as I removed one match from the box and waited for a signal.

"'Now,' bellowed Klaas, white eyed with a mad joy, 'light the bloody match and bring it here, quickly. I can hear gas escaping!'

"I stumbled forward, Sabrina, like a dazed animal. I was standing next to the pig and the stench was almost unbearable. Klaas had created a gaping hole in the swelled belly and a hiss of escaping gas was softly audible. I scraped the match against the box, and it snapped off. An angry mob behind me made a snake like sound and a grunt of indignation from Klaas made me quickly strike another. The flame took hold as Klaas plunged the knife into the small wound again and ripped the flesh open with a savage downward sweep of his bony wrist, his back a silver with a sweat sheen.

"'Now, light the bloody thing!' he yelled, backing off at high speed. I held my nose and pushed the match towards the gaping hole. The flame flickered and then suddenly and miraculously grew larger with a blue green halo. I stood so transfixed by the unique beauty of this phenomenon that I removed my fingers from my nose, almost oblivious to the ghastly stench and the angry hiss of escaping gas. From inside the pig, I heard a sound that resembled that emitted by an angry wasp trapped in a jar held close to an ear.

"The blast that spun me backwards was hot and acrid and the liquid that rained down upon me was hot, slippery like a dog's tongue and smelled of cabbage cooked with mince. The pig's stomach literally erupted with flame and a fine puree of nameless semi solid substance sprayed over the assembled group, dripping from the overhanging leaves and oozing into the water as a grey pink film that frothed in the waves. The porker was blown over onto its side, with a great flapping hole where the stomach had been, rank and smoldering in the hot breeze. I felt into my hair, finding lumps of waxy fat that clung on like maggots. My eyebrows were singed and lids glued near shut with the swine excrement. I crawled into the reeds and vomited, the odor almost engulfing me. Me and my rancid shadow, trying to find an honorable exit from the scene.

"'Look at Jaro, he's gone black!' shouted some wit and everyone gathered around me, while I tried to retch discreetly.

"And sure enough, my entire body has been splattered with an almost even coating of a dark brown green fatty exudate, which resisted all my attempts to remove.

"'God, you smell putrid,' sneered Klaas, forever the master of the obvious, throwing a clump of mud at me. The whole group took up the call to arms and I stood there, pig rancid and mud slung, trying to grin as I protected my face from the flying dirt. After a well aimed mud lump into my ear almost deafened me, I turned and ran, flinging myself into the river to avoid further humiliation.

"'Where the hell are my matches, Jaro?' someone shouted angrily from the bank and I laughed and laughed, while I drifted downstream, the African sky blue and kind above me.

"The water was soft and comforting, the current a gentle sweep underneath my aching body. I bobbed past the the black kids that stood silent on the bank, and waved to them with my greasy discoloured hand, they waved back, unsure yet curious. I wonder at this place sometimes, Sabrina. Heaven and hell seem to be mixed up here on earth. And they seem to take unfair turns in showing me their face. I found a sheltered bank, and there I rested for an hour, the smell hanging over me like a shroud. Finally I rose to my feet and made my way home furtively, moving from dingy alley to darkened doorway, to knock at last plaintively on the door.

"Father roughly pushed my shivering stinking frame into the bathroom, whilst Mother prepared to scour my tormented skin with scalding water and soap, slipping on her yellow kitchen gloves without the slightest trace of a smile. I spent the rest of the night reading and nibbling on Kamosh's ear. I miss you Sabrina, and I miss those rogue roosters."

o o o

Chapter Thirty-three

Waiting is Hell, but Heaven is Waiting

"Dear Jaroslav," began the familiar script, delivered into my hands by my unhappy Father, the house still reeked with stench of my misadventure, "what a remarkable tale, poor angel. Boys can be a delight on their own, but when they form a pack they can be worse than the lowest of the beasts. I've seen an old Jewish woman pelted with stones and chased out from the village where she had lived for sixty years, by a group of generally sweet boys that, prior to the German invasion, would greet her on the street and help her with her bags. Once the Nazis had made the torment of the outsider fair game, the boys formed bored packs against the weak and the helpless, sometimes under the quietly approving eyes of their parents.

"You ask about the mischievous dance between heaven and hell, my boy? Let Aunt Sabrina tell you a cautionary tale, sweet Jaro. There was once a man named Bedrich who believed that only through suffering, penance and denial would he reach heaven when he died. Every Sunday he would go to his church and kneel there in silent prayer. He chose the most austere of churches for his worship, one where the floors were bare, the walls thin, the priest a gnarled and hunched miser that fixed the many holes in the old walls with paper and board. Not many people visited this cold and musty church and the priest would be seen scowling down the main road at the village, a pure yet friendless figure. Bedrich felt the cold floor through his sparse knees, and reveled in the ache that was almost pleasurable. His hands on the hard rough wood of the bench before him, he would kneel there for hours, amongst a ragged congregation. The pew was his shelter. The bleak light shone the stained glass windows, and the wind moaned through the hollows. The Sunday mass was a tight lipped reading of the scriptures, followed by a a rhetorical question and answer analysis of the text. The audience coughed and wheezed in response to the gaunt priest's cerebral display, white faces stoic in their approval of his litany. After each sermon, the priest stood outside the church door and ashen faced, mumbled his thanks to the morose procession of believers that shuffled past him. No one caught his eye, nor shook his hand.

"Bedrich would walk home in his sensible shoes, to a flat that contained sparse furnishings and a bronchial parrot. The central heating would make friendly noises in the dim lounge and the man sat there nibbling on weak tea and lightly buttered toast, reading the Sunday paper and dozing in his armchair. The only company he had the sneezing parrot, the clock that ticked and the heating which chortled. All in all, a happy gathering. Bedrich's knees clicked when he cautiously arose to refill the kettle and to tap on the parrot's cage with a dry biscuit. And so it went on for many a year. Under Death's Hand, the congregation thinned out and the priest's voice developed a tremor that spoke of old age. The church groaned in winter assailed by harsh winds that blew the dust around, the particles slowly dancing in the pale sunlight above the man's head. He developed a cough not unlike that of his parrot. The bird sat glazed eyed on his perch silent in his senility, barely moving in his cage.

"The man buried the bird on a Tuesday. It had simply stopped moving. Not a wheeze left its decrepit beak and the seed trough lay untouched for days. Bedrich put his glasses on, and slowly pushing his nose towards the cage, peered unblinkingly at the shrunken bird. The parrot sat still. The man inserted a chewed pencil through the bars of the cage and gave his old a friend a soft poke. The bird did not blink, staring at him as he opened up the cage and tenderly removed the cold parrot. He held it close to his glasses. Life had passed, and the sad matted feathers felt cold in his hands. He took the bird to the cross that hung over the fireplace. Sweet suffering Jesus gazed down through varnished eyes. The man rubbed the parrot's head gently against the savior's gaunt wooden cheek.

"'Fly well, my bird,' he whispered, 'wait for me there on the other side.' He closed his eyes, and for a moment there a tear hung unformed, but quickly dissipated when he cleared his throat. He carefully folded pink tissue paper to line the bottom of a shoebox and placed the little corpse into the makeshift coffin.

"Rather be rooster than a parrot my gentle boy, that's what Aunt Sabrina preaches. Much more fun. Anyway, the story goes on.

"He buried it in the garden, quite close to the gnome with the chipped ear. At least the bird would enjoy some company on cold winter nights, he thought. The gnome was ever smiling, holding an equally happy fish under his arm. Back at home, the teapot called cheerfully and he looked up, glad for the distraction. He was terrible at saying goodbye and it was raining. His neck was wet with the rain and his glasses were steamed from the effort of burying the shoe box. The box that had the words "Size 7" cheerfully emblazoned on all the sides in extravagantly large lettering. The man retired to a nice cup of tea and a quiet night.

"He died a few days later. Pneumonia, they said. The church lost another believer and the priest's voice now echoed more stridently across the almost empty building on Sundays. The man's soul wafted upwards, leaving earth's mad, sad spin behind. Higher and higher he soared, and the air grew soft and delicate. At last, he appeared at the Gates of Heaven and looked around expectantly. Whilst he was alive, he had rehearsed his entrance speech to St. Peter many times, often loudly to the wide-eyed parrot that bowed and raised his head in consternation at the volume of delivery. Here at Heaven's Gate there was no one to be seen. The Gates stood open, a huge visitor's book lay idly on a table, pen sleeping on the spine between two white pages.

"'Hello,' he called, sheepishly in a small voice. No point in making a poor first impression. 'Hello, is there anyone here?'

"Polite rhetoric, dear Jaro, for there was no one there at all.

"He stood in the shadows of the nightly Pearly Gates for a while, nervous yet impatient. He pinched his hand in self reproach. He did not want to enter Eternity fidgeting. He was about to sit down and timidly wait to be let in, speech or no speech, when he thought that he heard a sound, a bare note perhaps, floating towards him from beyond the entrance.

"He stood up and ventured towards the gates. Sure enough there was distant music in the air, that caressed his grey ears and made him frown. Soft as a dandelion blown by a wind the notes danced across the wide celestial meadows and across gentle slopes that lay behind the gate. Looking around furtively and half expecting a Punitive Voice calling upon him to stop, our round shouldered hero quietly shuffled into Heaven. There was not a soul in sight as he walked up the mild hill, the note became a song and soon he could distinguish between the various instruments at play. A flute led a cheerful melody underneath which numerous drums throbbed and pulsed. His frown deepened. Back in life he would enjoy the hymns sung to the mournful sound of the church organ, played by the octogenarian Miss. Derbishaw, now deceased. He came to the summit and the warm wind smelt of roses. He took out his handkerchief and mopped his furrowed brow. The sun had a strange purple tinge and the grass was as bouncy as a new born pup. He stood still, marveling at the expanse around him. A valley full of butterflies lay beneath his gaze, with a river that chuckled silver. A fish jumped somewhere in the water and he could hear the splash of its body.

"The music continued to coax his ears. A guitar had joined in, and the he felt his body move involuntarily in response to the gay melody. He grimaced and made his way down the valley towards the source of the sound. A bright bird flew past his head and he purposefully quickened his pace, casting wary eyes around him. The beating of many wings high above him made him start. He was expecting angels to appear to lead him to his judgment and the sound made his heart leap up in his chest. A flock of wildly coloured exotic birds circled in the sky, playful and noisy. The birds chased each other through the air, nipping at tails, oddly in time to the tune that flowed over the land. The musical crescendos were met by joyous chirps from the excited air above him. He thought that he recognized his old parrot amongst them, swooping and cackling like a young chick. Its once sad wilted plumage had been restored and the tail feathers that sagged so sadly in the cage were now vigorous and majestic.

"He called out to his old companion, and the parrot paused in his swoops, broke away from the garish throng and circled slowly in the sky above him. Pollen hung in the air above our Bedrich, as the parrot made his graceful glides. There seemed to be a mutual recognition between them and time seemed to stand still. Then the parrot, as though following the prompts of some inner voice let out a euphoric cackle, and abruptly turned and wheeled away to join his flock. The man continued on his way, determined to find the origin of the song.

"Louder and louder it grew as he crossed the river, stumbled through a forest buzzing with fat bumblebees and waded through a luminous sunflower plantation. Distant voices had now taken up the song and his heart beat faster and hot in his chest as he half stumbled and half ran towards the sound that now seemed to fill every fibre of his being. He entered upon a huge meadow and at the far end, in the shadow of mighty oaks, he saw a huge gathering of many people, all wearing light clothes and barefoot. Children ran hither and dither, with flowers in their hair as laughter filled the air.

"He walked towards the crowd slowly. Women were dancing around a circle of musicians, couples were stealing away to kiss in the shadows and dogs scampered around an open kitchen, where chefs prepared a huge feast. There were golden pillows on the lawn on which many lay smiling, tables laden with great trays of fruits, wine and breads. Dragonflies followed the man as he approached the gathering, darting around his ears. He brushed them away with irritation. People noticed this stooped apparition making his way towards them and children were sent to welcome the stranger to the feast. A lively stampede of urchins ran up and grabbed his hands, some hanging onto his belt cheekily, others pulling him along, forward towards the celebration. The band, in salutation of the newcomer's arrival, broke into a deliriously wild gypsy tango, with violins blazing an irresistible tune across the meadow. Everyone joined in a hand clapping, thigh slapping dance. The men whistled, the girls spun on the grass and the pollen flew around them on a sun drenched breeze. Dragged onwards by his young entourage, Bedrich finally arrived at the edge of the sea of merry dancers. Women attempted to embrace him. Men came to him, smiling and with open faces, warm smiles and cups of wine on offer. He stood still. Shook away the children, who cringed towards their mothers. The band played on. A circle of bright-eyed inquisitive folk formed around him. He shook his head. A knowing smile lit up his thin features.

"'No,' he shouted, 'I will not be tempted. I will not fall to your artifice. This is a test of my Faith, a Final show of Loyalty to a God that does not tolerate the Trappings of the Flesh, nor the shallowness of idle play.' The band stopped playing and the chefs put down their trays. Not a sound was heard as he continued, red in the face and brandishing a skinny fist towards them all. He continued bellowing at the crowd.

""I will not be Swayed by the Demons that tempt me here with that what I have resisted all my life. Away with you, this is not the Heaven that I have been prepared for! This is surely some foul final test of my faith. Hard Work, Sacrifice, Abstinence, these are the keys to paradise. Give me that what I deserve. Give me what I have earned in all my time on earth. Take me to a place where I have peace and dignity and keep your children's playground for children.
I curse you for attempting to lure me, my soul is unblemished by desire. Get behind me, Satan. I am not about to take up your mantle.'

"He crossed himself and fell to his knees on the puppy grass. Whispering incantations, Hail Mary's and Our Father's he rubbed his eyes furiously, attempting to wipe away the vision of confused faces and shocked stares that surrounded him. He hated the grass, the ground and flowers whose scent mocked his anguish. He lay there, a small figure in an extraordinarily beautiful landscape.

"The crowd watched him with concern, mothers holding their children tightly, in silence. Then a voice boomed from behind the throng, amused yet mildly scornful.

"'Who are you, sir, and what do you seek here?'

"The words hung in the air like smoke as the man looked up and peered past the throng to behold the figure of a portly white haired man, resplendent on an ornate couch, surrounded by animals of every type. Propped up on a large saffron coloured pillow, the impressive fellow rested in the shade of an ancient oak three, festooned with a multitude of colourful birds.

"'Eternal Peace and Rest,' choked out our Bedrich, 'that is what I have surely earned, by my lifelong abstinence from the cursed wickedness of the world.'

"'My boy, you were given a gift and did not even open it's wrappings,' boomed the voice and above the parrots cackled.

"'You can have all the joy and the peace, and much much more if you would choose to stay. Or you could try another place more closer to your beliefs, a little more in line with your thinking, perhaps?' offered the elderly gentleman.

"Nodding furiously our sad hero got up and for the first time, smiled into that blessed sunshine. With a shrug and a sigh, the white haired one clapped his hands, slowly and deliberately three times and the birds surged into the air, noisy and brightly magnificent. It quickly grew darker and a chill wind swept through the valley.

"Bedrich woke up with the same cold air gliding up his trouser leg. He was kneeling in the old familiar rough pew, and the church around him creaked with age. The thin light barely passed through the stained glass windows, and in the thick gloom he could see others, stooped over in prayer. One old man in front of him turned his head towards him slightly, nodded a greeting and gave a huge wink, before resuming his silent devotions. His shock of white hair made Bedrich frown. That old rogue seems oddly familiar, he thought to himself. The gnarled priest shuffled in. 'Let us stand,' he said in a dignified voice. The congregation stood, and the man felt as though his soul had finally found its peace.

"Not every one respects the gift of life in the same way, my young Jaro. There are those that seek to cage the animals, or pin the butterflies to a board. We send spaceships and satellites out there to seek out life in the dark of space, and spend billions in the hope of finding even the tiniest of species, a strand of existence, and yet scorn each other, the opposite sex, other races and nature itself. Can you imagine the world headlines if a bed bug, or a flea or whatever lives in the ear of a flea was found on some distant star ? Clamour and celebration all around. Someone sometime ago said that 'hell is other people.' That is why evil can rub shoulders with the good on earth. The choice is ultimately a simple one, my boy. And that is to either live in love or to live in fear. I have lived long and have seen what fear does to people and to nations. You are far from home as a result of such a turmoil. But rejoice, for your Aunt Sabrina has sent you a present for your thirteenth birthday. Something very special and that which is so near and dear to both of us. Watch for the postman, my dear. And let me know if you like it."

I put down the letter and lay on my bed, listening to the sound of adult voices outside my room. Father's voice raised in a defensive bleat, Mother's shrill in a ratatat counter attack. I watched the plastic models of space craft that hung from the ceiling on threads, above my bed, slowly spinning around on the warm evening breeze until I fell asleep.

o o o

Chapter Thirty-four

Vigil

My sense of hearing grew wildly acute in in the two weeks leading up to my thirteenth birthday. I became so attuned to the unique sound of the postman's bicycle that I would spring up and bolt towards the postbox at the barest distant chink of a loose chain or a groan of a poorly oiled pedal. My parents grew exasperated at these sudden unexplained exits, followed by my long faced return. Often I would clamber out of my chair halfway through another of Father's monologues, which normally took the shape of soliloquy on the eternal Black Problem.

Two days before my birthday, I heard the unmistakable sound of the postman's tires crunching the gravel outside the house and was about to leap up like a ferret when Father rapidly stood up, wagged a finger at my agitated face and archly said "Let me check the post today, dear boy. You eat that omelette before it cools."

He disappeared before I had a chance to splutter my indignation. He came back beaming and holding an oddly shaped parcel, the length of a large shoe box.

"Well, lets see where this is from," he raised the gift to his ear and shook it slowly from side to side. I could have murdered him in that moment.

"Strange smell, " he said, eyebrows furrowing deeply, "what is Sabrina sending you? It reeks of cheese. You don't even like cheese, do you?" and he shook the box again.

"No, I don't even like cheese, but I would like to hold my gift, if you don't mind." I said in a poorly disguised growl.

"Touchy, touchy, my sweet son. I'm afraid that you will have to wait a bit longer to get your cheese. I'll put it safely with the other gifts, birthday boy."

I tried to look at him with love, earnestly attempted to put fear and loathing far away and to celebrate life in all of its guises and cunning paradoxes.

"Sabrina, where are you now?" I thought.

"Ha ha, Jaroslav. You look as though I've taken away your favourite puppy. You'll have to change your attitude, my child, if you want some special presents on the day."

"I don't want any special presents. I want that present." I pointed. "The cheese."

Their laughter followed me into the garden, where I sat glaring at the passing clouds. The postman saw me and cheerfully rang his bicycle bell, waving a suntanned hand. I waved back, attempting to smile. The days passed by like lumbering oxen. At school, the boys would run past me laughing and holding their noses.

"Piggy smell. Piggy fart," they would call, and I walked on by, nose in the air. Around the corner, out of sight of prying eyes, I would sniff at my clothing, blow onto my open hand and inhale deeply. Nothing but the sweet smell of books and wine gums met my quivering nostrils. I was not convinced. I did take to near compulsive washing at break times and would emerge from the ablution block with rose tinted hands and a glowing pink scrubbed face.

At home I crept from room to room, sniffing loudly, attempting to find the hidden gift by the pungent trail. To no avail, for Father had secreted it away, in some cunning breathless nook. The day arrived and I sat staring at the clock on the classroom wall. When the final bell chimed and all the boys rose to file out of the school gate, I clambered past apologizing and ignoring the occasional kick in my excited direction. Thirteen years old and in a sweat, I tore down the road towards home. I was almost flattened by a brown army truck that passed. I looked up and saw the pink-faced soldiers sitting in the back, in two neat rows facing each other. One flicked a cigarette towards me and it arched through the dusty air, to land with a gasp of sparks in the gutter nearby. I ran on and crashed through our front door. The house was silent and I stood there panting and wet with perspiration.

On the kitchen table someone had painstakingly spelled out the words "happy birthday, sweet 13" using dried spiced meat, my favourite snack, akin to the American "jerky" product yet more wildly spiced. I approached this odd sight slowly. The meat letters lay there glistening with fat. I was irritated at the lack of clamour and colour that I so expected to highlight my special day, so irritated that I ate the dried delicacy of the table in an instant, munching mindlessly. I wanted that parcel.

Wiping my oily hands on my shirt-front I set about once more, in peering into the most incongruous places for that gift. Mother and Father arrived at sunset, both looking very smug. By then I had angrily examined every closet, crawled desperately under every bed and looked through every large box in the garage.

"Did you enjoy your gift, on the kitchen table, birthday pup?" my Father said kindly, stroking my hair. They stood there, arm in arm, serene. And empty handed. I nodded numbly, trying to hide my disappointment with the alphabet meat birthday gift from my nearest and dearest.

"And now for the mystery cheese from Sabrina," he announced, madly cheerful, and disappeared to his car. I heard the truck door being opened and loudly shut. The cunning devil had hidden it in his rusty vehicle, and had driven around with it for two sun scoured days. He returned, beaming and offered the weathered parcel to me. As I reached out for it, he raised it abruptly to his ear, shaking it.

"Well, it's definitely not chocolates," he said, frowning, "smells more like tripe if you ask me." He handed it over ceremoniously.

I swallowed hard, mouth dried out with the salty meat gluttony. The parcel felt heavy and the wrapping paper had faded in the heat of the van. My name and address appeared as a pale blue tattoo scrawled with childlike swirls across the brown body of my gift. I tore at the cruel layers and the paper fell away in tightly wound sheets. The smell that unfurled from the secret depths was mixture of a long forgotten floral old woman's perfume riding on the crest of marshy murky vapour. With a mad shake I unfurled the last veil. I held up the dead rooster by it's gnarled feet, laughing wildly. Around the scrawny neck hung a mottled envelope on golden ribbon, an Olympic medal of love. My startled parents retreated away from me, as I advanced upon them, holding the unblinking cadaver before me like a standard.

"Father," I whispered quietly, and took great delight in watching his eyes grow wider with my stealthy approach, the bird held aloft. "What do you smell? The grave yard, my friend, the unquiet grave." I laughed out wildly. I could feel the gristle strands that filled my teeth. He jumped back, knocking over a porcelain vase.

Mother glared at him. With small apologetic sounds, he knelt to pick up the broken pieces, the Great Bird cold and merciless above him. Definitely the best birthday gift that I had received thus far. Mother pointed to the verandah and hissed "Out. Away with that foul dead thing. A monster of a gift, what was Sabrina thinking? Poor soul must be senile, sending a stuffed rooster to a sensitive boy. Take it away, far from me. Look how you've scared your fool of a father."

I did look, and took great pleasure watching the man on his knees, sweating to pick up the last fragments of porcelain.

"Maybe she'll send me a dried out carp for my fourteenth birthday?" I teased innocently, but her expression became quite witch like and I made my hasty escape to the stillness of the porch.

The ribbon untied, the envelope a breath in my hand, the bird looked naked without his adornment. I felt a momentary surge of remorse at separating the two new friends that had journeyed so far to bring me joy. But separate them I did, and made myself comfortable in the armchair that sat dusty and cat friendly on the porch.

"Dear beloved Jaro," began the crumpled letter, "I hope that the rooster hasn't been damaged during the long journey to you and that his stuffed presence is not going to make your parents angry. Let your old friend watch over you. I wish that it could be me being unwrapped to stand smelling of mildew before you, but the flame red rooster can be my representative in Africa. Thank you for your letters and I can read from them that you are growing up to be an unusual and magical boy, who has the gift of seeing the world as through a kaleidoscope. I knew that you, of all people, would delight in the receipt of such a singular and, perchance, odd gift. The poor bird met his end when the river rose during the last flood. It rained and it rained as though the world had grown tired of dust and empty skies. The first drops that fell were almost gold with pollen and wood smoke. I caught one in my mouth when I stood outside emptying my night pot onto the grave, and it tasted of resin and soot. The showers that followed beat down on the roof for days. The yard had quickly turned to a green grey mash and there were buckets all over the house to catch the drippings from the ceiling. The roosters ceremoniously filled in and perched quietly on their favourite pieces of furniture. Each bird has a place and that is how I know that all is well and that no one is missing.

"That night, there was a sad gap in the throng that strode in from the gale, dripping and sneezing as only mad roosters can do. I waited for the straggler to arrive, and kept moving from steamy window to window in the hope that I would see a forlorn figure waiting patiently somewhere outside in the murk. I strained my old ears for the sound of a bronchial sneeze, a whimsy of a rooster call, but to no avail. Exasperated, I put on my scarf, hoisted on the gumboots and took a very large swig from the plum brandy. Squinting against the foul wind that blew leaves into the house the instant that I forced open the door, I went to find that lost animal.

"The night was an enemy, mud pools had formed everywhere and I slipped and splashed my way around the miserable yard, calling out wildly, torch light illuminating a fraction of the space before me. The wind cut my words out of the air as I stumbled on, peering into the well, shining the light into the disused kennel, under the broken down tractor on which you loved to play. The sound of the river in a froth stopped me in my tracks and I ran down the embankment, skidding down the grass like child, until I reached the mad waters.

"It's strange how our stories are entwined by rivers, my gentle boy. The fishermen would leave the tied up nets safe and high on the shore, but now I could see that the raging water had risen high up on the sandy bank, and the nets were half immersed in the rogue current. What drove me to haul the nets in, when my mind was full of wet birds in trees, I will never know, but blood calls to blood sometimes across the gulf of logic and reason. Luck and not wisdom guided my hands on that savage night and I pulled and heaved the nets in, wondering at my own lunacy until a familiar claw emerged from the wet sheen of the material. I threw myself at this bundle wrapped in netting. The beak was open the feathers were as wild as mane of a lion. The poor thing had become entangled, a land – fish in a trap, drowned in the foamy waves.

"I carried the old clucker home. Inside the roosters had started to doze, with gentle steam rising from their little bodies. I placed their drowned friend onto his favourite chair, to complete the circle for the last time. The roosters gazed at me. With kindness, I thought. I lit many candles and positioned them around the room. The birds smelt of grass and seed and I smelt of mud and leaves. We sat there for an hour or two, listening to the rain. Birds' heads rose to blink and then sank back onto their soft chests. I went to bed, feeling both light and sad, a wild mixture of contradictory emotions .

"The next day the rooster was taken to Zlin for stuffing. A man with a white mustache arrived on a motorcycle with a side car into which we carefully laid the gentle beast. He shook my hand and promised to perform the taxidermy with utter reverence, proudly showing me a photo album filled with glass eyed fogs, birds and even a turkey. The remaining roosters sat on the disused tractor, sneering in our direction. The motorcycle roared away, the man hooting his horn cheerfully. A tiny tear blurred the landscape for a second or two.

"Look after the old warrior, Jaro. A piece of the old world, the world that can stand over your bed in Africa. And try to keep the moths or weevils or whatever infestations come your way down there from nibbling at his proud plumage. I promise to not to send you any more stuffed roosters but I did feel that at least one red devil would bring both a smile to your face and perhaps a small tremble to your heart, as I have now. Do keep on writing those sweet letters and never fear to tell me those secrets that scare the parents. I love you and hold you close, my boy. And don't forget, where wisdom fails, luck steps in."

I put down the letter and watched as the long shadows grew across the lawn, silently closing the curtain on my thirteenth birthday. Armed with the unblinking bird, I returned to the house.

o o o

Chapter Thirty-five

The Carp as an Albatross

My Father had many Czech friends, expatriates that would arrive at the house with boxes of beer and their laughter would echo into the night as they sat together under the great African sky.

Many of the men had left their families behind, arriving as steely eyed immigrants stripped down to the bone that dutifully sent home part of their monthly incomes. Others simply turned their backs on the past and became lonely pariahs that packed together, filling bars that had a Eurocentric flavour, with dusty deer horns and yellowing pictures of castles and forests. They would arrive at our home with a motley succession of local women and I would watch them from my bedroom after I had turned my lights off. Someone once even appeared at one of these gatherings with a black woman, both of them drunk and laughing. They seemed very happy together, but left soon and that never happened again. My Father would try and impress these new acquaintances with his wit and banter. I cringed behind the curtains. Behind me, up on the cupboard stood my rooster, proudly on his pedestal, with small glassy eyes forever watchful.

Three days before Christmas I was bundled into the much dented van, filled with red faced Czechs. Fishing rods were everywhere and every time I moved someone would growl a warning at me, lest I injured one of these prize tools. Beers were opened with a foamy snap and the van filled up with cheap cigarette smoke as we waited for Father to arrive. Carp was hotly discussed all around me, as my migraine grew hooves and claws.

"Carp," said one rheumy eyed enthusiast, "can read your mind. No, truly, it can." He shouted over the laughter that rocked the rusty springs of the van, "it is not your everyday dullard of a fish. It watches you, observes your manner, how you stand, what you wear, even what aftershave you are wearing." More howls of merriment, punctured by random wild coughing.

"The fish is a creature of legend, and we all know about the Golden Carp Of Prague, its unique power to grant wishes and to ensnare a timid lover's heart." We all nodded sagely. At that moment my father bounded in, apologizing fiercely in all directions for being late and we set off towards the local lake to hunt for the mystical fish.

"Christmas is nothing without a fine carp soup, steaming up the kitchen. Can you imagine not dining on a succulent carp fillet, fried in batter, washed down by frothy headed beer?" he spoke slowly, as though in a culinary trance. The van grew silent, a communal reverence stoked up by his words. We all shared a half dream of the perfect carp dish. In the corner seat, a fat man sighed. Africans on bicycles waved at us as we passed, the dust obscuring their shiny faces for a brief moment until it settled on the summer land.

"I remember when I first tasted my first carp cutlet," he continued as though recounting an opium dream, "the war had made everything scarce. Shoelaces, tobacco and meat were fought over luxuries. One day I walked into the kitchen, hungry as a young lion but too shy to ask for even a nibble, for that would earn me a solid crack around the skull."

He looked at me through the rear-view mirror, and I turned to stare at the fertile vegetation that we were passing through. The audience in the van sat back in respectful silence as the story unraveled.

"My mother sat very comfortably in her favourite reed rocker and seemed to be peeling onions from a basin in her lap. Next to her was a large wooden bucket in which what appeared to be floating turnips, bobbed slowly in some slimy water. She called to me and her face was a huge smiling moon.

"Come and see what I have for our supper, my boy" she cackled and I approached with trepidation for she had a wickedly cruel sense of humour, until she got struck down by religion in her later years. She had a carving knife in her one hand, her veins were red and blue as she shaved the object that she grasped in her other. I must have looked numb with confusion because suddenly as though exasperated, she lifted the possible onion to my face. I drew back startled to see that it was actually a fish head that she was shaving with such painstaking gusto. The poor fish had every vague nuance of flesh removed and I beheld a perverted version of Hamlet's skull before my bulging eyes. She howled with laughter as she dropped the cleaned head into the bucket with a splash, and rummaged beneath the surface for another fleshy morsel to peel. I was overcome by a violent nausea and left the house to walk in the soothing snow that waited softly outside." he paused, face peaceful as he held the steering wheel. I felt a great pang of love for him then, his vulnerability echoing within my small chest.

"I came home to find that the scene of horror had been replaced by a crackle of a happy fire, a table laden with steaming pots and an ornate silver serving dish. I felt foolish in having run away from what was in essence a joke at the expense of my overwrought sensibilities. The family gathered and glasses were raised, and in that instant the war seemed very far away from that table. The serving dish lid was raised with a flourish and the most extraordinarily beautiful carp cutlets were revealed. Golden batter gleamed with oil and the aroma that filled that humble room had the power to woo a king of his throne. A kindly local had managed to steal a barrow load of carp heads from the kitchen of the German garrison that was nearby. Mother had toiled for many hours to scrape off the fine succulent meat, and had boiled up the bony remains with carrots and potatoes for our soup. The flesh was mixed with sage, flour and garlic, held together with egg white and constituted into a cutlet shape before being battered and fried. The result was the softest, most luxurious flesh upon which any mortal hoped to feast upon.

I will never look at a carp's head without remembering the warmth and otherworldly joy that the meal gave me that night. Many may scoff and bray at the thought of such a dinner, but I tell you this," he paused, and the silence in the moving car was a living thing, "that those scrapings sang an anthem that most chefs would sell their souls to the devil for!" And he hooted the horn.

We all jumped up in our seats and cursed him with much mirth and merriment, but I could tell that the story had left an indelible mark on everyone's imagination that day. An old black man passing by waved from his bicycle, but the hoot was not intended for him and we looked the other way, visions of golden carp cutlets hanging in the air above our heads. The vehicle rumbled on and the passengers sat in a glassy-eyed stupor. My father caught my eye in the rear view mirror and winked. I smiled and for a moment the world was a place of great joy and unbroken skies.

The sun was setting as the van slowed to a rest at the side of a large dam, the last rays of light stirring up an orange haze over the quiet water. We emerged as one crumpled mass, that creaked apart into listless men and one boy. Rods were baited and with cosy rugs unfurled, a fire was lit. I sat back on a log watching the men rubbing their hands in gleeful anticipation at catching a fat fish.

"A bottle of plum to the one that bags the biggest monster!" shouted a stout man with a nose as warty as a cucumber, brandishing a flagon of brandy. The group hissed like snakes at his jovial volume. The sacred fish had ears at the back of its scaly head, grimly reminded Father. The fire crackled as the moon appeared and the group sat round shouldered and peaceful, all eyes on the rods that pointed at the dark waters. Stars peered out and a bottle of whiskey was passed around. Much nodding of appreciation and raising of glasses ensued. Someone sliced large glistening chunks of a smoked ham. The crowd, bored by the company of the silent rods, gathered around the fire, drinking beer.

I sat a little distance away from them, watching my small rod quietly. The noise from around the fire grew louder and louder. An excellent joke led to the much thigh slapping and appreciative bellows, carp long forgotten. The bait remained untouched by the many eared celebrated fish. Men staggered past me to urinate in the bushes close to my rod. I gritted my teeth as they tousled my hair and pulled my ear in a merry way. More wood was flung onto the flames and the heat made my skin stretch and ache. I reeled in my line and set off to find a more sheltered nook.

Father called after me, but broke off to join in an old Prague sing along. A banjo was strummed wildly and some red faced fool had found two spoons to beat together. Everybody was having a great time. I sat in the reeds, the shadows of gesticulating figures dancing on the darkened green leaves.

"Watch out for snakes, young Jaro. You don't want to sit on a puff adder," someone called after me needlessly. The noise was sufficient enough to drive away bears, let alone a timid snake, I thought. Hours passed, and the African night settled in. Father staggered across past the dying fire to drape a blanket over my shoulder and retired to snore fitfully on a rug some distance away.

Plum brandy hung in the air over the camp-site and the men slept in a happy group around red embers. I yawned, grateful for the wordless peace that settled over the gathering. A splash in the middle of the lake made me sit up. I rubbed my eyes and stood up. For a moment I saw a shape in the distant glow of the moon on the water, a dark outline that rose up momentarily and sank quickly.

It looked like a large rooster crop, that briefly flapped above the shiny surface of the lake. I felt as though a cold knife blade had quickly pierced my heart, and blinked. At that moment the rod end gently swayed as though blown by an invisible breeze, and suddenly curved down. I released the reel and the line unwound quickly. I waited for a few seconds before I closed the line feed and yanked the rod up. Behind me someone in a heap of bodies farted musically and I laughed out loudly as I cranked in the line. There was a mild resistance, with the nylon tugging in the opposite direction, out towards the unseen depths of the lake. The line came in, water spraying of the reel as I excitedly wound in the catch. A flurry of foam and a small carp looked up at me from the muddy shallows.

I paused in my triumphant toil, my sweat cooling in the night air. It had the gentlest face that blessed a Sacred Fish. I saw a small thing gasping up at me in the shallows, nylon line raising a gummy upper lip into a mad smile. Behind me I heard someone stirring and yawning loudly. I grabbed the fish that flapped weakly and tried to remove the hook that glinted maliciously out of the corner of the mouth. The tail flapped against the grass as I twisted and turned the steel, the point jabbing me cruelly until we were both covered with my blood. Cursing, I cut the line and pushed the hook through the now larger ragged hole. The gills moved like bellows and a voice bellowed out my name as I flung the poor thing away from me as though it was made of red hot metal. A tiny splash, and I turned to face Father standing there in the rosy dawn blinking with a sheepish grin.

"What's happened to you?" he mumbled, looking like hell, nodding at my blood streaked hand.

"A fish bit me," I said sarcastically, and he sighed as he turned away, to walk back to a recently revitalized camp fire.

Bedraggled figures were standing in the smoke, staring morosely into the fragile flames. A sorry sight, I thought as I sucked on my punctured thumbs, the taste of metal fusing with smell of mud on my pale skin. We drove back in the silence that follows all failed fishermen. Carp cutlets fading in the glare of the new day. Father placed a cassette into the player and we all joined him in a ragged heavily accented rendition of Yellow Submarine, until the tape jammed at around the third chorus. Mother watched us from the patio and smiled as we wearily emerged from the van. Crumpled carpless men and a mud caked boy. Her humour survived until someone dropped an empty brandy bottle onto the driveway. She glared at the pile of broken glass that glinted cheerfully in the African sun. She turned her back on the paltry group and dislocated an ornamental Santa when she slammed the main door. All eyes turned to Father, who nervously hummed another chorus of Yellow Submarine.

o o o

Chapter Thirty-six

Bad Gifts Exchanged Here

Christmas came in wearing a clown suit that year. Father went out and bought a fish, Mother crumbed and fried it in a pale imitation of the Legendary Carp. I was asked to bath and to don my formal clothes that lay neatly arranged on the bed. My hair was combed vigorously whist Father, equally immaculate with eyes and cuff-links agleam, played the one dusty Czech Christmas record at full volume. We sat on the patio carving the non carp. Father beamed at us magnificently and held Mother's hand. The sweat dripped down my nose and onto my salad, but I dared not undo my top button. My tie felt like a garrotte around my neck. The sunset was a screaming masterpiece of purples and reds as the evening crept in. Mushroom coloured moths flew in and out of the candles. The smell of their singed wings gave the gathering an almost cathedral like essence. I could see Father truly enjoying the ceremony. I fidgeted until the dessert arrived. We rose and knelt around the Christmas tree. My eyes streamed as the garrotte grew tighter with each movement as I opened up my gift. I had learn to dread these occasions, the birthdays, Christmases, days which would normally be longed for, nay, pined for with a fury, had become through woeful experience, simply absurd apostrophes in my calendar.

Father was especially drawn to choosing presents for me that seemed to be intended for someone else. When I turned seven, I was presented with a hunting knife that was capable of skinning a moose. Within moments of receiving this weapon, I had managed to stab a hole into my thigh while whittling a stick. The doctor that stitched up my wound grumbled under his breath and cast dark glances at the family that stood there watching the process, still wearing their birthday hats. On my eighth birthday, he surprised me with a bicycle that was obviously made for an adult. My feet barely touched the pedals as I wobbled down the road, merely to fall into a hedge a few meters away from once again astonished well wishers.

Now, I as I removed the glossy wrapping material I felt an almost perverse joy of having my suspicions confirmed. "The Young Carpenter's Kit" included a pencil, ruler, a saw and sundry instruments that guaranteed a precise smooth cut to any plank that the aspiring handyman selected. I was known, admired and sometimes, even ridiculed for being a bookish boy, more at peace in the quiet sanctuary of a dusty library than on the rugby field or in some woodshed, with fresh sawdust in my hair carving out an ashtray for Papa.

"Thank you, Father," I said brightly and loudly and ran over to give him a hug.

"Now it's your turn to open that special gift from me," I crowed, pulling him along towards the blinking Christmas tree.

"That one," I croaked, pointing, whilst the tie quietly turned into a boa constrictor around my neck. He knelt and fumbled with the ribbon, excited and keen to rip open that badly wrapped box. Suddenly he paused and stood up, holding the gift, my present, to the light.

"What is it?" Bewilderment staunched his politeness.

"It's a beer decanter in the shape of a famous statue, The famous Pissing Boy of Brussels." Behind me I heard Mother cluck her tongue with disapproval, but I continued, smiling enthusiastically, playing the part of the over zealous informant.

"You unscrew the Pissing Boy, like so," I grabbed the decanter from his shocked hands, and demonstrated as slow as a magician pulling out a budgerigar from an unsuspecting ear.

"Then you pour your favourite beer in to the receptacle, like so." I swept up a freshly opened bottle from the dining room table, "and then you replace the Pissing Boy, screw him on tightly, no spilling in the house, if you please.

And then you hold your favourite jug, mug or Steiner before his very small penis, which actually is a spout, and there, you push the secret button at the back and the Boy will deliver a shower of beer into your glass. Brilliant, is it not ? Batteries fit snugly in the back to drive the pump. Took me ages to find it. And I know that you will love it." I gave him another hug, stepped back and let a joyous arc of beer froth from the little man into a glass.

"And there we have it" I said, raising the glass to him. "Your first glass of decanted beer from the famous Pissing Boy." He took a sip, watching me carefully. I kept on nodding at him like a lunatic.

"Well? Well, is it great? Is it fun? Does it taste better?" I could feel him being mildly worn down by my earnest dogged clamour.

"It is quite wonderful" he replied, cautiously, "truly a surprise. What a gift, so unusual."

"See, I knew that you would love it. I know you." I crept up to him, and whispered loudly, so that Mother would hear. "I know you." I repeated, and gave him a huge wink, laughing wildly, pleased with my theatre. "A little gift from me." Mother laughed too, albeit nervously. Father sipped his beer shyly.

"That's what I love about this family," I added, allowing a hint of sentimentality to creep into my voice, "it's the depth to which we know each other."

"You have always been an odd child," announced my Mother, but there was love in her voice and my mayhem and mischief evaporated and I suddenly felt an urge to put my face into her hair and to stand there for a century. Instead, I turned to open her gift to me. A bathing costume. I held it to my cheek to feel the warmth and smoothness of new cloth.

"Your old one stank like a dead pig, so I threw it out, foul thing that it was. It's funny, you don't seem to go down to the river as often as you used to."

I blushed at that, and mumbled something about having too many studies to fret away my hours down at the river. I never told them about the pig experience, merely fabricated a banal tale of falling into a dirty hole in a forest. I missed that river but was afraid of the wild boys that played there. The memory was a sour thing to me and in the school yard I tended to seek companionship with the less popular, marginalized types. Father stood around toying with the Pissing Boy. I hoped that the Bad Gift Exchange Society had had its last meeting that Christmas, but as Sabrina used to say, only those with illusions can be disillusioned and mine were still in their infancy.

o o o

Chapter Thirty-seven

Fear

"Dear Sabrina, I am sorry that I have been so quiet recently. It's been quite a turbulent time here in the sweaty tropics. Firstly I had my Young Carpenter's Kit confiscated by Father, only a few months after Christmas. He said that he had grown tired of seeing his furniture handicapped by my sawing and gouging. The Pissing Boy stands dusty and idle on the mantlepiece and beer is drank entirely from a bottle. At school the days are a dirge interrupted by weekends, but yesterday was very different and quite exciting.

"The headmaster quietly crept into our history class and whispered softly into the ear of the history teacher and they both nodded and frowned earnestly in our direction. The headmaster left quickly and we sat in silence, the sound of his footsteps echoing in the corridor outside. The history teacher drew in his breadth and speaking with great gravity, informed us that although the school day was nearly done, we were to remain at our desks. Public transport was temporarily interrupted by a protest march in the city centre. There was looting and shooting, the police were attempting to grasp control of the situation. We glanced at each other, sensing adventure and joyous chaos. It was not safe, he continued over our our swelling wave of clamour, for any pupil to attempt to go home via the city, either by bus or on foot. Emergency transport had been organized. The kitchen canteen would reopen and tea would be served. We swarmed out into the corridor where a couple of teachers were making a brave effort to usher an outpouring of boys towards the canteen.

"'It's the blacks,' shouted a tall boy, 'I heard it on the radio, the blacks are marching in protest against their schooling and the police are sending reinforcements with dogs and tear gas.'

"'Maybe we should join them, we could do with a better school lunch.' I teased him, but someone behind me failed to appreciate my humour and I was pushed over my suitcase, falling heavily. A burly brute, bristling with red hair and acne leant over me, spitting out 'You won't be laughing when they cut your head off, funny man. I hope that the army bombs them all.' And he gave me a kick that I managed to fend of with my lunch pail. Garlic polony and rye bread flew across the polished floor.

"'Who's throwing food around?' shouted an angry voice from somewhere behind the crowd watching my torment. A bearded teacher pushed his way into the circle, glaring around him feverishly.

"'Jaro, sir. He threw his lunch at us,' whined the foul red head, suddenly transformed into an angelic being, 'he said that the Blacks deserve better treatment and that our time here is up.' There was common gasp of astonishment and the teacher grabbed me by my scrawny arm.

"'What you need, my boy,' his nose was almost rubbing against my own as he fumed out his dank words, 'is a dose of the cane followed by a stint in the army. Fortunately for you, you are too young for the uniform. But not too young for the cane.' And he dragged me down the corridor, holding the remains of a garlic polony sandwich in one hand as potent evidence of my traitorous ways. For a moment I closed my eyes and had an instant daydream wherein the school walls were scaled by a thousand fierce black people who would burn and hack their way to rescue me from my oppressors. I blinked as he marched me into the headmaster's office and pushed me towards the man behind the mahogany desk.

"'This boy has been saying provocative anarchic things against the school and the government and has befouled the canteen by hurling his foreign foods at his fellow pupils.' The fuming in my ear was a hot wind of malice and indignation.

I stammered and spluttered a defence but the headmaster merely silenced me with a kindly gesture.

"'Thank you, Mr. Jansen. Leave him with me, I'll get to the bottom of this." He rose to his feet. The ruffian teacher made his exit, growling. The headmaster contemplated me for tremulous moment.

"'Kalac, is it ?'

"I nodded emphatically. 'Yes. That it is.'

"He smiled at the response.

"'I think that I know your father, a plumber, is he not?' Again, great confirmation from me.

"'He fixed a huge leak in my bathroom. Remarkable work. Quick, efficient, cheap and a truly a master of his trade. Maybe you too will grow up to be a master plumber, like your dad.'

"I shrugged foolishly. As you know Sabrina, there is more possibility of me becoming the star of the Bolshoi Ballet than a remarkably quick and efficient master of plumbing.

"'All that could possibly be, in this great country of ours,' he continued, speaking as though to himself. 'A country where freedom can almost be taken for granted and where the daily comforts, which must seem strange and new to you, coming from a land where these things are non existent, can almost be held in contempt. Here, you can rest assured, there is a future for anyone willing to work hard, for any person that respects the laws and the government of this land. We have sun and gold and beautiful schools full of fresh young things with a future so rosy that we are the envy of many other countries.' Here he paused to stare out of the window. A seagull flew past and he turned to me and placed a hand on my shoulder. 'I am certain that you can be part of this great place. Your father chose well to bring your family here. I know that it may seem a little strange sometimes and perhaps a bit lonely, but you have my word, as Headmaster of this fine school and yes, your friend, that if you pull up your socks and try to integrate more with your fellow pupils, play a bit of rugby, join the chess team, I am sure that with time your rewards will come. You, my boy, may well astonish us all with your abilities and skills. Take a candy,' he pushed a bowl of confectionery towards me who stood staring at him with amazement, 'in fact, take a handful. You can you know, because now you are in a country that is generous with those that it cares for.'

"He gave me a deep nod. I nervously took a handful of candy and put them in my pocket.

"'Now, go and join your friends and don't forget: great things await you.' He waved me out with a smile and I stood outside the door, staring into nothing. I walked slowly back towards the canteen. My classmates seemed wary of me as I reached into my pocket and dropped the handful of crushed confectionery onto the table in front of them.

"'Sorry about the garlic polony,' I said, 'I don't know what came over me.'

A bell was sounded and blue uniformed policeman appeared, led towards the centre of the assembly by the bristle faced teacher. All was well, order had been restored, town was to be avoided but the bus service was again operational, he announced. Road blocks would ensure safe passage and the glass would be swept up.

"I sat on the bus, in the back seat with the rear window sun warm on my back. My friends were laughing and shooting elastic bands at each other. Town was behind us and suburbia welcomed our return. The bus driver seemed anxious and I could see his pale face reflected in the large rear view mirror. No one else paid him much attention, did they not notice his sweat and look of terror. The bus accelerated and as we lurched around a corner I stole a glance behind me. In the distance a wild faced mass of people were chasing after the bus, arms raised, teeth shining white in black faces, voices too far to heard over the grind of the heavy engine. The bus turned sharply left at a pedestrian crossing, barely pausing to stop. More grating of gears and frightened backward glances from the driver.

"I kept on looking behind me, but only green lawns and ornate houses greeted my weary eyes. I pinched myself, unsure of what I had seen.

"It had been a day of odd visions and near dreams. The driver watched me intently. Police sirens were whining in the distance but their noise seemed to reassure the passengers, who swapped game cards, farted and scratched in their bags for apples. I sat there clutching my satchel sucking absent mindedly on the last sweet, my gift from the principal.

"Sabrina, was it you that used to quote the line of 'those that the gods wish to destroy, they first make mad?' At that moment, on a sunny bus ride through manicured lawns, past the smiling mother pushing the be ribboned pram through the streets and waving at the driver as he putty faced raced on, we all seemed destined to that madness. At home, Mother and Father sat in stony silence, listening to the soothing voice on the radio. 'Minor disturbance', 'under control' and 'troublemakers held in custody' seemed to soothe their senses, because when the classical music that heralded the end of the news bellowed out, they rose to their feet and continued with their chores, and their arguments about the leaking taps in the kitchen.

"I went upstairs to my room and sat there idly toying with the stuffed red rooster, until the dusk fell softly across us all. At supper Father raised a toast to peace being restored by the quick action of the police.

"'Those ungrateful swine, demanding god knows what rights should be grateful that they live in a democracy. Back home,' he said, almost proudly, 'they would be dragging rocks in the Gulag by now, along with their sons.'

"The following day news headlines showed pictures of youths carrying a boy shot in the protest. The faces that shouted their rage out of the picture were almost identical to those that bayed after the bus. I shuddered and went to school where the conveyor belt predictability soon erased any ripples of chaos. The most immediately significant outcome of the previous day's events was that I had made a new, red headed enemy."

Chapter Thirty-eight

Antidote

"'My beloved Jaroslav,' I read her reply a few weeks later, 'you are truly living in strange times in an odd place. And that headmaster of yours sounds like a complete lunatic. My late husband met many such as he in the trenches of the First World War. He liked to amuse me with tales of their bright eyed unquestioning bravery as they scrambled up over the wire singing into the screaming bullets and choking gas of No Man's Land. Not many came home and those that did were twisted up by rage at their own blindness. Such men are dangerous when they are in charge of others.

"A neighbour came over to me yesterday insisting that I watch the news with her. We sat down, strudel in the oven and plum brandy tipple in our hands, and I must confess that my blood ran cold seeing those children gunned down in cold blood with the dust and the helicopters and the tanks creating a scene from Dante's Circle. Perhaps the State television has an axe to grind with anything to do with the West and over exaggerates the news when it has a chance to sling mud over the Iron Curtain, but I pray that you are all well.

"Your father has always been quite pig headed in the way he forces his views upon other people and you three being in that dangerous place seems another example of his blind will. I miss you and I worry for your safety and the strudel got burnt because I was so upset. The neighbour, Madame Bilkova is an old duck that comes visiting every now and then, when the weather is good. Hunched up with rheumatism, her reputation as a psychic and teller of fortunes stretches far and wide. The Mayor of Prague even had a tea reading with her and by all accounts he left the room pale around the gills with a green sweat. And sure enough, within a month he was replaced by some Russian stooge and was never heard of again. Although that's a fairly common occurrence here these days.

"Her great skill is especially noticeable when she is asked to do 'spit readings', which I take to be her ability to predict whether you will go bald, die of cancer and how many years lie between you and the Grim Reaper.

"After watching the distressing news she calmed me down with more plum brandy and a warm hand to my forehead.

"She suggested a 'spit reading' and in a wild moment, I agreed. Creaking mightily, she went back home to fetch her divining potions and books. I had to lie down on the rug and with the fire crackling in the grate next to me, I took a great swig of foul liquid that tasted of liquorice and mushroom. Soon my saliva turned to an oily froth and she started to sing, or more precisely, to keen over me.

"Softly at first, like a faraway wind, but soon it grew disturbingly loud something that hovered between a groan and a hum. I tried to swallow the oily mass that threatened to well up over tightly clenched lips, but the old duck indicated that I release it into a blue ceramic bowl that she had placed beside me.

"With a mild blush or two, I happily complied and she nodded her approval, intoning rhythmically all the while. I lay there staring up at the ceiling, strangely at peace with the world, the images from the news fading into a haze that blended in with all my other memories and thoughts.

"'Like rain falling into the night sea.' I sighed out loudly, and giggled self consciously. I had not meant to share the words with anyone, but the nodding and smiling face above me shone with tenderness. A warm gnarled hand crept into mine. We remained in that position together for perhaps ten minutes, until she slowly removed her hand and picked up the blue spittoon. I sat up, both curious and amused. My head felt as light as a fun fair balloon and I yawned deliciously, the way a cat does in the glow of the midday sun. From her breast pocket, she took a tiny mirror and held it towards me. I craned my head to see a mad reflection of myself, hair in disarray and with eyes as big as saucers. She dipped the mirror into the liquid and stirred slowly, anticlockwise, watching me without a blink. I held my breath as she stood up with a dry creaking of ancient joints, and positioned herself by the fire, fanning the flames with the moist mirror, from side to side. The room had the odor of sweet liquorice and sweat. The saliva dried quickly and she held the now dull mirror up to the light. A lone rooster called, somewhere far away. The fire continued its merry crackle as she slowly looked up at me and croaked out words that blew a cold breath upon my heart.

"'You are in a desperate stress, my friend and neighbour.' I sat up, head throbbing with strange dull ache. Keen for the words yet dreading their arrival. And come they did.

"'There is someone very close to you that you long for, and are in a dream with. That is a truly special relationship, not often found amongst people, even mothers are out of touch with their children, and lovers are often too lost in the idea of love to swim in the deep waters of complete selflessness. What I see here,' she said, holding up the scaly mirror, 'is a powerful bond that completes both your worlds. Do not dread for this child, my sister, for there is little in the world that can truly separate you from each other. The only danger that he faces is heartbreak and a loss of faith. There is no apparent physical harm that hovers over his head, merely an open soul and a free spirit and these can conspire together to make him lose his way, to vanquish his joy and to take away his shine. But that applies to all of us, in all times and in all places. The trick is to laugh, even while the walls are shaking with the fury of the storm outside. Laugh when the bestial madness of the world is scratching on your door.

"'Do I not see you, Sabrina, out of my window every day, even in a downpour as you pour out your chamber pot onto your dead husband's grave? Smiling like a young girl, mischief and mayhem tugging at your nightdress. I turn away from the window and suddenly all seems well with the world.

Send the boy love and faith and stories, soft words that spark up his life and he'll flourish.' She held me when I became a little weepy at that sweet speech, my far flung heart. She coughed, and to my amazement, continued. 'But I do see another in his life, striding forward to meet him in the gloom of what's to come. A girl, a most unique creature that will set his heart ablaze.'

"And suddenly it felt as though the entire room had become a frozen cave. A cold coil moved in my stomach, something that had sat there, still for so many years had now found a fertile soil in which to breathe and to grow. The old woman sensed my discomfort and lean over to plant a soft kiss to my wrinkled parchment of a forehead. I could see that she too was experiencing some inner commotion, for her skin had become unusually pale with silver blue sheen. She is a woman of a ruddy complexion with great pink mottling that suggest a frequent fondness for strong beverages. We looked at each other for many seconds, before I asked the most obvious question in the whole wide world.

"'Will he be all right?' My voice was like a bird trapped in a cellar. She placed the tiny mirror into her mouth, closed her eyes and all I could hear was her shallow breathing as she savored the future.

"'Yes. He'll be fine and he'll be good. But the path is strewn with thorns and many devils will nip at his ankles,' she said sagely, 'he must especially be wary of the Fly season. He has the purity of knight and that will be tested.'

"Then she went on, whispering about my destiny, and cautioned me about my habit of sleeping with the windows closed with the fire ablaze in the hearth. Croaked ominously about a black moon that would mark at the beginning of a blighted era. My hair stood on end as I listened to the foggy words. Which of course, sounded quite vague to me.

"There are devils at play in the world, there always were and always will be, and angels that arrive in the most oddest disguises. I have encountered many on my own road, but her words did make me frown. I am very partial to sleeping with the house snug and sealed, the smoke makes me have the most extraordinary dreams.

"I rose shakily to my feet, like a newly born animal. The room seemed exceptionally bright for that time of the night and I clutched at the table for support. She gently wiped the foam flecks from your Sabrina's hairy chin. We each took a huge swig of the ever faithful plum brandy and the warmth of the liquor melted away some of the icebergs that pressed against my heart. The old crone sat back sucking in air through her toothless mouth and set to finishing off the bottle.

"Obviously you will have to walk lightly and brightly, my sweet boy. And god knows how you will go about avoiding the fly season in the sweaty tropics where pigs blow up at the strike of a match.

"It would appear that you are to be blessed with young love. May your heart find joy and do let me know all the details, let the letters flow and fly. They do bring a great cheer to this old woman's solitary life. It is partly through you that I celebrate this mad dance called life. The devils and angels are our orchestra, I for one, cannot imagine an existence without them."

I re-read the last paragraph at least a half a dozen times. The words "young love" made more of an impact on me than the witches's circle talk of flies and angels. It occurred to me then that Sabrina would have loved to have been the fourth witch in Macbeth, sitting by a autumnal fire at the crossroads, waiting for the unwary traveler to pass by. My interaction with the opposite sex was minimal. None of my friends at school had girlfriends and we bluffly suffered the bored scorn and derision with which the older boys wished to anoint us. Our group was decreed as being both notoriously studious as well as ugly, and whilst other classmates paired off with the sundry sisters and cousins of the school community, we remained the shuffling bespectacled pariahs on the outskirts of the rutting herd.

Alienation likes company. I would catch myself staring at my friends' acne troubled skins, at their double chins, and I would happily weather the sour breeze of their halitosis in exchange for companionship. And I would feel serene that I was at least part of a group that wore their obvious undesirability on their sleeve. My thick glasses and stammer were badges that bound me to the group of the unlovable. Sabrina's letter had however somehow adjusted my view of myself. I was a knight, blessed with a glowing destiny, ordained to surmount those challenges that would cripple a lesser mortal. No longer content to live in dread of the topic, I decided to ask my father about girls.

o   o   o

Chapter Thirty-nine

Desire

"Women, my dear Jaro," he mused in the late afternoon sun, face flecked with the shadows of leaves of the tree above us. "Women think through their behinds."

He cast a crafty leer at me. This was obviously one of Father's favourite topics for discussion and my stumbling into adolescence was a signal for him that his prime listener had at last arrived. He had never previously devoted much time to matters that concerned me. School work and household chores were firmly delegated to Mother, and his role was to pontificate about politics, race and religion, often deep into the night. He would often ensnare my visitors into the itchy cage of his vast monologues, by offering them cups of tea and biscuits. As the hot beverage cooled, he would expound upon his world views, which often emerged from the wreckage of his broken English as ungainly irrational tirades. The visitors eventually dwindled, and those rare individuals who would timidly knock on the front door gently resisted every attempt to be lured in, proffering to wait, even in a downpour, until I emerged.

The word had spread that I had a Mad Father. Ignorance and malice gave birth to wild rumors of his eccentricity and armed the local bullies with new tools with which to torment me.

Unlike the usual jibes about my origins, which I easily deflected, the derision that grew around Father's apparent oddness burnt deep into my heart. The few friends that I had ceased to visit me at home, for fear of being cornered in some cabbage smelling drawing room and tormented by slabs of poor dictum punctuated by wildly passionate gesticulation. Father was lonely. Many of his friends had gone up in the world and had little time for the plumber with wild ideas and strange stories. Others he had managed to aggravate through his argumentative spirit. A few of the hard wearing faithful remained true and were entertained by his wit and eccentricity, but even these die-hards eventually formed relationships with local women who were of a more delicate disposition and found the wild eyed Czech disconcerting. Party invitations dwindled to a frail stream and the previous merry chatter of semi-sober groups that filled our garden on many a summer Saturday night was replaced by the mocking sounds of crickets that disturbed Father immensely as he tried to focus on his book, alone on the porch with his glass of red wine.

Mother busied herself with the housework and her correspondence course in accountancy. They had drifted apart over the four years in Africa and only occasionally would I see them smiling fondly at each other, as they used to in days of old. A house of outsiders, with a blood link that pulsed slow and dull. I had unwittingly become Father's ventriloquist dummy, sitting and nodding while he reminisced in the name of filial advice.

"I love women," he continued, staring wistfully out onto the garden that grew more shadowy with the passing of the sun, "they have brought me great joy and delight, but truly they show themselves to be a most fickle and contrary of species. It's a relief for me to hear you ask about women, young Jaro. I was starting to worry that the apple had rolled far from the tree, and that you would be stuck in books and childish things for longer than is healthy. Forever writing letters and disappearing into the mold of the town library to emerge dazed and confused and pale. Have you noticed how pale you have become of late? In Africa too, with all the other boys tanned, white-toothed and strong."

I blushed and clenched my fists, his words ripping at the cobweb of my self-worth.

"At your age, I already had a reputation with the girls. I was both envied and imitated by many boys and mothers would warn their daughters about me, which merely served to enrage the flame of their curiosity. Young conquests and young love, those words make me sigh. Happy memories are like treasures that no one can steal from you." I nodded for him to continue. For a moment there was stillness that hung heavily over us, and his face looked strangely hollow. Then he quickly remembered that he had a duty to fulfil, that a young man needing inspiration sat nearby, watching him intently. He took a large sip of red wine, suddenly smiling at the secret images that flickered across his inner screen. I felt an involuntary pang of envy pierce my stomach. I also wanted those images, my own versions, I needed to hold them in the grasp off my own memory. He must have sensed my silent process.

"You are lucky to have inherited my charm and humour you young dog," he said, "all that you need is to learn is the art of guile and to arm yourself with a repertoire of sweet words and white lies. Women flourish under such conditions. Be brave and never fear failure."

How odd, I thought, his words were echoing the contents of Sabrina's last letter.

"Zlin was an ugly industrial town, and the factories and workshops that belched out their foulness for six days a week were a scandal to the nose and eyes. But to a young fox such as I, these grime holes were lined with the brightest of jewels. Young girls came from far and wide to find work in Zlin, and lived in large, typically Iron Curtain granite apartment blocks that lined the roads like rotting giant's teeth. Sad sickly dumps that these were, on a good Saturday or Sunday in summer, the doors would open and disgorge bevies of laughing young things, with colourful scarves and short pants and sandals. Legs and smiles would be everywhere, and groups of girls would wander into the forests, and could be seen swimming in rivers or lying on tartan rugs out in in the parks, smoking and keeping a watchful eye out for boys. Let me tell you one thing that I have come to realize in this world of borders and rules. In such an environment, with the young women far from home, in a boring town filled with staring young men, it is only a matter of time before amorous mayhem becomes the norm.

"In fact there were so many girls in those tower blocks that on dance nights at the local bistros, many would dance arm in arm with their friends, simply because there were not enough men to go around. Many a married man fell to the siren charms of those factory girls, calling out to strangers from their balconies, giggling and edging each other on to greater acts of outrageous behaviour. The dormitories were inevitably supervised by ugly Russian women, but in many cases these would turn a blind eye to the girlish play, or would be too drunk to summon up an admonition.

"No man was allowed into these hives of lipstick, nicotine and the cheap transistor music that blared out from the windows. Underwear hung in delicious lines on the balconies and my friends and I would stand there gazing up at these soft sweet containers that danced so merrily from their pegs in the warm breeze of late summer. The wind caressed these elusive garments with invisible hands and down in the dusty road, our mouths were dry with longing. Perhaps at this moment, you are too young to know the sullen ache of desire that follows you home and wakes you up in the middle of the night. We watched from the street and would quickly walkaway when a girl appeared on the balcony to take in the dry washing or simply to feel the sun on her face.

"My best friend in those feverish days was Pavel, who was as shy then as you are today. His father was the postmaster. He walked around town with his chest puffed out like a pigeon, his brass buttons scrupulously polished daily by his equally pompous wife. Pavel grew up tongue tied and nervous, quick to jump at the slightest sound. I liked him because of his bookish knowledge and dexterity with words, and he admired my rebellious ways. One particularly sweaty day, we meandered out of town onto the road that led to a nearby river, keen to find an escape from the heat in its soft waters. Horseflies trailed after us and we took turns in swishing at them with the towels that we carried. The road wound gracefully through a glade and an occasional vehicle would roar past, covering us with pale brown dust as fine as icing sugar. Soon our faces and necks were streaked with rivulets of sweat and the horseflies sang cruel and determined songs in our ears. Thirsty and irritable, we trudged on.

"The house stood on an incline above the road with a neat healthy green lawn on which a girl sat on a swing, holding onto the chains, watching our approach. The chains creaked and she began moving slowly, forwards and backwards, skirt up high on her thighs, sandals threatening to fall from her delicate feet as she swung, so young and pliable, in that afternoon sun. She smiled as she rose and fell, each time the motion taking her to a higher level than before. One sandal fell to the ground and I stopped in my tracks, Pavel bumped into my back with his chin, too distracted to see anything besides the angelic figure before us, soaring and laughing, while we stood and gaped like fish on a slab."

Father paused to light a cigarette. The evening chill had slid in and through the open patio door we could heard Mother singing to herself in amongst kitchen sounds that suggested that supper was on its way. The breeze twirled a suggestion of roast pork around our nostrils. We looked at each other and smiled, and listened to the frail harmony for a while, in silence with our own thoughts. I could almost hear the chains clink and imagined the brown legs, the white socks that teased the air with their radiance. I sighed, and Father nodded.

"Yes, sigh away young man, as we did on that day, with the heat tickling the back of our necks. She eyed us with unabashed curiosity and tucking those legs beneath her seat, allowed the swing to slowly cease the magic arcs. We jostled clumsily forward, but the path had grown too narrow for the two of us. Stomach tight with tension, I crunched up the gravel path towards her, casting a guilty glance up at the windows of the house, fearing that some anonymous adult would rain disapproval upon my feverish head. Pavel sped up his gait in an effort to overtake me and I turned my head briefly to glare at him. He reluctantly fell into resentful shuffle behind me. The girl on the swing watched us with an amused expression. She was older than I had initially assumed, perhaps eighteen or so and I mumbled and stumbled over my words as I greeted her.

"'Good morning,' I croaked whilst Pavel giggled idiot like behind me. I could have strangled him at that point, seduction hates an audience.

"'Good morning back.' She trilled and smiled sweetly, revealing sharp white teeth. My fringe became matted to my forehead with sweat.

"'A stinker of a day,' I continued, quietly cursing myself for imitating an adult. There's nothing more ludicrous than a pale approximation, Jaro, and she knew it.

"'Indeed it is, a stinker. Why is your friend hiding behind you?' she purred, and I spun around to see the pathetic Pavel leering and kicking up the dust in my wake.

"'He's an idiot that follows me around,' I said unkindly and turned to face her.

"'Maybe your idiot friend and you would like some lemonade?' she suggested, and hopped off the swing and walked towards us.

"'Now that would be an utter pleasure and a treat.' I had found my tongue and had started to enjoy this unexpected banter.

"'Then wait here for me here,' she lowered her voice to a whisper, yet her eyes never left my own.

"'I'll get us a pitcher of heavenly juice. My brothers do not approve of young, handsome boys coming into the house.' I frowned and she ran up to me and gave me a grin. She was all freckles and dancing impishness as she spun on her heel and skipped towards the homestead. Pavel looked at me cow-eyed with amazement, and I shrugged nonchalantly.

"'We are lucky, so very very lucky, luck, luck, luck, lucky,' he crowed, and I nodded, deeply confused but determined to hide my dismay. She came back with a tray of glasses, a gleaming pitcher of fragrant juice and a bowl of candied fruit. We sat on the grass and munched and stole glances at each other. I told stories and Pavel shed his moronic exterior to reveal his wit and our merriment made the birds fly of the wire above our heads. She spoke of her dreams to be a performer and quietly sang us a little song that she composed. I sensed her watching us throughout the tiny recital, and beamed when we clapped. She snuggled in between us and there we sat together, thighs pressed against thighs, faces almost touching, breath hot. I lay back and stretched out fully on the lawn. The other two immediately did the same and we lay there, with her in the middle, talking softly. I was aware of her womanliness, of the languid strength and length of her limbs that nudged against me. She reached out and held both our hands. I had to grit my teeth to prevent myself from shaking. I wondered what Pavel was experiencing there in the distance on the other side of her. Somewhere, a window was slammed shut, the noise a burr in the instep of our joy.

"She raised herself up, and kneeling beautiful and magnificent over our flushed and startled faces, she gave us each a tender kiss on the lips. 'Let's meet somewhere else tomorrow, if you would like to see me again. It's been such an exciting afternoon.' Her whisper was both a balm and a lightning bolt that made me want to clutch handfuls of the glorious earth that steadied me then. 'Yes, of course,' we both stammered, 'where, when?'

"'Um, what about tomorrow at two in that little forest over there? The shady little brook.' she indicated with a graceful finger, towards a smattering of pines not too distant from the road.

"'The little brook, yes, yes. Shady is good, perfect and fantastic.' Pavel and I were back in Laurel and Hardy territory.

"She rose to her feet, and with a wiggle and a hop ran quickly back to the house. At the garden gate, she turned and blew us a kiss. And then she was gone."

"Come and eat, you two smelly males." Mother's voice was a bucket of cold water over my heated head. Father and I stood up, and suddenly it was as though we were dovetailed together as never before.

"More soon," he quietly assured me.

I sat through the supper in a stupor, picking at the shiny green cabbage, while Father spouted forth on the tired topic of the slothful nature of his black labour force, on the need for endless vigilance when it came to working with the poor and uneducated.

I listened with half an ear. This was not the story that I wanted to hear.

"And would you believe it, some opportunist swine stole the machete from the back of the pick up," he said. At that point, I looked up from my reverie. I had always coveted that dangerous shiny blade, used for hacking down clumps of bracken and "to scare away the snakes."

Father fancied himself as the hard living sun-battered white man in Africa, although his pink gleaming pate and hairy legs in short pants betrayed his firm Central European leanings. The socks and sandals combination did little to dilute the white man lost in Africa profile.

"The Panga?" I enquired, "Gone? I wonder who took that? It's a pretty nasty weapon to have wandering around."

"Must be that new Boy that started this week. Sullen brute, and always glowers at me when I ask him to carry my toolbox. Surly and contemptuous with his arse hanging out of his pants. Thank god that the other workers are not like that. Lazy they may be, smelling of beer and sweat from morning to night as they do, I trust them well enough not to steal my tools. But this one, he's mean as a snake and as silent. We'd have a hard time here if they were all like that. Backs up against the wall is where we would be. I'd rather go back home and face the Communists than to try and placate that amount of blind hate." He frowned. "Sometimes I worry about this country," he added, glumly.

Mother rose up abruptly and started to clear the table. "Hey, Mom, I haven't finished with my cabbage yet."

"I'm sorry, Jaro. There you go." Her voice glacial, as she placed my plate before me, with a bang, "and you can continue to make interesting patterns with it for another half an hour. I'm going to bed. To await the tread of the Pangaman." She narrowed her eyes at my Father, who shrank from her simmering wrath.

"I simply mentioned that the damn thing is missing." he bleated.

"I know. It's as simple as me misplacing my lipstick."

"Well, almost," he cried with relief, "I'll fire him as an example to the others. There are dozens of people out there," he waved at the window, through which night peeped in, "who will do his job with a face shining with gratitude and honesty to boot."

"Sometimes it's your use of language that scares me the most about you," she fumed and disappeared into the kitchen. I sat with my congealed cabbage, and tried to appear neutral. He turned to me and wrinkled his features into a clownish mask. "Didn't I tell you, they think through their behinds. Moody but so very pretty. Let's have a drink."

A bottle of red wine was produced and I was given a full cup. White porcelain with picture of a two bunnies sitting on a log, holding hands. I stared down at the dark liquid, and took a small sip. At fifteen, I was allowed a tiny amount of alcohol with supper, but a post meal cupful was truly a reward. Normally I would have quietly withdrawn to my room, where the golden rooster watched over me and Sabrina felt as close as my own heart. But I truly wanted to hear the end of the story. The girl on the swing held us both captive.

o o o

Chapter Forty

Swing High Swing Low Love

"We walked home slowly. The heat had subsided into a dull ache around us, and the countryside had paled to a blur. A common delirium possessed us, and as we meandered back through the valley I could see the excitement shining in Pavel's face. Rubbing our hands with conspiratorial glee, the tower blocks full of the factory girls where underwear fluttered so cheekily on lines now seemed meaningless in the magnitude of the moment. We had no time to hang around in the hope that a girl would call to us from a balcony. We had a Plan and a Time and a Rendezvous that was as real as the dust on our sandals. That night Pavel and I sat up into the late hours, obsessively discussing the next day's event. I opened up another bottle of beer stolen from my father's hoard and passed it onto Pavel who drank from it eagerly.

"Y'ou do realize, that we must take precaution,' he advised me, a trifle tipsy, for we had consumed at least four beers each, "we cannot afford to make a woman like that pregnant. We are after all, still at school." That was true and I nodded in agreement sagely.

"'We must get some condoms.' I announced, reveling in our almost instant leap into manhood. New horizons demanded a new jargon.

"'That's absolutely right. Tomorrow, first thing, we have to go shopping.' Pavel chuckled. After a moment of silence we realized that neither of us had any experience in these novel purchases and a sense of dread descended upon the room.

"My parents had already gone to bed and we dragged an old mattress and blankets out into the garden. Pavel and I talked foolishly into the dark, blowing cigarette smoke up at the stars, exhausted by our exuberance. Sleep stumbled in like a ragged tramp. We arose with the dew crisp on the lawn, two disheveled Casanovas that stood smiling nervously at each other in pale morning sun.Burnt toast and coffee odors wafted from the kitchen windows and we trooped in to breakfast, dank and crumpled yet exchanging secret smiles as the adults clucked and murmured their disapproval.

"It was a Saturday, I recall, and we hurried into the town before the shops grew too busy for such a discreet transaction. Our vigorous pace slowed down to a plod as we approached the street corner where Hruba's Chemist shop stood, doors cheerfully open to the summer glare. It was a haven for both the old and the young, offering sweets and medicine with equal aplomb and we had spent many happy hours there ourselves, paging through the magazines that lined the walls. On that sun filled morning the shop had taken on a distinctly sinister demeanor and to our wild and guilty imagination, the place throbbed with accusation. We paused and walked on by without looking left or right and found ourselves giggling girlishly in the safe haven of a nearby greengrocer, where we purchased a bag of grapes and stood in the street munching the crisp fruit forlornly, like cows at their cud. Pavel nudged me severely, and nodded his head in the direction of the chemist shop.

"'Well'? Are we or are we not going to do this? The place will be full of people soon, and somebody may recognize us, my parents aren't as lenient as yours, you know.' He was right. The shop was starting to receive far too many customers and we were starting to attract curious glances, skulking and spitting out grape seeds onto the road in our anxiety.

"'Come on then,' I growled, more to reassure myself than to spur him on, 'no eggs broken, no omelettes,' and we lurched forward together, like Siamese Twins joined by invisible skin. I stood behind a bent old crone that was fumbling with some weathered script, Mr. Hruba smiling encouragement kindly, yet keeping a keen eye on us. I put another grape into my mouth and held his gaze. The old woman finally found her prescription and shuffled off, not before giving me a leer and a nudge. At that point I was ready to dump my bag of grapes and bolt out of the shop. Everyone seemed to sense the true nature of our visit. At a poke in the back from the impatient Pavel, my mouth rasped out the words that I had practised so many times during the previous night.

"'We would like some condoms, please. Sir. A small packet would do.'

"'Of course,' he replied, 'are you both sixteen? Would you like a specific type, colour, texture or length? And talc soft or gently abrasive? Dampened or lined? Is it for home use or for outdoor purposes?'

"The questions all seemed quite odd and alien to me, but the last inquiry made me bellow out with laughter, and he joined in, with a staccato shrill yelps of mirth. This was turning out better than I had anticipated and Pavel joined me at the counter, a bit perplexed by the sudden bloom of frivolity that had sprung up in the desert of our initial dread. Mr. Hruba reached into a secret place beneath the counter and ceremoniously placed a tiny packet before us. We stared at the offering with amazement. The epicentre of nocturnal rumination all reduced to this shiny packet that called upon us to celebrate our new status as Men. Pavel picked it up and scrutinized the garish packaging.

"'This,' he said with gravity, 'is a ticket to the circus.' The three of us craned our heads together, the item in his hand held aloft as though a Sacrament and there was a solemn silence. Broken by the sound of another bevy of wrinkled women entering the shop, cackling like ancient geese.

"Were you not embarrassed about being found out, discovered ánd jeered at?" I piped up from the couch, swimming in the warm sea of his words that rose and fell upon my blushing ears, savoring the pull of a forbidden tide of secrets shared.

"No, and yet again yes, I was and Pavel was, but then Mr. Hruba gave us a wink of approval behind the counter and all seemed well again. We strutted past the old crones like young peacocks and stood outside the shop, examining our prize. The packet shone with neon red lights and tinsel in the radiance of the day. A hot coal in the palm of my hand, and one that would ignite even greater fires. We ran laughing, wild and gleeful through the crowded street filled with blurred faces and their hatchet frowns. Hooting with mirth as we nearly collided at a street corner with a bevy of fresh young girls in their starched town frocks, with blond hair that shone like halos in the brilliance of midday. Their wrinkled chaperone snarled at us but we were already gone, rushing to sit on a park bench overlooking the lake, lungs aching from the ecstatic charge through alleys and up into foothills. I looked at Pavel and his face was full of light and dried sweat. He raised his eyebrows at me I crinkled up my face gnomishly and our laughter pealed up to the heavens. And for that unusual moment even the reason for our mad behaviour flickered out into insignificance. Adventure and mischief were the spurs in the side of our joy.

"'Now,' I said, assuming the role of the leader, for I had the magic parcel in my pocket, 'we have to prepare the setting for the meeting. I think a shower and a fine fresh shirt is what is needed. We can't meet her like a couple of tramps. This is a woman, not some schoolyard princess.' He agreed enthusiastically, both of us forgetting that upon our first encounter with the siren we were covered with a fine layer of white dust and our hair was matted and rank.

"'And we should prepare a comfortable place for us to sit or to lie down on,' I added, earnest and wise. A great silence descended upon us at that point and we listened to the sound of the fat bees that flitted through the bushes nearby.

"'In fact, I think that we should hurry up and get ready.' I rose and he quickly jumped up.

"'It's only eleven o'clock,' he whined. 'We're only supposed to meet her at two.'

"'Exactly,' I said, imperiously, 'we have to get ready.' And I strode off, full of purpose and vision. He followed me at a trot, grumbling all the way to my house. We showered and scrubbed each other's backs with a wooden brush. I examined my tiny array of shirts hanging in the cupboard and flung the least glamorous item at him.

"'This is more of your style,' I urged , 'the stripe pattern really suits you. Offsets your milky skin. Brings out the rugged man in you. And make sure that you do not sweat all over it.' He squinted into the mirror unsure of the advice, the shirt held crumpled in his pink fists. A moth flew up and circled around his head. He sneezed and the insect flew away in an erratic spiral. We dressed quietly with shy glances at the clock whose hands knew no pause. Our hair combed back, oiled slick and aromatic, we looked like a singing duo. All that was lacking were floral shirts and guitars.

"'Bring the blanket,' I commanded. Pavel started to pull off the bed cover. A teddy bear tumbled to the floor. I sucked air in through clenched teeth.

"'That blanket, you fool,' I hissed,pointing to a tattered scrap that lay folded at the bottom of the clothing cupboard. He picked it up hastily.

"'Now,' I said, kicking the bear under the bed, 'let's go and meet that minx.'

"The road back to the girl on the swing seemed somehow longer and stonier than before. I cursed the dust that made a mockery of my shoe polish but my humour was lifted by the sigh of Pavel attempting to wear my oversized shirt with panache and grace. Already the sweat had seeped through the thick fabric, and dark patches were forming underneath his armpits. He avoided my stare and kept his fists firmly clenched in the pockets of his trousers, the condom packet tight in his grasp. We arrived at the rendezvous point, early and tense. The swing stood still, the house behind it loomed large and silent. A black bird cried sharply from the branches of a nearby oak and we both took an involuntary step back from the uninviting scene.

"'I told you that we were stupidly early,' grumbled Pavel, 'we look like desperate dogs, hanging around some dustbin. Let's go and find a quiet spot where we can at least have a smoke.' He turned quickly, keen to retrace his steps.

"'Not so fast, big boy,' I drawled, 'the reason for us being here so bloody early, is to make sure that we create a boudoir, somewhere out of sight, for our lovely bride. There, under those trees. That will do.' I pointed to a shady spot in the distance, 'let's go and have a look.'

"We trotted there, relieved to be away from the brooding menace of the house and grounds. The trees formed a canopy, the grass in the shade was soft and bouncy. The swing could be seen in the near distance, gently swaying in the summer breeze.

"Pavel nodded encouragement. 'Let's make a mattress out of this grass, it's so sprightly. She's going to love the secret bedroom.' He removed his shirt and hung it from a branch. I was amused. He flung himself into the task of tearing up clumps of grass making an impressive layer. With the morose blanket on top, he crafted a makeshift bed that was truly springy and enveloping. We lay there for a while, blowing cigarette smoke up into the branches that hung over our love nest.

"'Two o' clock,' I announced, picking a leaf out of the oiled luxury that was my hair, 'time to leave boyhood behind, methinks, Pavel.'

"For a moment his face looked young, pale and glum. A similar surge of emotions ran through me, but then we cackled with excitement and ran down the road, Pavel fumbling with the buttons on his shirt. The day was bright with sun and promise as we loitered breathlessly by the swing. Even Pavel looked uncharacteristically scrubbed and fetching, teeth white and lips moist with expectation as we chatted, with ever frequent consultation of the watch hand. At last there was a movement that broke the spell of expectation. A curtain twitched briefly in an upper floor window and we both turned our heads to stare, two boys burning with a common fever.

"'Maybe we should simply ring the bell?' offered Pavel, hoarsely.

"'Hmm, that could be a bit embarrassing if her family are home. A couple of youngsters dressed for the ball, at two in the afternoon, looks a little suspect. And besides, you've got hair oil running down your face. We'll wait out here. It's more seemly.' I had no desire to be quizzed by the strangers that lived in the house. An interrogation, with us shuffling out our secret guilts into a lounge carpet while hostile eyes looked for chinks in our armour, was the last thing that I had on my mind for that day. Another curtain moved, in different window. We stood rooted to the spot like Easter Island statues. A pause and another curtain shook, momentarily. Only this time the motion was a little too symmetrical and sustained to be a mere consequence of someone momentarily peering down to look at us, two fools staring up.

"'What kind of a game is this?' I mumbled, and Pavel grunted his irritability. I was about to continue, when the sudden sound of a bolt being slid and a creak of the front door opening silenced his reply. The girl emerged, radiantly beautiful in green dress, with her sunglasses fashionably perched upon her head. Pavel and I surged ahead to meet her but stopped abruptly at the sight of the devilishly handsome man that followed her. The couple stood in the doorway, barely disguising their mirth.

"'Are you here with a school outing?' the man asked waggishly, placing his foul arm around her waist. She gazed up into his face with adoration, and giggled at his wit.

"'Or are you, perchance collecting old clothes and wares?' and this stirred up more barely contained merriment from the girl, who looked everywhere but at us.

"'We had an arrangement,' I said with steel in my voice, my face flushed scarlet, 'to meet and...' my tongue stumbled and stopped. Behind me, Pavel gave me an encouraging cough.

"'And what? To do what ? You two, with her?' The suave fool brayed, slapping his thighs. The girl hid her face in her hands and shook with laughter. I felt like ripping away those hands and slapping her rouged cheeks.

"'To be together, to have fun. To, you know, to...' My anger was a bird that clawed it's way up in my chest, seeking light, seeking air.

"'No, I don't know what you are stammering about,' he sneered, advancing upon me. I moved quickly to meet him and he stepped back, astonished at my fury and my fist shot out as though from nowhere and he fell to his knees, holding the bloody nose that wept crimson into the dust. I was young but street wise, tough and built like a whip.

"To screw, you slug, to hump. With that slut. The slut on the swing.' Pavel chortled and kicked dirt into the bewildered face. The girl stooped over him, her lush hair trailing in the muck and the blood. She looked up at us and hissed 'You two are pathetic, brutish pigs. We were only having a laugh at your stupid naivety. Look at yourselves, gutter grease spit and bile, what would posses me to touch you?' Her face was a curse and we drew back, shocked.

"'You mocked us, jeered at us, toyed with us...' I began, in our defence.

"'Get away from here, go back to where you come from. If you want a woman, find some factory whore. I never want to see you loitering here again. Filthy animals.'

"'Hang on,' began Pavel, always a step out of synch with any event. I turned away and his words died on his lips.

"'Come, let's leave this mess,' I mumbled, shaking my head and he nodded. We walked away without a backward glance, bitter and sad. We sat together on the bench, once again, watching the river. Only this time there was little to look forward to.

"'I still have the condoms,' said Pavel brightly.

"'Another time, Pavel. At this moment, I would feel safer walking through a forest of vipers barefoot than to place my trust in some hussy.' His eyes grew wide and then he howled with laughter, which was deliriously infectious and I joined in, rejoicing in the release. The world had dropped a veil for us that day and we caught a glimpse of its true face. And so you see, young Jaro, you have to walk tall in this life, because without a doubt derision and false women will come to you. Take a page out of your odd Father's diary, friends are more important than some flighty errand, some pursuit of a pair of golden thighs at the end of the rainbow."

I thought about that for a moment or two. He had no true friends here, under the African skies where the setting sun glowed red and the red soil smelt of jasmine and petrol. Where he rode in the work van, alone in the cab, while black faces stared from their positions in the back with the toolboxes, the shovels and gear.

"Yes, I hear all that, but what about love? You love Mother, don't you? Aren't you glad that you have us and that we are together?" There was a deadly pause, and suddenly I cursed myself for asking the question because the answer did not appear quickly, nor spontaneously and now we were captives in the spotlight of my creation.

"Yes, of course I do," The words came slowly and, I sensed, with hesitation. Then came the hammer blow. "But to be honest, I sometimes do wonder if I should have left you both back there, in Czechoslovakia. And came out here on my own, like many others did, you know, and sent the money back home, faithfully, month by month."

"Like the others?" The tears threatened to come, and my voice shook as I blinked behind my thick lenses, "how many send money back home to their families? Mother told me of these 'newly single' men. She meets a lot of them at the Immigration Department. They have new girlfriends and new things and drink and forget the past. They will never see their families again, so they make new ones here."

"It was just a thought, Jaro, don't get so upset about it. Just sharing a thought, just as I shared the story with you, you're almost sixteen now, I trust you enough to see things in context." His tone was kind and soothing and he placed his strong heavy arm over my shoulder. I nodded, glasses skew on my face under the pressure of the arm around my neck, wondering what the context was.

Chapter Forty-one

A Man in a Van and a Glimpse of Heaven

"Dear Sabrina, I miss you and the rooster gang. Are they still aflapping on this earth, they seem pretty immortal barring their companion that watches over me here in the exciting sub-tropics? The excitement reached a new height on Tuesday when Father discovered a black man hiding behind our garden shed. Father bellowed at him like a bull and when the man turned to run, he managed to grab him and wrestled him to the ground, swearing and shouting for Mother to call the police. She dropped the chicken fillet that she was battering for lunch and ran to dial the number frantically, egg mix running down her arms and over the gleaming telephone. Outside the men rolled around in the dirt for a while until Father managed to twist the black body into a submissive position, and sat on the man's back, growling and snarling like a dog. He kept on shouting at Mother, urging her to hurry and she shrieked back her responses.They had a high volume argument that cut through the walls and my eardrums. I felt a pang for the black man, lying there, buried under a beefy body and a tirade of full volume Czech.

"There is an unwritten law in these parts, a common understanding that once the African labourers complete their work in the white suburbs for the day, they disappear like ghosts, back into their townships and are not seen on the streets until the next day. One or two villages up north still celebrate an official nightly curfew. Suburbia is a white haven in between the hours of 7 pm and 6 am and the police patrol these streets with gusto. To find an African person hiding behind your shed after seven o'clock in the evening constitutes something of a crisis because the chances are that he is up to no good, and recently a few of the local houses had bicycles and washing stolen from the yards. Ghosts should remain intangible. That law keeps the peace between the worlds, the worlds of us and them.

"Father held the man down and when the police came they congratulated him for his vigilance. The staff sergeant and Father stood drinking iced tea on the porch while the young constable pushed the black man into the back of the vehicle and slammed the steel door hard enough to make the local dogs bark in a chorus. The black guy watched me through the thick wire mesh unblinkingly. The blue light from the roof of the police car flashed like a perverse lighthouse and soon locals dropped their barbecue tongs, gathered up their six packs of beer and started to throng around the street outside our house. Women with towels wrapped around suntan oil gleaming bodies, sandals half-fastened in their rush from invisible poolsides to mill and to stare.

"Father called me to move away from the van and the constable ran his nightstick against the mesh playfully. The man inside the van spat like a cat. The cop laughed and turned his back on the face behind the wire. The neighbourhood had gathered around our driveway and I shrank back into the shadows of the patio, away from the swagger and curses of the men that stood there in front of the vehicle, pointing at the sweaty black face that scowled back at them. The flashing light created a dreamy strobe effect on which the crowd bathed in the setting sun. More handshaking and the vehicle finally sped into the dusk. Father went to meet the mob, and for a brief drop in time he was a welcome addition to the community, his thick accent forgiven, the socks in open shoes forgotten. Beers were opened and bottles clinked. I slid into the house, glad to be free of the raucous throng, the high pitched brays of the women and guffaws of the men. He sauntered in humming and Mother gave him a proud hug. I avoided his attempts to ruffle my hair and he looked at me, hurt at being rejected in his moment of triumph. I could smell the sweat that clung to him from his impromptu wrestling match. All I wanted was to bolt into my room and to read myself out of the situation around me.

"I should be glad that Father is seen as a hero by the police and the neighbourhood, because the word will spread through my school and I will no doubt be blessed with some hand me down respect, but I would have preferred it if he had let the man go. Such laurels feel like emblems of hollow victories. I still doubt that he was the laundry thief, and one of the kids who had his bicycle stolen had actually forgotten that a friend had borrowed it for a day. That fact died a very quick death in the seemingly endless repeats of the story of How the Weird Czech Fellow Subdued the Black Threat.

"I read somewhere recently, Sabrina, that anonymity is the best disguise, but that certainly did not help the man in the back of the van. I stole quietly up the stairs, glad to shut out the clamour and laughter that seethed in the street below. Closing the door, my bedroom felt like a raft on some dark sea, with the sound of mad birds wafting in on a secret tide. I turned on the radio to drown out the muffled voices, the drone of Father repeating his heroic tale in ever expansive detail. I had lost my desire for the comfort of a book and felt oddly sad and listless. A young and a keelless thing adrift in the dark. I lay on the bed, the light growing dim with the dying of the day, the tinny music from the speakers soothing my senses. The pale red outline of your drowned stuffed rooster on the cupboard above my bed soon faded into the dark and for a moment or two I drifted into soft sleep. I woke up into blessed silence and lay there listening for evidence that the last thrill seeker had vanished from the street outside and that life had regained its composure. The stillness was reassuring and I rose to open the window to let the sweet florid nocturnal wind roll into the room. I stood there for a while, watching the lights come on, in the darkened suburbia that spread out across the valley beneath our house. The street lamps outside showed no trace of the day's chaos and I was about to return to room when my gaze chanced to linger upon a movement on a balcony of the house across the street. A woman was standing there, in the dim moonlight and I could see the red trail of her cigarette as she expressed herself animatedly at an unseen figure that stood in the shadows of the balcony.

"What struck me like the flap of a rooster wing, Sabrina, was the wild mane of her red hair and the low cut of her dress, her back almost naked as she turned to light another cigarette. I vaguely knew the woman as a single mother of boy in a junior grade, and that she had a schoolground reputation for being unusually fond of both men and drink. The son would blush and disappear whenever the topic of his mother arose in the din of the lunch time ribaldry and I always felt a pang for him on those occasions. I know what it's like to have an odd side of your family exposed so crudely. I tended to avoid her in the streets, partly out of an unspoken fealty with the boy and also partly because she tended towards very revealing clothing that unsettled me strangely.

"Now I stood in the darkness, watching her movements with a fascination undiluted by social graces. A siren sound in some distant part of the valley made me retreat into the warm entrails of my room, but my heart was beating hard in my chest and my blood sang in my ears. Inspired, yet near blind in the gloom, I dug around inside an old toy chest, in amongst the broken soldiers and scruffy bears, until at last my frenzied fingers felt the cold comfort of the metal binoculars. Another poorly conceived birthday gift, destined to lie forlorn and dusty until this moment of illumination. Keeping my ears pitched for the clammy sound of my parents calling for me, I leapt back to my vantage point by the curtains and focused the grimy lenses. Her back was a golden flow of tight muscles as she leant back and laughed derisively to the man that had joined her in the light on the balcony. I strained to hear her voice, the cruelty of her mirth apparent in the manner in which her partner stood cowed and resentful by her side, his face a rigid mask in the twilight. I suppose that there are many ways of getting to know the least, tiny part of the map that is the opposite sex, Sabrina, when you are young and blundering and be-speckled like me, but at that point I felt the delirium of discovery, and it did not come out of the pages of a greasy magazine passed around the Geography Room,whilst the teacher was out.

"It may seem odd, but the reality of the interaction distant and dubious as it was, felt more delicious than hoping that a 14 year girl would dance with me at a teenage party. So judge me not, dear Aunt, for I have been shy and I have been a bit lonely here, in this crazy land. I watched, sitting on the edge of my bed, partially obscured by the curtains that eddied and flowed in the current of the evening breeze, the binoculars trembling in my hand. The man on the balcony turned from her abruptly and I confess to a sudden sense of relief as he stormed out of my vision, to emerge out of a front door which he slammed shut so forcefully that the violence made me duck behind my curtain, lest in a moment of instinct heightened by obvious anger he would spot me, up above suburbia, wide eyed and watchful in the dark, half owl, half mouse. The sound of a large vehicle skidding away in a frenzy of rubber prompted my return to the viewing station.

"She was gazing directly up at my window, and I once again retreated into the shadows, my hands wet with sweat, the metal of the scopes now a slippery burden that I dropped onto the bed, from where it bounced and landed on the wooden floor with a clatter. An eyepiece rolled off and I scampered after it on all fours.

"'Jaro?' came the predictable sound of my name being called by an irate and inquisitive parent. 'What's going on? Supper's ready, where are you?' Mother's voice was a wasp in my ear.

"I quickly flung the pieces of the binoculars under the duvet. Leapt across the room to switch on the piercing light of normality, and opened the bedroom door to call out 'I'm coming.'

"Heart beating wildly, I cast a reluctant farewell to the window, where the curtains billowed seductively in the scented air. I descended the stairs to be greeted by a half a dozen neighbours crowded around the dinner table, glasses raised to Father standing face red with false humility, the centre of attention. Mother in apron, appearing with a tray laden with food, the guests clamouring to help themselves.

"'Your Father is a real hero, a Ghost catcher of note.' A burly man beamed at me, barely pausing to add another sliver of ham to his plate. Everyone laughed wildly at that. 'Ghost Buster, ghost catcher.' They bayed, and Father performed a cumbersome curtsey which led to more applause and hooting from the throng. I sat down, and avoiding eye contact, ate quickly. The noise around rose and crashed and at a climatic calling for yet another round of toasts, I gracefully slid out of my chair and carried my dishes to the kitchen.

"I was a shadow that slid up the stairs and as the bedroom door shut behind me, the darkness warmed my heart like the hand of an old friend. My pulse beating in my ears, I moved to the window, silver moonlight a soft welcome to my return. The balcony was sadly empty. Her windows glowed with dull light and up above the roof the stars softly speckled the sky. No graceful figure, arched and assured, awaited my hungry eye. I felt cold in that summer night, my face as flushed as Father's, but before my heart could drop further into some dark inner sea, she walked into the spotlight of her lounge. She poured herself a drink and once again disappeared from view, to re-emerge in the bedroom with a twirl. Dancing to music that I could not hear, she spun around unsteadily, her drink in one hand, her long hair a free flowing mass of ringlets that bounced and teased me cheekily. She refilled her glass and swirled around the room. A lone figure dancing, watched by a lone figure that sat hunched and trembling in his room. She swayed and writhed and I ached to hear the song which seduced her into this lonely rapture. At last she stopped, and put her glass down on some invisible table and stood watching herself in a long mirror for what seemed like an eternity. She reached up to loosen the ribbon that held up her summer dress, and I wanted to stand up and applaud, Sabrina.

"Some devil interfered in the moment for suddenly she paused and turned around and advanced frowning towards the window. Standing there, kissed by a common breeze that linked us, her shape a silhouette in the burning light behind her, she looked directly up at me. I was safely concealed in the shadows, yet I felt her gaze grab my soul and threaten to steal it away. And god knows that I would have, at that moment, given it up without a murmur. The street was an abyss between us, as with a deft movement she quickly closed the curtains. She moved quickly from room to room, and one by one the lights went out, leaving me gaping at a grey slab of a building that stood scowling back at me. Only a dim glow of her bedroom bespoke of the tenderness that lay within. I remained standing, a watchful sentinel framed by night. I picked up the binoculars again, and idly scanned the blackened windows for one last time, for my disappointment had ushered in exhaustion in its wake.

"To my utter horror and dismay I focused on her face staring back at me from her kitchen window. The wily minx had crept back in the dark to catch me in my moment of exposure. There are no words to describe the dread that assailed me as I flung myself to the floor of my room, a man struck by lightning would feel less vulnerable and foolish in that instant. I could not drag myself back to confirm my shocking discovery, for I was convinced that she would be there, awaiting my return. Instead, I simply lay on my bed, breathing quietly lest some evil wind drove the sounds of my misery to her ears. Minutes passed, and I was starting to feel a little more at ease, having convinced myself that my guilt had played tricks upon my senses, and that my presence at the window could be excused by a myriad reasons.

"At fifteen, the world damns you as a mass of hormones in turmoil, and I bow my head in shame at my behaviour, Sabrina. But in that instant as I lay there I knew why a thousand ships were launched to Troy and why men spilt their blood into the soil in the name of beauty and life. I was starting to fade into sleep, stretched out as I was on the soft raft of my bed, when the grating crackle of a radio, somewhere in the street below dragged my terror back to me, tenfold and wormy. A blue police light flashed strobe patterns on my wall, and I crept to that dreaded location by the window and cringed to see a police vehicle parked on the curb outside our house. A quick glance across the way, towards the Minx's window revealed a stoic darkness that brought some relief to my shredded nerves. I was convinced that they had come for me. Itching to arrest the bookish pimply pervert that leered at older woman in the privacy of their boudoir. I could already feel the cold hand of the law on my nape. Disgrace and Derision would be my constant companions, with both Luck and Wisdom shaking their heads in disbelief. School would either cease or enter a new circle of Hell. My young lust my yoke of shame. I listened at my door but there were no footsteps up the stairs, and no angry fumbling with my door handle and no pool of outraged faces that spun around me like carousel horses.

"Instead the sound from the front porch of Father welcoming the young constable back, the black man safely locked away, the neighbourhood vigilantes having a party celebrating another day of safety in paradise. Suddenly my guilt vanished, and for the first time on that florid day I smiled and went back to the muse called sleep. You are truly the one to understand the mad carpet that people weave as their lives, Sabrina. Oh to run with the roosters and to hear the happy sound of the carp flapping in the warm mud of a lake in summer. I understand why you love the farm and the forest so dearly. Send me some words to make sense of this jumble, of this clamour and clatter that waits for me every time that I open my eyes in the morning."

○ ○ ○

Chapter Forty-two

Sabrina's Youthful Folly

"Dear Jaro, what a mad story, my boy, and I am so glad for your honesty and for your faith in this old crone that creaks from dawn to dusk, attempting to avoid both the Reaper and the rooster beaks with a swish of my moldy apron. Some secrets are sadly a little too fragile to share with our moral guardians, an open heart deserves good company. It's quite remarkable watching you grow at a distance, and I love your story telling, it holds me captive, line by bewildering line.

"I know little about the place that you find yourself in, and of the politics and the laws that surround you. It all seems to be quite bizarre, even to me, the old hen clucking behind her Iron Curtain, and I burn a candle for you all every Tuesday night, as I pray for your safety and joy.

"Be glad that you are not growing up here, in the land of Fear and Longing, for the Communists are not the kindest of taskmasters and a knock on the door at midnight is often the sound of the end. By now you would be some builder's apprentice, eating a pork and rye bread lunch on some dank building site, your beautiful mind fogged by premature misery. Your father knew well to take you away from here. Better to live on your feet than to die on your knees, my love, although it would appear from your letters that a great many people there around you seem to be servants on their knees in their own land. One wonders how long such a system can last before someone gets truly angry, and people get hurt. Hence the Tuesday night candle burning ritual, may long you prosper, my boy.

"Your story of trembling desire made me smile and cry, because it blew away the dust of an old memory that I have kept buried away in the basement of my head for so many decades. I cannot recall how long since I last even lightly lingered on the sorry saga of my unrequited love for an older, married man. He was lean and wiry fellow, with a smile that stopped my heart whenever I went to his butchery to stand in the eternal queue that was our lot in the war years. I was a foolish quietly romantic girl, full of secret longings that grew out of stories from the books that I so cravenly consumed in moments stolen from my household chores, in the dark of the night when the rest of the family snored out their sleep. Tales of young maids whisked away to a sumptuous life by a passing cavalier on a coal black horse, to castles filled with fruit and song and light. A spark in the gloom of my drudgery, the books with their magical words gave me hope and cheer in those fearful times.

"The butcher was notoriously good looking and many of my friends would whisper of his veined hands that carved the bare scraps of meat, the gypsy eyes that stroked their bodies while they stood frozen at his counter, breathless with longing, pink with shy desire. I always kept my head bowed as he cheerfully whistled, attempting to block out the effect that his graceful movements behind the counter had on my quivering frame. I would quickly grab the cool paper parcel that contained the allocated ration of some sad offcut from his delicate hands with their delectably tapering fingers, and bolting out into the sunlit safety of the street outside, I would stand there and shiver like a cat out in the rain.

"His wife was a severe woman, who no doubt had her patience infinitely tested by the daily bevy of giggling girls that appeared in the butchery, their eyes hungry for a flash of promise in his dark handsome face, that smiled as he carved out the portions. She often stood in the shop doorway, chatting with the mothers and the crones, her arms folded in a proprietary manner as she watched her man as he worked. Occasionally he would look up and blow her a kiss which made the women chortle and nudge at each other. The young girls hated her and she knew it. She treated them with glacial queen like contempt. She obviously did not regard me as a threat to her kingdom and often spoke gently to me, the shuffling nervous bird that I was, with my workman's shoes and cumbersome feet.

"There were rumours floating around that he had had an illicit liaison with a whorish factory supervisor a few years previously, which may have explained the weary watchfulness of his basilisk wife. I was partially glad to have escaped her suspicions, yet was mildly irked that my lumpy plainness had rendered me apparently invisible to his attention. I found solace in the pictures of beautiful nymphs that appeared in the books that were piled up high next to my bed and on some quiet nights, while the wind blew softly in the trees outside, I would lock my door and light a candle which I placed next to my long mirror. I would sit there with my hair loose and wild like a witch, watching the glow dance across my neck and I would unbutton my night dress, letting the halo of light stroke my bare shoulders. Sometimes I would feel free and strong enough to do anything, free to shout out my name to the wind that whistled a nameless tune in the branches outside. But I always ended up resisting the temptation. At other times I would simply sit there in forlorn silence and wish that the wind would carry me away to a better place, where ugly girls had as much place in the sun as anybody else.

"One day I decided on some mischievous whim to test the hand of fate. I awoke from a troubled sleep, racked with a mad longing for his touch. My face in the mirror flushed with guilt as I combed my straggly hair, while my delirious fancies hung over me like ether. I longed for the tiniest scrap of his acknowledgment, craved a glance that was a silent nod to my womanhood. Yes, my Jaro, I do know what it is to watch and to wish upon a distant star. Crazy foolish thing as I was, and caught up in the current of my secret desires, I stood up and tied my hair back, and shaved my long neglected upper lip, for as you know I have always been cursed by that hair that belongs to some other person, some Mexican fellow who misses his mustache. My ears have been the redeeming feature of my otherwise forgettable face and the earrings that I chose on that hazy morning hung like twin braziers from my long lobes. Next came the lipstick, and the flash of the crimson sheen when I licked my lips made me want to sing like a siren, bawdy and wild. I did not wear a brassiere that day, and the stockings choked my thighs, those sorry pale thighs that quivered with tales of too many strudels, for I have always had a sweet tooth. The dress I wore was a flimsy garment, festooned with ribbons and little bows, more appropriate for the theatre than for a visit to your local butcher.

"A' half a kilogram of your best horse meat, sir." I practiced those words in the mirror, the lipstick made them sound quite lurid.

For that was the most common cut available, in those sad old days. I examined myself dispassionately in the glass and my heart sank for standing before me in the mirror was a witchy doll, an apprentice palm reader at the fair. I shook off my fears and covered myself up with drab coat. Instantly I felt a relief. A lumpy girl in a shoddy coat, safely invisible again.

I crept out as stealthy as a wisp and walked swiftly to the butcher shop, afraid that fear would overwhelm my sense of purpose and that I would bolt away like a frightened colt. Yet I walked with my head held high, as proud as a mare. While inside I was a raging sea of doubt and desire. I felt like a woman possessed and I enjoyed the sensation, so new and so forbidden it felt to me, as I bustled down the street. There were people already waiting outside the butchery, and the town clock struck eight times as I joined the queue. I cursed my own urgency, dreading the prospect of standing around in the street in front of a closed shop, with the world spying on me.

"My earrings swayed on my nervous head. A sound of a key, the grind of a lock resisting, and the butchery door opened. The butcher's wife welcomed us inside the cool emporium. I feigned exasperation at the early morning heat and slipped off my coat. The breeze touched my skin, and I could smell the floral floor polish. I shivered. I ignored the hum of voices behind me as I waited behind an old man that wheezed and coughed into a foul handkerchief. Peering over his shoulder I caught sight of the handsome butcher, smiling and nodding as he took an order. Out of the corner of my eye I could see the wife who stood frozen in the doorway, watching me like a snake, her face hard. I made a small sound of panic, more of a hiss than a croak. The old man in front of me heard me, and turning around to me offered me his place at the counter. I shook my head, suddenly hating my own visibility.

"'There, beautiful lady, I insist.' And he stood back to reveal the smiling face of the butcher, who nodded at me kindly.

"I teetered forward. His gaze made me warm and soft and my earrings were dancing all around my ears as I whispered the magical words 'A half a kilogram of your best horse meat, sir. Is the horse fresh today?'

"Behind me I heard the unmistakable sound of his wife approaching. She appeared at the counter, nonchalantly pretending to wipe away at some spot with a red cloth. 'Fresh as the dew, my love.' She replied for him.

"They both stood staring at me as the blood rushed to my face. I mumbled something about needing a good cut. He place a hunk of meat in front of me me. 'Fresh.' he said.

"'Like a virgin.' the wife added, and he and I looked at her. Her mouth was tight and the eyes bored into me like acid. I felt a wave of hate crash over me. Our mutual contempt met in a sick tandem. Behind me, the old man chortled.

"'What's your name, sweet girl?' The butcher's voice soothed me, and I moved closer to the counter.

"'Sabrina. Could you wrap it up for me, in a double sheet?' I suddenly reveled in our tiny dialogue for I knew that the harridan seethed behind her frozen mask behind me.

"'Of course, I will. I don't want the meat to stain your dress.' His words made me tremble afresh and again elicited a wet sound from the old fool of a man lurking close.

"'Going to a wedding?' the caustic rasp of the wife made me drop my coat. Gazing up, I saw her as I had never seen her before. Old, bitter and unkind. I cherished the moment and in a low slow purr, I faced the butcher again, replied 'Maybe, if I am asked.'

"The silence that filled the butchery was a melody that made me smile then, as it does even now that the memory has been unearthed. Seconds ticked by, the shop was still enough to hear a pin drop, and then the reply came.

"'Well, you forgot to shave your upper lip properly, my dear.' The wife moved between me and the counter, hands on her ample hips.

"'All that I lack for, is a proper razor, madam.' And we stood there, face to face, while the butcher suddenly let out a peal of thunderous laughter. 'She's right, Magda, you need more than a shave to make you edible.'

"I looked at him, and then back at her again and I felt like the queen of a castle. I shone like your Helen of Troy, my Jaro. I pushed past her bulk and he placed the neatly wrapped parcel into my hand. And gave it a squeeze. I turned on my heel and the crowd parted as I made my way slowly to the doorway. At the entrance, I turned around, purely to catch one last glimpse of the happy couple.

"'See you tomorrow,' I trilled, and he grinned.

"'Looking forward,' he shouted.

"His wife, pale with rage, made no reply. I went back the next day. And the next. I went there as me. Lumpy clumpy me. My hair in disarray, in my oversized men's shoes. The wife, the gargoyle at the door, eventually withdrew, claiming nausea at the sight of me. Scared of my tongue, which as you well know is an organ of fire. He kept on grinning and every time that he saw me his smile grew broader. And each time that I went there, he gave me larger portions. Inevitably, he would place the grease proof package into my hand and squeeze my fingers with his warm strength, and we would linger in that hazy moment together. It was a heady time for me, those excursions to the butcher, and I would lie on my bed staring up at the ceiling, whilst the oily aromas of the evening meal prepared by my mother rose up from the kitchen below, and teased me gently, whispering of warm hands that held mine.

"Until one day, the package from the butcher contained more than a generous slice of horse meat. Daydreaming as usual in the sweaty darkness of my room, with my eyes blissfully closed, I was tracing the outlines of my face, softly with my fingers, lingering on my lips, stroking my cheek and I was about to sigh my soulful sigh for the thousandth time, when door crashed open and my mother towered over me. I blinked against the corrosive light as she pushed a foul moist scrap of paper into my face.

"'What have you done?' she wailed, 'how could you be so stupid? And with a married man, in a small town where everyone just watches and talks and laughs at a clumsy cow making eyes at the well known seducer? You have humiliated me and the family and yet you simply lie there, in your moon calf reverie, gaping at me. Read this abomination.' Her voice shook and tears glistened like stars in her face.

"I sat up and took the grimy note from her trembling hand. Writing, pale and smeared, a jumble of lines in runny blue. The paper reeked of garlic and sweated oil onto my hand.

"'I can't see the words clearly,' I whined. She grabbed the paper from me, and nudging me aside with a growl, turned on the bedside light, glaring at me, and read out those sad and private words, her voice as strident as it was imperious. Standing over me, with the torturous blaze of the lamp illuminating her frame, the words fell like dead birds from her lips. I have kept the note, and it has survived with me for so many years. For along with your writing it is one of the few treasures to which I return, time and time again.

"'Beautiful Sabrina, you may not know how you have touched my soul, with your elegance, intelligence and charm, but I can no longer remain silent in my adoration of you. Your youth and innocent grace have served to remove my jaded middle-aged disdain of all thing fresh and supple. I have grown young again, fed by the gentleness and girlish wisdom that you exude with such a spring like abundance. In so many sweet ways, you have discreetly touched a part of my heart that has long remained frozen, my boyhood magic forced to live in silent captivity within the confines of my adulthood, where the walls are composed of a loveless marriage, while I slice dead flesh for a living.

I ask nothing more from you than an understanding that I am applauding you, celebrating you, rejoicing in you. What you have is so deliriously precious and so extraordinarily rare, an alchemy of spirit and humour in a goblet of compassion. All girls have life and youth on their side, but none seem to honour it more than you, my star.' My mother's voice softened to a near whisper and I cautiously glanced up at her. She caught my eye and flashed me a quick nervous smile. She settled beside me on my crumpled bed. I could feel her trembling imperceptibly, and I placed my arms around her.

"She smiled at me shyly and returned to scrutinize the letter. I watched her intently as she continued to read. 'Some may view this heart driven letter as further evidence that confirms my already tainted reputation, but I trust that your instinct and integrity allows you to understand these words. I wish only to offer my thanks to you for having trust in me and sharing your pure, unprejudiced joy with a man that many see as a pariah. I sorely hope that this letter is found before you prepare the meat, my dear. Your friend and admirer from the butchery. P.S. We have a special on the ox tongue tomorrow, but you need to come early, for the word spreads quickly.'

"At that mother and I laughed and she held me tightly. her cheeks were wet when she rubbed her face against mine. 'Dont ever let anyone read or know of this letter, Sabrina. People are vindictive and stupid and dangerous, at the best of times. Please promise me that. I want you to keep it, it is a very special gift, but do not even whisper of it to anyone. Promise me that. Promise?' Her face was pressed close to mine, her grip strong and her eyes were large and dark.

"'I promise.' I mumbled, and I kept that promise, until now, dear Jaro. The letter has lain secretly in amongst the yellowing pages of Winnie the Pooh for almost five decades, undisturbed by this gangly woman, who pours out the contents of her chamberpot onto her husband's grave each morning. Nothing more happened between myself and the butcher. Somehow, my desire for him faded in my triumph over his wife. He treated me with utter care and kindness whenever I went there. In his eyes I could see a man longing for a mere nod from me to light a way in his darkness but I did not want to be his release. People need people to grow with and to learn from, but dependance can be the ultimate weakness. Eventually I fell in love with a young man, who later left me for another. The butchery closed suddenly one June. The blue veined butcher was a devout anti-Communist, living on borrowed time. The wife moved away. Escaped to England eventually, I later heard.

"I know what naïve, obsessive desire tastes like, my joy. It tastes likes lemon slivers dipped in cream, with a greenness that makes you weak at the knees, egg white beaten to a frothy frenzy with the mildest sprinkling of bitter chocolate. Air and promise, a sigh that you can eat. It can turn your heart inside out. Sometimes it brings fruits that are not the sweetest though. But I can't tell you to be careful in your love. All in all these are precious times in one's life and yet they are also those that can cause remorse in later years, through introspection and wisdom. Still, I did enjoy sharing the tale with you, we both can and do learn from each other. I feel pity for the butcher's wife now, possibly because I now only turn heads as a source of amusement, now that my mustache has turned snowy white and resists any razor. And my need to be desired has turned into ashes that rest with my memories.

"But I have you writing to me, so beautiful and so steadfast in your reaching out across the continents, and the old house keeps me on my feet. There is always some disaster, either of man-made or avian origins knocking on my creaky door. We are here but for a little while, my boy, and dwelling on the past can make me cry, sometimes, when no one is watching. So write on. The letters are my periscope into your world, and I reread them often."

o o o

Chapter Forty-three

A Fall from Grace

"I have somehow made two red headed enemies at school. Two boys that were once my friends and somehow felt rejected by me and now that they have swelled up and play loud waterpolo, they have taken to pushing me around whenever opportunity allows. I hate going to the public baths where they strut about, but go there nonetheless to seek solitude from the heat and from family in the waters. And more often then not, as I slide into the calming blue, the inevitable shout of 'there he is!' heralds the end of my peace. Two heavy splashes followed by the heart stopping sight of twin heads bobbing towards me, scowling with red rage as they thrash the waters, I am frequently tormented by this duo. The waterpolo training has made them strong and canny with under water kicks and neck locks and I limp home bruised and wet and wary of public places.

"The situation was getting progessively worse and my fear of sudden attack made me stand alongside the black people that sat on the railings outside the pool complex, watching the happy white people swimming and tanning. Up on my perch, I would scour the crowd for the flash of red hair that spelt danger to me. Father sometimes takes me swimming and the red heads lurk around revelling in my distress. Whenever he disappears to the public toilets or to buy us ice cream I silently curse him, because the grinning brutes are encouraged to draw nearer, and to flex their freckled muscles at me. Grateful for his return, I bound up and meet him and devour ice cream cone nervously, one eye open for the bullies that scowl and posture, the small angry mob of two that brood as they tan.

"Pointing up at the black faces that sat stoic and watchful on railings above the pool area, Father sometimes grinds his teeth and looks glum. 'One day, those people up there will be allowed to swim here, and that is truly going to be a pity.' That sentence is a slow knife to the stomach, but I am never sure if it was his prophecy or the obvious fear in the prophet's tone that turns the invisible blade so adroitly in my innards.

"The black faces gaze down upon us, basilisks against the lurid blue of the African sky. I once nervously waved to them thinking that a friendly overture may be recalled at the Day Of Judgement that is so ominously hinted at by Father. A sharp elbow to my skinny ribs made me drop my hand. 'Ignore them, you fool,' Father hissed from the corner of his mouth, 'otherwise they will think that you're mocking them.' I looked at him confused, but a flash of anger in his eyes silenced any further debate.

"I think that ignoring the polished ebony faces that hovered so vividly above us is tantamount to an outrageous mockery. A denial of the person's existence feels like a sin to me, Sabrina, and sometimes, at home, I feel a little bit like those poor souls on that rail. I feel like a barely tolerated nuisance. Last week I was in the school urinal, quickly having a pee between classes, when the red heads came roaring around the corner, kicked my suitcase aside and half-nelsoned me into the gurgling toilet bowl. I reached out but my hand slipped on the wet tiles and I fell, glasses flying, elbow first into the narrow pissy trough. The sleeve of my jersey soaking up the water like a sponge, I blinked at the blurred faces laughing above me. A bell rang and they scuttled off to class. I gathered up my belongings, wrung out my sleeve and glowing with the flush of embarrasment, I ran after them. The classroom door was closed. I was late. With a timid knock, I pushed open the door to enter a silent room filled with staring boys and frowning teacher. I closed the door gently behind me. For a few seconds there was a ponderous silence and just as I was drawing breath to explain my late arrival, the whole room exploded with laughter. The water trickled from my crumpled sleeve onto the floor, and I shivered.

"'Jaro, you are like a wet puppy, please sit down, but try not to drip on anyone, and no I do not want to know what happened to you. Again.' The teacher was being kind and as I struggled into an empty bench. The red heads sat together, sharing one sneer.

"I went to the Science Lab at lunchtime. It was joyfully empty and I quietly opened up the wooded case where the scissors and scalpel blades were kept. I took one tiny blade, as shiny as a fish and crept out. After school, I sliced a small groove into the straw of the outside rim of my boater. We have to wear these stupid English hats here, Sabrina, which must date back at least half a century, here in the tropical heat where the even the police strut around in shorts and long socks. The boater is one of the most expensive items of the school uniform, and to lose or to break one is tantamount to a catastrophe. I placed the scalpel into the shallow groove with only the slightest glint of the blade exposed. I had watched many spy films at the local cinema, and loved the shoes that flipped out a blade when the heel was clicked, to hack into the leg of the assasin that was busy throttling you.

"I was not sure of what I intended to do, but my hidden friend gave me comfort as I made my way home. I always follow the same sunny route, down the lane where the jackarandas buzz with insects and fill the air with their fragrance, which is bliss to a weary schoolboy. The red headed boys stood stony faced in the shadows of the trees at the end of the lane. Business as usual. I walked towards them, refusing to be intimidated by the chest hair that poked out from unbuttoned shirts, nor by the muscles straining through sweaty dank clothing. They moved towards me, each a mirror image of the other. Cruel Tweedledum and nasty Tweedledee.

"'Pissy boy, sissy boy. Time for a bit of medicine, lets see you laugh your way out of this one,' they chortled.

"The thugs split up, one on either side of me, and I know the old school trick where one boy talks to you, whist another quietly kneels behind you in a fetal postion. A nudge or a push from the talkative brute sends you falling over backwards into the dirt. Haha. what playground fun.

"'Please, don't hurt me again. I just want to go home,' I pleaded, but suddenly I saw a way out of this tight spot.

"'Whatever you do, don't break my boater. Anything but that, my mother will kill me, if the boater gets damaged.'

"I took the boater off my head, in a show of attempting to protect it.

"'The boater? Your mommy will kill you, if it's busted? Well, I'll kill you if you don't hand it over chop chop, do you hear me?' The rusty cur growled and his friend leered.

"'You can't break it. No, please, don't, I'll have to pay for it out of my own pocket!' This was true, Mother had grown tired of replacing my boaters.

"I stepped back and they moved forward, fat hands reaching out for the trophy. I timidly offered it to the nearest one, and as he grabbed at the rim I quickly yanked it back, a picture of nervous dread. He suddenly stopped, frowned and opened his hand. Brute beast number two grunted and lurched back. He saw the long gaping wound dripping with thick sticky red waves that formed glutinous rivers down his fingers as the sun blazed and the bumblebees hung fat and heavy in the flowers above our heads. Taking advantage of the shocking spectacle, I, with a magician's deftness, quickly removed the hungry blade from its straw groove.

"'What the hell, what did you do to him?' cried the red head suddenly pale , whilst his bloody twin sat down, teeth grating against the sight of his juices departing with such abundance.

"'I've no idea what happened. You saw, I did not do anything. It must be the straw. Straw can cut you like a knife, even grass blades can nick you.'

"'Oh, just bugger off, Jaro. I don't want to see your rat face. Go. Away. Now.' He croaked at me, frightened and mesmerised by the lurid gape of the wound and bent over to tend to his friend. I felt a great pang of pity for them both. We used to be friends, sharing popcorn in the silver light of a darkened cinema, swapping comic books for sweets. A world weariness came over me, made my heart shrink. I nodded, blank-faced and wide-eyed. And gratefully retreated. At home, I shivered for an hour, through the crackle of the afternoon heat. They have never tormented me since that afternoon. Avoided me in the corridors at school, and swam away from me at the baths."

o o o

Chapter Forty-four

Growing pains. And yet there is more to tell, Sabrina

The summer holidays came along with their long sultry days and nights thick with mosquitos. I grew tired of gluing together model airplanes from kits, and the well thumbed books on my shelves gathered soft dust that hung like a palor in the air. Time stood still and my listlessness grew. My friends were few and were mostly a timid bunch that entertained themselves with endless board games and exhausting chess tournaments, or with idle prattle about girls that hardly knew of their existence. I was smarting for an adventure of a different hue. I found myself dreamily drifting towards my bedroom window, quietly hoping to catch a glimpse of the woman next door, the whisky drinking lone dancer that had disturbed me so profoundly.

"Dear Sabrina, one morning, when the blue sky yawned luxuriously at me through the curtains, I once again made my sleepy pilgrimage to the window. There she sat sunning herself in a deck chair, the woman next door voluptuous and serene in her yellow bikini in the garden outside her apartment. A magazine on her lap, skin that shone with oil, even at a distance. My parents had gone to work and the house was still but for the sudden beating of my heart and the dry hot air that rasped in my lungs. I felt wild euphoric sense of abandonment, alone with my prize, free from the inane prying eyes of adults. Clad in my pyjamas, blue with little red squirrels, I crept into Father's bedroom, which had a better view of the street outside. Mother and Father have separate bedrooms now, Sabrina, after a recent incident of late night bickering and general foot stomping that had something to do with his regular excessive drinking. I think that we are all bored and lonely here, in the land of dubious opportunity.

"But at that moment I was neither bored nor lonely as I peered through the window. She stretched out, a golden cat with astonishingly long tapering legs, her breasts heavy in the cups of yellow. A telegraph pole obscured my view and my frustration grew. I wanted to drink the vision in, craved to savor this rare sight of tanned flesh. Somewhere in another part of the leafy suburbs my friends were no doubt setting up the chess boards for another rousing day long tournament.

"Suddenly I had a wild idea. Our house is narrow and high, with a Swiss style roof. There is a trapdoor in the ceiling, allowing access into the space under the roof. Father sometimes goes there to adjust the hot water cylinder. I thought that a higher vantage point would enable me to get a clear view of the gift laid out so supine and splendid before me. I ran downstairs and lumbered up bearing a short ladder borrowed from the library, which I positioned below the trapdoor. A quick leap into my room and the faithful binoculars were around my neck.

"Frantic with excitement at breaking so many rules at once, I clambered up onto the shaky ladder and pushed the hatch aside, dust and wood chips falling onto my feverish face. I dragged myself up into the aperture and my pyjama sleeve snagged on a bent nail as I tumbled into the murky space. A savage tearing of cloth and I was free, to tiptoe along a wooden beam towards a fissure of light between the roof and the wall that promised a fine viewing port. My sleeve hung in tatters, and so utterly transfixed was I upon the source of the light that I, for a fraction of a second forgot Father's warning when walking around in those spaces. 'Never step off the beam, otherwise you'll fall through the thin ceiling and break your neck.'

"Yes, Sabrina, I stepped off the beam, and as I did not only did his words come flooding back, the floor creaked with a sound a gunshot and broke underneath my slight weight. I fell through the ceiling like a hanged man falls through the fatal trapdoor once the lever is pulled. As luck would have it, I had chosen to crash through the wafer thin ceiling over the staircase that led to the ground floor, so that the drop was double the height. As I fell, I managed to grab onto the solid beam with one hand and dangled over the staircase, wild-eyed and sweaty. Below me, a few pieces of ceiling material crashed down the stairs and the dust swirled around my ears.

"Surely there some saints that protect the naïve and the lusty, and on that day they all joined forces to spare me from a sticky end. Panting and almost mad with fright, I managed to hoist myself back into the darkness of that accursed place and I crawled back to my original entrance and slid quickly down to the ladder and to the safety of the carpeted floor. I stood there for a while, the object of my desire long forgotten. Above me was a huge hole in the ceiling. Below me was a staircase littered with debris and dust. This was not going to be another languid day in the sun. I closed my eyes and for a moment I was playing chess against a spotty teenager and all was well. I had six hours to repair the hole before my parents came home from work. I showered, dressed and grabbed my measuring tape.

"With teeth grating reluctance I clambered up again and hurriedly measured the area of the boy sized hole in the ceiling. Reluctantly I emptied out my piggy bank onto the bed. My pityful savings lay there in a small pile and I crammed a few notes into my pocket and cycled through the heat to the hardware shop. I purchased a thin wooden board that would fit snugly into the partition of the ceiling that I had fallen through. A pot of white paint to blend in with it took the remainder of my savings. No one would be wiser to my morning's mischief. I cycled back with my load, the board wobbling under one arm, with the wind challenging my red faced progress with playful gusts. Black children ran alongside me laughing and tugging at the board. I tried to kick them away lest they damaged my precious jigsaw piece of a ceiling. I arrived at home, a shaky nervous wreck.

"I painted over the bland neutral grey of the board, with an even coat of brilliant white and stood back, pleased with my efforts. Downstairs, the clock chimed twice. I was well within my deadline. I placed the board into a wind free corner of the yard and waited for the paint to dry. An hour later, I replaced the broken partition with the new Jaro version. I gazed up and what I saw filled my heart with dread. The ceiling was painted a sullen matt white whilst my new addition glowed with a happy glossy brilliance. A luminous polished square on a pale dusty chess board.

"My partition won the beauty prize, shining down at me from amongst all the other morose wallflower partitions that stood around her. A glossy strumpet in a church of the matt dull and faithful. I would be discovered, quizzed and no doubt, punished. There was already enough tension in the house to make life unpleasant, and my act of apparent vandalism would add a further discordant note to our common dirge.

"As I trembled there, in a helpless rage against myself, the clock chimed three times, and suddenly I had an ingenious idea. I drew all the curtains and closed the doors leading out into that accursed passage, creating a blissfully faded twilight in which the gloss glare on the ceiling was reduced to a pleasing innocent dullness and all was at last well. The adults came home and I cringed whenever anyone went upstairs to the twilight floor, but nothing was said and miraculously, peace reigned in the house.

"Each day I grew more calm for not a word was spoken about the novel new dingy ambience of the first floor. A month later, I was deeply absorbed in a book, when a knock on the bedroom door made me sit upright.

"'Yes? What is it?' I was not happy with anyone lingering outside my door, right underneath my source of guilt.

"'It's only me.' Father pushed open the door and stood there, nodding at me.

"'What is it?' my voice trembled, the swine stood seemingly transfixed in the doorway. I ached for him to move in or out, simply to get away from that spot. All he needed was to look up and all my careful handiwork would be for naught.

"'Just seeing how you are. Good book?' he asked, pointing at my adventure anthology.

"'Brilliant book, absolutely riveting. Come and have a look at these illustrations.' I flashed a page at him, hoping to lure him in away from his post. He did not move. In fact, he seemed determined to stand there and smile at me.

"'Look at this new model aeroplane that I put together yesterday, the glue's almost dry,' I said desperately, quietly begging him to enter. I saw myself as one of those mommy birds that pretends to have a broken wing and hobbles around pathetically, hoping to lure the predator away from her nest. This predator was not taking the bait. His smiling and nodding was getting to me, Sabrina, and a total of two minutes of silence passed, with me squirming quietly in my skin and him all a grin but not moving an inch. Until he suddenly pointed up, yes up there, behind him and he softly asked those words which were potent enough to drive me to jump out of the window, in my imagination, and to run to the hills.

"'What actually happened there?'

"I sleep walked to his side and innocently gazed up into the gloom that was the ceiling.

"'There.' He pointed to my whore of a partition, the one that I studiously avoided in looking at, whenever I descended the stairs.

"'Oh! Umm… that was a bit of an accident… you see…' I blushed and faltered and prepared for the worst.

"'Say no more, you little rascal. It was so sweet of you to fix it, and in such a clever, naïve way. We saw the bright new partition on that very first day that you must have repaired it and realized that you must have got bored with your endless books and decided to play in the secret spaces of the attic. So inventive, we thought and agile, no doubt. Not a trace of dust nor wood anywhere, we were really amused, and watching you closing the doors so obsessively, maintaining the twilight state of the passage was truly a stroke of genius. Sleep tight, young Jaro,' and he ruffled my hair and left. Whistling as he descended to no doubt share his mirth at my plight with Mother.

"'And please, would you kindly leave the lights on in the passage from now onwards, I'm a bit tired of falling down the stairs. Ha ha.'

"It's a strange experience to have your up downed and your down upped, Sabrina. I was so convinced that the axe would fall mightily upon my scrawny neck, and deservingly so, too. Instead, my hair was stroked and praise was sung. Quite shocking to have your fears toyed with. I felt foolish and small, a child stuck in a lumbering adolescent's body."

o o o

Chapter Forty-five

State Calling

"What is it?" The envelope was brown, made out of cheap paper. On the back an uninspiring official stamp in blue, the ink smeared.

"You know what it is, open the damn thing." Father's kindly words were not making the situation more palatable. I grimaced and sliced at the flap with a dull jam knife.

"Here, let me do it." Father took the official document and tore away one side, revealing a single white page, emblazoned with a childish crest of some buck standing nose to nose on their hind legs with a bird flapping it's wings above them.

"Yes, here we go, young Jaro," Father read out, in an official voice. "Now that he has successfully reached killing age, our sixteen year old is invited for a minimum period of two years, yes, two years only, to serve in the ranks of our revered and feared defence force. Presently having their asses kicked on some nameless border or other, by servants of Stalinism, clad only in loincloths." He looked up at me, but I was not smiling. "You're quite safe for now, my son, but they know where you live." He seemed to be enjoying my anxious expression. "As long as you are at school or in college, they won't come for you. It's a small price to pay for living here, you know in the sun, with sea and the sky and the easy life. Two years is like smoking a cigarette, it's over before it's even begun. I spent a year in the mines digging up coal amongst the poison gas, and a year in the Wondrous Warsaw Pact Penal division, digging trenches and hauling firewood for the State.

Look at us now, in the Land of Milk and Honey. So chin up, study and stop looking so fretful. Here, smell my fist. Come on smell these old knuckles, tell me soldier boy, what do you smell?" I advanced my nostrils towards the scarred fist, and inhaled deeply. "Rabbit pie?" I asked, and turned away before he could respond.

Until that moment, it was quite easy to discount the army road blocks on the highways, the screening of bags at the entrances of supermarkets, and to ignore the plastic models of Russian mines glued to the walls of the post office, with the dual entrances, one for white folk and the other for the rest of the population. It was easy too, to scorn at the Saturday afternoon radio oozing with the balmy charms of Aunt Esme, who read out poorly written yet earnest letters of loved ones, sending warmth and hope to their boys "Somewhere on the Border" followed by the inevitable soppy West Coast ballad and adverts for wholewheat rusks. The Border seemed both intangible and pervasive, in this ominous Land Of Oz where civilized order was the myth maintained by force.

The milk smelt sour as I a threw the envelope into the trash can. Nationalization of the Czechs meant conscription for their progeny, and Father's jovial apathy made me sick to my stomach. I was firmly invited to help to put out fires that I did not start. Two more years at school would give me some respite from the hands that reached for my throat, and threatened to send me to the nameless places that Aunt Esme so glibly mentioned on her Saturday radio programmes.

A few days later I dressed up to go to a Punk Party, and examined my miserable wardrobe for appropriately outlandish accessories. With my farmer boy fringe and thick spectacles I already felt a trifle handicapped in the anarchist department. The homely jerseys and sensible trousers that hung there in the wardrobe before me were as threatening as silkworms. Frustrated, I rummaged through my T-shirt collection and rejoiced when I unearthed an old tattered tank top with the national flag emblazoned upon it, with the words "I love". I cleverly ironed two small Nazi lightning bolts discreetly into the centre of the sacred emblem, and happily bounced down the stairs to bid farewell to the parents.

"What is that thing that you're wearing?" Father roared like a bull, pointing to my chest. Mother shuffled up, peering myopically at me.

"It's a t-shirt, I'm off to a Punk Party," I replied proud of the reaction that the simple addition of two pieces of cloth to an old rag had provoked.

"You are not, I repeat, not going out like that. No bloody way do I work hard to keep you in books and model aircraft kits for you to jeopardize our safety here. Do you know what they will do if they see you like that? They'll jail me, or have us investigated. You know nothing, swaggering adolescent. We are here by the grace of Their Kindness and we have to be Respectful of their Laws, whether we agree with them or not. I spent thirty years with the Communists breathing down my neck, to the point where I left everything behind to give you a free and a better life, for a chance to be something more than a plumber like me. And now you put on a red flag to a bull shirt and go out laughing into the streets. To a kiddie party! Remove that shirt instantly. Now! Now!" I did not budge, and stood scowling at him in a Punkish way.

"Gee, Dad, can you listen to yourself, just for a moment? You have just confirmed the very reason that I am wearing this rag. Why keep quiet about a system that is so intolerant of playful criticism? You seem to have taken us out of a frying pan into the fire. Rather to die on your feet than to live on your knees is what I say."

"And what precisely do you know about living, my boy? Stuck in your garret with your books and endless letters to that witch Sabrina? Get that thing off you before I wallop you one." He advanced upon me, his face a mask of rage, the Grave Yard fist raised.

I retreated backwards, almost knocking over my bewildered mother. Reluctantly, and with a bitter slowness, I peeled off the shirt.

"I'll go and put on something more appropriate, shall I?" I asked archly, "Perhaps the good old faithful Donald Duck number from the happy days of my youth. That will surely guarantee our sleeping safely in our beds at night?"

Turning on my heel, and with nose proudly in the air, I sneered past his red face, half naked and indignant. I dragged on the Donald shirt and did not look in the mirror. At the party I reluctantly took my usual place amongst the uninteresting and the unlovable boys that skulked around the periphery of the jollity. Nursing our fizzy cheap wine, the halitosis and acne brigade looked on as the exotic boys and girls danced to abrasive punk music. "Great shirt, Jaro." drawled a blond body builder type, and his companions laughed.

"It's a relic." I tried to be witty but they had already returned to their conversation. I cursed Father's fear and my own lack of ingenuity. I should have worn the offending article underneath Donald, when I left the icy sea of home. Unleashed it upon the cynical beautiful people at the party. Goodbye, pimply wallflowers, hello credibility. Yet it was not to be. I would have to remain a closet anarchist. And one that had never been kissed. By anyone under forty. Life seemed to be moving very slowly for my liking. The disturbing aspect that trailed after me as I went home, later that night, was that Father's words had scared me more than I initially realized, and that our place in the sun was not altogether assured to be either a lasting or happy one. I crept up the stairs to my sanctuary of books and to a stuffed rooster. I stood in front of the mirror, mussed up my hair in a wild fashion and removed my glasses. Even then, the blurred figure that gazed back at me did not look in the slightest interesting, radical nor kissable. Time is a leaden yoke that I wear.

o o o

Chapter Forty Six

Help Needed

"I'm going to take you to a brothel as soon as you hit seventeen," Father announced one evening, soon after our political wrestling match. We were sitting in frosty silence on the porch, I glumly turning the pages of a textbook of algebra, the formulae as abstract as cuniform to a penguin. I was grateful for the distraction, yet horrified at the prospect. He raised a glass of red wine in my direction, and gave me a conspiratorial smile. "Yes, I have been thinking that maybe all your ideas are symptoms of a simple frustration. You are obviously quite hormonal, and you never go out on dates. Your friends are a poxy menagerie of milk fed types. Of little use to you, your giggling tribe obsessed with board games and adventure stories. You will be Virgins into your twenties, no doubt. What you need is a crash course in the carnal that will fuzz away those shallow provocative ideas behind which you hide. When I was your age I was already well in the game. Mothers would warn their daughters about me, which enflamed the attraction. The War had made us grow up quick and hard with little time to waste in playing scrabble.

Back in those days, if a man was cursed with the clap, he had to report the fact to the local police, who would give him a certificate to take to the doctor. You had to disclose all the private details to some beaky pen pusher. Spill the beans on the partner, demanding to know everything, the names, times and dates. No certificate, no treatment. Quite demeaning. Harsh times indeed. Communism did not look kindly on what was classified as a Western disease. Then and only then would some quack take a magnifying glass to your abused privates." He sighed at the memory. I closed the book, and sat in uneasy silence. I could sense that his memories were making him sad. Maudlin even. Perchance something to do with his fate, in being relegated to a single bed as a married man. With an obtuse child, staring on as he retraced his footsteps down the tunnel of his life.

"I remember meeting an older woman in a supermarket," he continued whimsically, his voice soft and oddly vulnerable. At this point I sat up, keen to hear more. He noticed my enthusiasm and chuckled. "She caught my eye, a gamely wench, all bouncy blouse and skirts and blond hair, carrying a basket of greens. We struck up a conversation around something trivial, the lack of cheese in the store or something. The Communist Paradise often failed to deliver the essentials, one week there was a glut of rice, the next week one couldn't find a rice grain in the Republic. The same went for meat, shoes and floor polish. Anyway, she lived alone, and invited me home on some pretext or other and the moment that we crossed the threshold of her tiny apartment, we tumbled onto the couch. Nothing like a well traveled horse, I say, that knows the road. I lay back expectantly, while she disappeared into the bathroom to as she politely described "make herself ready." I was about to light a second cigarette when a discrete regular splashing sound that originated from behind the bathroom door made me frown. I slid off the bed as quiet as a cat, and gently opened the door, just a tiny bit, curious to see the source of this mild disruption of our previously heated collision. She had raised those saucy skirts to reveal ample pink thighs and sat astride a large metal bucket. Frantically rubbing herself between her legs with a sponge that was plunged repeatedly back into the moss green liquid that threatened to splash out of the shaky container."

"What was in the bucket? It sounds quite bizarre," I asked, bewildered.

"Oh, no doubt some medicinal concoction designed to sanitize the inflamed areas, but I must confess that the sight disturbed me greatly, and I closed that door and made a hasty departure. I should have stayed, but the vision dampened my ardor completely, and I didn't have the heart to pretend otherwise. I chose to rather be unkind than to be embarrassed by her disappointment. Young and imperious, that's what I was and it doesn't sit well with me, even now, in retrospect. So mark it in your diary, my young scamp, the brothel date with your old man, at seventeen. That'll give you a more of a nudge down the path of true enlightenment than any of those novels that you hide in, and far better than any advice that mad Sabrina might offer."

Suddenly I realised that perhaps his contempt for Sabrina stemmed from some silent jealousy that he harboured, disgruntled at the letters that we exchanged so frequently and with such passion. I made up some tepid excuse and left him sitting there, alone in the darkness of the porch, with his wine and his memories of the blond and her bucket. I dreaded the very thought of him dragging me off to some house of ill repute, pushing me forward into some harlot's den, and then crowing about his achievement to his drinking hole cronies. A vision of him pounding at some paid for flesh, perhaps a few metres from my own state of distress, turned my stomach. I resolved to sabotage his promise, via a discreet word in Mother's ear.

A few days later, whilst standing next to her, drying the dishes that she washed, I gently broached the subject of the future brothel rendevouz. As anticipated, she slammed down her sponge and hissed like a basket of snakes.

"Over my dead body will he drag you to some syphilitic floozy. So bloody typical of him, a man with no taste and obviously little respect for neither you nor for me. Let me assure you, you are not going down the same sorry path that he has been on all his life. Why do you think that we have separate bedrooms these days. I'm fed up with his adolscent ways, and thank God that you spoke up. I would hate to be cursed with two sordid hyenas, one infernal beast is surely punishment enough for whatever sin I must have commited."

Father popped his head around the kitchen door. "What's all the shouting about? I'm trying to read a book, you know. A man needs his peace, surely that's little to demand." I shrugged my shoulders with bemused innocence. He turned around and left making clucking sounds with his tongue as he returned to his leisurely reading.

Mother growled under her breath as she slammed the dishes around and I took some delight in her ferocity. Sabrina was avenged and my neck was out of the sticky brothel noose. Lascivious as I was, and most willing to risk life and limb in sneaking a peek at the woman next door, I was not willing to risk the humiliation of being paraded as Virgin Lamb before some ravaged She Wolf. Choice, after all, is the ultimate freedom.

There were strident voices arguing in the lounge that night. I lay in bed, trying to shut out the muted yet abrasive clamour, and eventually fell into troubled sleep. In the morning the house was silent as I crept down the stairs. At the breakfast table Father glanced up from his paper and scowled at me. "Judas," he whispered as I nibbled at the toast. A low growl from Mother silenced him immediately.

Nothing more was said. Not a word from any of us, and I gulped down the food and hastily withdrew from the corrosive silence. It was quite obvious that the looming threat of the brothel visit had passed. But with it so too vanished the boyish intimacy that had been forged between Father and myself over the years. And confirmed the need for separate bedrooms to which the parents retired after the day was done. A line from Shakespeare comforted me in my guilt at driving a wedge in the already well-formed gulf between my parents. "Why do you dress me / In borrowed robes?" pleaded poor Macbeth. I was not going to be a stumbling replica of Father. Blinded by desires, blown by the wind of my hormones, I realized then that some advice could be more toxic to me than a mouthful of cyanide.

o o o

Chapter Forty-seven

Love Struck

"Dear Sabrina, my faithful confidant, find yourself a comfy chair, open up the plum brandy, and celebrate the Spring with me, for I am in Love. Yes, for the first time in my life have I chanced to meet a butterfly softly gliding amongst the raucous smelly mortals that have surrounded me for almost two decades. And no, it is not the whisky guzzling fallen vixen from next door, to whom I owe a great deal of stolen pleasures and a myriad of bruises. It is a girl, the sweetest most delicate frond of young womanhood that a boy can dare to hold. I am so happy to write these words, Sabrina, and yet they might read as though gleaned from the pages of a medieval romantic novel. I am both shy and ecstatic to share these gurgling feelings with you.

"Her name is Vashti, and she is a true pale English rose who blushed wildly pink when we first met down by the river's edge last week. She was walking along the promenade with her mother as I wobbled by on my bicycle, ringing my bell cheerfully, with my glasses sliding down my nose at every bump. They called to me and offered me a drink of apple juice from a hip flask. We sat on a bench together watching the river as it sighed and foamed towards the sea. They had recently arrived from England and although delighting in the climate and the flowers that whisper of paradise, had found the locals a trifle coarse and somewhat lacking in culture. She had an older brother who had enrolled in a local high school. My school, it turned out. Soon we discovered a mutual love of books and theatre and

I sat between the two ladies on that bench in the sun, the happiest of men. I was invited for lunch at their home and marvelled at their fullsome library, and almost cried when mother and daughter entertained me by a repertoire of celestial melodies performed on piano and violin.

"Vashti Cransen-Day is her full name, and with her golden hair falling across the fretboard of the instrument that she held so lightly with pale hands, I felt my inner darkness cracking with a new dawn. I sat there in that elegant living room, holding my breath as the girls giggled at me and goaded each other to even greater feats of virtuosity. At the end they collapsed onto the rug, mother and daughter laughing and tickling each other, while I grinned like a madman, the tea cold in the cup that I clung to in my delerium. The cocker spaniel wagged his orange tail at me as I took my leave, and a peck on the cheeks from most perfect hostesses made me want to dance and sing as I cycled home through the shady lanes of blue gum trees.

"The moon came out and I gazed up at the pristine silver blue paleness, at that pearl in the sky: the Vashti hued moon. I smiled at the thought. Across the darkened street, the whiskey woman stood on her balcony, watching me in my lunar rapture and called out something to me, but her words died mid-flight in the space between our worlds. Violin's song and the etheric Vashti had smitten me. I felt like a man taken out from a desert and lowered gently into a silver warm spring, bathed with dabbled light and lilting song, to drift in the genteel currents, washed clean of the heart-deep debris.

"At school, I made tentative enquiries about the family. Much to the derisive amusement of my colleagues. 'Cransen-Day? Ha ha, the Ghost we call him, a true English oddity. As pale as the Grim Reaper, and about as amusing. In fact he's as odd as you are Jaro. And he has a Ghostly Sister that's even milkier,' sneered one oaf.

"'Something wrong with that family. Milky English types. His sister's a bit of a freak. Rumour has it that they have no melanin pigments, some kind of gene defect, no doubt. Interbreeding, I would suspect was at play,' laughed another.

"The descriptions were not flattering and I quickly toned down my investigations. The Ghost was seen sitting quietly in the corner of the playground at break-time, but I was too shy to approach him in front of the easily amused and cruel boys. I watched him from a distance. Tall and creaky of limb, his unearthly pallor was truly incongruous amongst the sun drenched gardens and the bronzed rugged schoolboys that avoided him so earnestly. He nibbled quietly on a pork pie. I stood there quite mesmerised by his composure, a pale spectre in the tropics, and I felt a great upwelling of empathy towards this castaway, for this ungainly link to my Vashti. During science class, I tore out a scrap of notepaper and wrote the tiny yet pertinent missive, in my best handwriting. 'I am a friend and admirer of Vashti. Would you kindly ask her to call me? Much warmth, Jaro in the 10th Grade,' and included the telephone number of my home. A silly thing to do, no doubt, Sabrina, yet I needed him to be part of my connection to her. And I ached for her to call me.

I saw him again a few hours later, at the end of the school day, just as he was leaving. A forlorn figure jostled aside by the mob of boys streaming out of the gate.

"I gently tapped him on the shoulder and he turned to me and snarled 'Bugger off.' I nodded and smiled and pressed the letter into his pale hand. He took it from me and frowned down at the soiled scap peevishly. 'I can't make out your ludicrous handwriting. What does it say ?' His English accent was deliciously detached and elegant.

"A passing lump of a boy elbowed me out of his way, 'Out of the way, freak,' and I nearly stumbled into the Ghost, apologising automatically to both. 'Um,' I began, 'it's really meant for your sister. I'm a friend of hers, and I would like her to call me. My name is Jaro, and I met her, along with your sweet mother along the promenade, a few days ago. Would you be so kind and give her this illegible message?' He took a step back and looked at me, and then he scrutinized the letter again. And then he laughed, warmly and freely. I shuffled and grinned and shuffled again.

"'You are truly the most unusual bird in this sad place, Jaro. Of course I'll give it to her, she spoke well of you, as did Mother. It's a pleasure to make your acquaintance, old man.'" His eyes were soft and blue, and his smile was quite astonishingly vivid in his drawn, bloodless face. We beamed at each other. Two birds of a feather sitting on the same lonely branch.

"'Well, I look forward to seeing you around,' he said, and shook my hand formally. I stood back and blinked, and the only words that I could summon up as a reply were 'Thank you.'

"At home I sat staring at the phone. Father, who has become increasingly deaf over the years, has rigged up a system of warning lights linked to the telephone, that flash bright orange at the first ring. Many a visitor has spilled their tea at the startling display, their consternation further entrenched by Father's bellowing into the receiver. Sadly, very few people bellow back for him to hear the reason for the call. Increasingly, very few people call home at all. As luck would have, the phone rang and the lights flashed just as Father was passing.

"'Hello, hello, hello,' he shouted into the mouthpiece and I wanted to crawl beneath the carpet with soul scouring embarressment.

"'It's for you,' he shouted, in English, waving the instrument at me, 'some Bushman on the phone for you.'

"I grabbed the telephone from his clumsy hand, and he looked at me with reproach, mildly offended by my exasperation.

"The words that flowed into my ear, caressed my abraded senses and I felt my face burn with pleasure. Father, noting the phenomenon of my changing pallor, hung around, folding papers, rearranging his desk, his dull ears straining, but he could not hear soft Vashti inviting me to a picnic. Gentle Vashti laughing at my Father's bull like behaviour. True Vashti sending me a warm hug. I replaced the receiver and flushed with joy, hugged him as he sat slumped in a chair, pretending to scrutinize some bills.

'You buffalo you,' I whispered. He tilted his head back and smiled at me with confusion.

"'Me? A buffalo? What do you mean? Who was that? It was the softest voice that I had ever heard. A schoolmate of yours, I take it.'

"'No, it was a Tiny Bushman, Father, with the smallest of voices.'

"He grunted at that, but was pleased with the unprecedented display of affection, so rare to all of us in that house. So, dear Aunt, I'm off to a picnic. A first date, the first one in my odd, and knotty life. Send me your blessings, and your wisdom and wish me luck, Sabrina."

o o o

Chapter Forty-eight

Goral Was A Painter

"Such wondrous news, I glow with pleasure at your joy. You deserve the very best, my boy. May she be the most delicate of companions to you, and her family sounds quite delightful. It's long since I have heard you be so enraptured with life. Sometimes, I confess that I find your stories a trifle disturbing, and they leave me feeling helpless, for reaching out to you is so hampered by both distance and a foul postal service. Well done for finally finding someone of your own kind in that stange and wild place.

"Sometimes, I wish that some of the rumours that seem to persist around me, that I am a witch steeped in the dark arts, were indeed true. I would harness a chariot of roosters and have them flap me over the mountains and across the burning African plains to you. But alas, I am but a poor old woman that spins yarns to you at a distance. Threads of tales like the string that helped young Theseus back to safety after fighting the Minotaur in the maze. And for you, in this time of bliss, my joy is a cautionary story of love and desire.

"Goral was a great painter, blessed with a true maverick spirit. An enigmatic man, living in austere isolation, his work had gained him enormous international acclaim and notoriety over decades. Critics and skeptics were cowed in their preconceptions of his style, for he would confound all by a seemingly inexhaustible ability to flit from genre to genre in a manner that was deliriously contemptuous of public expectation. His Hades phase, with its acrylics that screamed of rancid damnation, with scenes of torment and savagery, would be followed by a period during which he crafted breathtakingly beautiful sculptures of trees and of fantastic birds. As soon as the art world had settled in and smugly incorporated these wild deviations into private collections, and he had yet again become the darling of the auctioneers, Goral would disappear for months or perhaps for even a year, and return to the cruel and fickle spotlight of the critics with a wild new tangent. Paintings that mocked all previous notions of his own style, or wood carvings that scorned the predictable profiling that a captive audience craved. Each phase would harness an outraged response from the clients and agents that had grew complacent and wealthy from his previous triumphs. 'Factories are for reproduction. If you seek standardization of style and of content, buy a German automobile,' he was quoted in one rare interview. He challenged the loyalty of even his most ardent fans with his obstinate reluctance to conform to a common predictable strategy. Great debates grew around his almost compulsive digressions in style and content, yet one common denominator existed across all the clamour that ensued with every new exhibition. The work was always truly remarkable and perversely iconic. Goral the Glassblower using the finest hairs of silica to make his singing, ringing installation that stood four meters high and scattered light across the room. The giant and regal leaf crucifix that dripped water slowly over the onlooker. The mill stone sized torture wheel filled with animal skulls, upon which a naked man effigy climbed, teeth bared with effort, the hands bleeding raw and livid. The three hundred miniatures in oil, each depicting an an anatomically precise fraction of the human heart, the capillaries glittering with miniscule portions of the Milky Way.

"He turned protagonists into antagonists, detractors into protectors, critics into humbled song smiths keening his praise. And then, with nary a backward glance he would reverse the process, again and again. 'I am not a prisoner of a formula and those that reject my freedom reject their own,' he was reported in stating, during the same interview. Forever risking absurdity, free from compromise, that is the path most artists stray away from, dear heart. True faith in the expression of his soul made him impervious to the barbed reviews and to the mud slinging that were the inevitable consequences of his cathartic outpourings.

"In a world that applauded the Emperor's New Clothes, he vociferously shouted "I am naked." There is something quite delicious about a rebel with a cause, the fearless warrior for passion. In many ways, he reminded me of the mischievous zen monk, Ikky, who challenged the austerity of spiritual faith by little acts of devilment. He would be the one that chose the apple from the bottom of the carefully constructed pile at the market, to be chased down the street by the irate vendor. The imp that hid the monks robes while they were bathing in the lake. He showed that play and audacity were as important in the development of a healthy soul as was piety and reverence.

"Children loved to hear the tales of his trickery and good humour, whilst adults would shake their heads at his frivolity. There is nothing more life robbing than a man that cannot laugh at himself. It is in the same spirit that I pour out my night water onto my dead husband's grave, and besides, the smell keeps the roosters from digging there. Those cackling birds brimming over with own special mischief. Stay true to your pale love, my boy. Derision and poisonous tongues can blind you to the gift that you hold in your hands. Vashti trusts you. First love is a blessed thing that can either gently or violently, shape you for the rest of your life. The story of Goral will follow in my next letter to you."

o o o

Chapter Forty Nine

Picnic Amongst The Stars

The basket was packed to the brim, the contents covered with a gaily lurid pink cloth. I stood in the kitchen, eying it with mounting apprehension as Vashti's mother swathed us both in suntan lotion. The Ghostly brother watched us with amused interest from the doorway, smoking a cigarette.

"Now you do look like twins," he drawled and a quick glance into a mirror revealed my face that was luminous with sun block ointment.

"Isn't that a little excessive?" I asked, rubbing at an irksome drop on my nose. They all laughed and Vashti with a delicate finger drew tiny graceful circles in the lotion on my face.

"Wait until you see my bonnet," she sang as she disappeared into the cool shade of the lounge, and quickly returned wearing a lilac sun bonnet, festooned with pink ribbons. She smiled brightly at me as her mother tied a huge bow under her chin.

"There. Perfect. Mary and her Beautiful Lamb."

"Beware the Big Bad Wolf." the brother muttered, grinning.

I picked up the giant basket. "I will protect the picnic and Mary with my life," I said manfully. We held hands as we left them waving at us from the doorway. A gloriously odd couple, forever exchanging warm glances. In the shadow of the bonnet, her eyes were a sparkling blue and I felt that I could wrestle tigers to keep her safe and happy. Her palm was gloriously warm and she smelt of violets as we made our way down the path to the river. I tried to extinguish the memory of the exploding pig from my mind, for I had not ventured back to the yellow water's edge since that odious day. I would still, upon occasion, wake up with that choking stench in my nostrils. I suppressed an involuntary shudder in the heat of the day, and Vashti grasped my hand tightly. I gripped the basket handle with renewed vigor. We were within sight of the water that seethed and frothed in the distance when a boy on a bicycle came careering around a dusty corner. A muscular fellow, one that I recognized from the schoolyard. I tensed and quickly looked at Vashti. She was oblivious of the cyclist and was naming all the flowers that swayed delicate and vivid in the afternoon breeze. She knew them all by name, some even by their Latin origins and was enraptured with this pursuit, when the oaf braked wildly in front of us, showering Mary and the Lamb with an arc of dust.

"Oh, sorry," he shouted, "didn't see you two there. Casper and Goofy on their way to the market."

"Bugger off," I croaked, in a watery imitation of her brother. He merely laughed, and pedaled off into the shimmering heat. We stood there staring after him and then she astonished me by drawing close and whispering. "You are my Goofy. Covered with dust. A precious clever nugget amongst the grey pebbles." And she kissed me. Softly, on the lips grimy with African dust, with her bonnet peak nuzzling my forehead. I closed my eyes, and let the millstone of the basket drop from my clammy hand. It fell, turned over and a boiled egg rolled out into the gravel at our feet. We stood there, lip to lip, not daring to part. Her blue eyes never left mine. I dared to hold her by her wrists and the day became a mist that stopped the clocks and made the sun our golden audience. I stepped on the egg and her laughter was a tiny bell. We picked up the pieces together, her bonnet pecking at me like a duck's beak as we hunched over the debris.

The walk to the river's edge was strewn with wild flowers and I cast back many a nervous glance but the cycling ape did not return to resume his torment of us.

We sat in the shade of a magnificent weeping willow tree, shoulder to shoulder watching the river burble by, as she carefully removed her headpiece, wondrous blond locks tumbling out onto her sweet neck, as pale as a swan's crest. The tip of her nose had grown sun kissed pink and she dabbed her forehead with a moist florid handkerchief, while I looked on transfixed by the porcelain smoothness of her skin. She caught my glance, and timidly placed her arm around me. I, cumbersome as a startled colt, put my trembling arm around her and we rested there, beneath the willow, heads inclined towards each other, her soft hair blowing across my face. I closed my eyes and breathed in her gentle perfume, the lemon, rose and barley water fragrances that swirled around me, held me aloft with invisible hands and made my head swirl.

Her head on my shoulder, her breath grew slow and deep and the arm holding me fell softly to the sand, and I knew that she had fallen asleep. Daring to open one eye, just a fraction of a guilty crack, I took the opportunity to study her serene features, drinking in the light that danced of her lips, rejoicing in the tiny flickers of her elegant lashes as she drifted in the afternoon sleep, a small delicate girl as white as icing sugar. At last she stirred and shook her hair loose and free and glanced up at the sun that was squinting down at us through the leafy roof of the willow tree. She slowly stood up and suddenly with girlish glee, clapped her hands at the sight of the basket, lying there so forlorn and dejected in the grass. She ran around on those tiny feet , unfolding cloths, arranging plates and glasses, food appearing out of the seemingly bottomless basket, to await our pleasure. I watched her with amazement as she picked orange flowers from a nearby shrub and scattered them on the table cloth.

We feasted well on ham and pineapple and cornbread, washed down by beetroot red wine, that Vashti had cunningly purloined from her brother. Boiled eggs and cheese followed by strawberries. This was as foreign to me as a singing carp. The air and her joy fused with the food and wine to make me want to dance and sing. Or to swim. Emboldened by her presence I decided that it was time for me to lay exploding pigs to rest. I jumped up and took her hands in mine and pulled her up onto her feet. "Come, sweet girl, let's go and run in the shallows. Wouldn't it be great fun to dive in and swim on a day like this? I often used to come here with my friends and it's wonderfully safe."

Her frown blocked out the sun. It was the first time that I saw her disturbed and anxious. "I'm sorry to be such a nuisance," she spoke softly, "but I have to be quite careful around places of infection. It's a long and boring story, Jaro, but my constitution is not as it should be. Easily burnt by the sun, quick to get sick, that's me. Yes, the pale English Rose, here in the tropics amongst the rough tough bronzed locals that can go anywhere, eat anything and be the pictures of health. That's one reason that we came here, you know. Both my brother and I are painfully, idiotically prone to colds and asthma, and England is a rank and dank place at the best of times. Of course, the sad little joke is that this place simply drips with flowers and pollen, but at least it's dry and otherwise quite accommodating. As long as you drench yourself in good sunblock each day, all will be well. I know, it's not fair on you either, to be handicapped by this relic of Victorian wanness. But you go and swim, I'll watch you from the sidelines." She studied my face intently for a reaction.

I shook my head, and smiled, silent in my sudden shock and confusion. "I'm not very fond of the sun myself, either. And rarely hang around those bronzed locals, who seem to regard me and my brother as some kind of pale exotic animals. The fool on the bike is just one of the many white kids that are spoilt rotten, don't read anything and find our kind quite hilarious and odd. So here's to the pale and to the strange." I raised a dusty wine glass to her.

She raised hers and moved towards me, under that leafy canopy where the light dappled her skin .She placed her forehead against mine and stared into my eyes unblinkingly. "Damn right," she purred, "let them all bugger off." And kissed me right through to my soul.

o o o

Chapter Fifty

A Friend In Deed

"The elusive artist had a wealthy and astute patron in the form of a Doctor Fastnner. The good doctor was both a friend and adviser to the legendary Goral, standing as a solid buffer between the frequent public outrage that the mercurial provocateur engendered. It was Fatssner's great ability in pouring rational oil on emotive troubled waters that enabled Goral to indulge his Loki – like muse. Fastnner was widely respected as a knowlegeable highly instinctive entrepreneur, a veritable dowsing stick for quality that many less confidant investors followed. The two men knew each other well and there was true unspoken bond between them. It was, after all, Fastnner who as a young moneyed gentleman had chanced upon the wondrous talent that smouldered within Goral's soul, and for nearly three decades remained a loyal and patient protector of the sometimes obtuse loner.

"The men were both visionaries in their own spheres, their union as unique as it was enviable, made watertight by the glue of trust and honesty. Goral lived simply yet worked almost ceaselessly, a man seemingly possessed by an all consuming hunger to see his inner worlds fleshed out in glass, oils and metal. Travel, good food and relationships meant little to the artist. His voice would tremble with the torrent of new ideas, his long grey locks shaking with the agitation at the very mention of a wife or a lover. Life offered but a brief chance for his endless inner vistas to be made manifest, and he cursed the god that had limited him to a single pair of hands and possibly eight decades of breath.

"Fastnner was a family man, a devoted husband and a lover of all fine things. His dinner parties were sumptuous affairs with long tables festooned with exquisite cutlery, exotic foods and guests who were to wear fancy dress, clinking glasses while a string quartet serenaded their boisterous merriment. Goral would often shun an invitation to these lavish celebrations, for time was not his friend, but nonetheless, his jovial patron insisted that on every such occasion a seat be made available and held vacant in the hope of summoning up the recluse. Banquo's Chair it was called, and it caused much mirth amongst the guests. The two men would meet at intimate coffee houses in the city, and there in the soothing anonymity of the sheltered booth they would laugh and drink together, their friendship impervious to the distant clamour of the outside world. Kindred spirits in a different guise, many watched the union with both envy and with pity. The corpulent and brash businessman revelling in the intensity and passion of the stooped wild-eyed artist. Goral quietly enjoyed the humour and the playful nonchalance with which Fastnner approached the seemingly voracious and emotionally shallow art fraternity. Their bond was a rare alloy that had weathered the corrosive elements of time and ego. Fastnner had learnt to avoid discussions concerning family, love and matters sexual with Goral. Such conversational gambits were often rebuffed with a glacial stare and a caustic remark and the men would sit there in mild embarrassed silence, each one hating themselves for causing discomfort to the other. And their friendship may have survived until the grave separated them, were it not for the tiny devilish voice that began to whisper in Fastnner's ear.

"Perhaps it was the same voice that urges a boy to strike the forbidden match and deliriously watch it burn a scrap of paper, away from the condemning eyes of the guardians of order. The gnawing rodent of an idea that desires nothing more than itself to be made flesh. Most artists use malleable material as expressions of themselves. They heat, beat, stroke and mix these into emblems of their will, and display them for all to see. Others, sometimes unconsciously, use people as the raw material on which to carve out their will."

o o o

Chapter Fifty-one

Love Spirals

"Dear Sabrina, weeks have passed since that dusty first kiss in the road, with the egg broken at my feet, and I am the happiest boy in the world. Also, the most intrigued one, for your story of Goral has captivated me entirely, and I have read extracts of the tale to Vashti, who finds it wondrously enriching. I hope that you do not mind me taking this liberty, for our letters have always been a sacred space between us, and perhaps you may feel that the presence of a third party, even as a peripheral guest, may disturb the intimacy somewhat. You are my muse and my Confession Booth, my wise Aunt. She is my earthly passion, for which I silently prayed, over the past few frosty years in this odd and fractious country. We spend sweet hours together, reading aloud from our favourite books and she strokes my gawky face as I plough through Voltaire, listening intently to the trials of Candide as he struggles in a world ravaged by chaos and greed.

I'm not a great public speaker, years of silence at Father's tales have made me quite insular in terms of sharing my thoughts vocally, but under her patient wing I have grown to trust my own voice. Her mother plies us with tea and biscuits and often sits in the corner of the lounge, quietly knitting whilst the words fly around the room like fragile butterflies. Vashti has a most melodious lilt and her reading of Edgar Allan Poe soothes my nervous state as a narrator. Her hand in mine, the afternoons pass by like smoke and I return home heady with words to recount the stories to Mother, who seems most distracted these days. She often asks me to repeat a sentence or two, and when I finally finish describing the events of The Black Cat, for example, she sits there blinking at me, toying with a the napkin or rubbing at an invisible spot on the table. I am determined that the peace and joy that I encounter in the company of Vashti and her family does not evaporate at the threshold of my own official sanctuary.

But keeping the spirit alive seems to be difficult under our roof. Father has little time for tales that involve other people beside himself, always leaves when I begin my faltering description. I dared to ask Mother what the matter was, and why we sit like two prisoners, sharing a cell, with my words crippled by the father's habitual exits from what could be, in theory at least, a rare moment of closeness between the three of us. She gazed at me, long and hard and then her chin trembled and a lone tear popped out and slid down her smooth cheek.

"'There is a joke, back home that may explain the situation, dear boy' she said, her own voice tired and low. 'A man died, and upon entering Heaven, a kindly angel approached him. 'What was the last moment of grief that you experienced, just before you died?' asked the beatific one, placing a comforting hand on the man's shoulder. 'I can help you with a wish, in order to restore some joy to the world that you have left behind.'

"'My pig, who loved me dearly and followed me like a puppy, sensed that I was ill and grew small and thin and eventually died before me.' replied the man.

"'Would you like me to send your widow a new, healthy pig?' offered the angel.

"'No, I want my neighbour's pig to die as well.' answered the man with a scowl. The angel shook his head and departed, leaving the man to find his peace in heaven, alone.'

"When I heard the 'joke' I reached out and took her hand in mine, and gave it a warm squeeze. A new trick that I had gleaned from Vashti and her family, who were forever honouring each other with such displays of affection. Mother's hand lay there on the table as inert as a glove. Then all at once. she sighed as she squeezed mine back. Perhaps my recent discovery of the power that is contained within a warm seam of intimacy between people could help thaw out the glacier that had become our home. I do not want my spirit to grow old and cold before my body dies, Sabrina. And I never want envy and frustration to make me numb to the beauty of the world.And I pray to the stuffed rooster that watches over me, that I will always have an open ear to the stories of others. What happened to Goral?"

o o o

Chapter Fifty-two

Goral's Challenge

"Fastnner had a dream. In the dream he sat in a golden chariot, pulled by a dozen plumed horses and the streets of the city were lined with people holding bunches of brightly coloured flowers. Young girls stood on balconies, in their finest dresses, craning their delicate necks for a better view of the street below. There was a tremor of excitement in the air and everyone gazed in a reverent silence at the chariot that slowly and majestically made its way up the street towards them. Fastnner sat back in his ermine lined seat, and smiled serenely. The chariot driver, his livery a rich maroon, applied his whip to the backs of the horses and the golden wheels rang gaily on the freshly washed cobbled streets.

"The crowd murmured as one as the ornate vehicle approached, the early morning light glinting off the shiny metal. Fastnner stood up, smiling magnanimously to receive their adoration, his hand held aloft in a regal greeting. They looked at him through blank eyes. The carriage passed through the throng, without a single acknowledgment from even the lowliest of the onlookers. Everybody stood gazing beyond him, away from the magnificent horses, at something that he could not see from his triumphant perch. He snarled an order at the driver and he pulled at the traces. The vehicle slowed and stopped. Fastnner, his face a livid pink, turned around and gaped at the figure that appeared in the distance behind him.

"Goral walked down the long avenue, seemingly oblivious of the huge crowd that watched his slow deliberate tread. As he looked up and blinked, the silent audience let out a welcoming roar and the children rushed towards him with the adults throwing their hats wildly into the air. A band appeared out of the bustle and started up a merry brass tango. Goral smiled and embraced the nearest dancing child. Women sighed and men blew out their chests with pride and Fastnner was pushed aside as the townsfolk moved forward to meet the humble artist. The horses whinnied and the driver grinned as Goral was raised upon shoulders and carried past the carriage and into a banqueting hall. The joyous throng followed the artist and suddenly the streets were empty. Fastnner felt cold and tired.

"He awoke and looked around. His splendid bedroom felt vast and empty as a tomb. The morning light was soft with dancing dust, but in his heart he had little joy for his comforts. Cold and clammy, he lay there breathing hard. His breath had the sour reek of fetid envy. Yet somewhere in the midst of his self loathing, an idea bubbled from the rank back waters of his mind, and it quickly grew into a lurid sea of scheming. He gazed up at the ceiling and for a brief moment, he could still hear the laughter of his children, echoing down the long corridors. His secret smile was not for them.

"He summoned his man servant. Invitations must be sent out, forthwith. To all his friends and the more noteworthy of his clients. A few select journalists from the art world were to be included on the list. Fastnner was turning sixty within a month and knew that no one would resist such an invitation. And Goral was to be announced as Guest Of Honour at his birthday celebrations. The servant left hastily to spread the news. Fastnner upon called the artist and after encountering some expected resistance, managed to cajole the recluse in accepting the role. Fastnner clapped his hands together with joy and hummed gaily around the house.

"The month passed quickly and on the day of the celebrations an army of chefs arrived. The mansion was filled to the brim with exotic flowers in huge scented abundance. Candles were lit by the score and an orchestra tuned their instruments underneath a huge mural, painted by Goral some years before. Pyres were lit in the gardens, their crackling glow reflecting in the carp pond as the guests arrived in their droves. A Highlander in full regalia, piped the well wishers up from the garden area and into the house, the strains of the bagpipes echoing into the night. A herd of bright-eyed goats, their golden bells clanging as they grazed, tethered on the sumptuous lawn. Ribbons fluttered from their horns as a servant, dressed up as an ancient herder played his flute to the animals. A silver suited trapeze walker, his wire illuminated by giant Catherine Wheels, moved slowly above the guests, the smoke from the combustion at times swallowing up the moon that hovered above them all. Many gathered beneath to point up to the silver figure and to applaud his sure footed silent progress across the invisible path. A fountain of champagne bubbled at the entrance of the grand home and Fastnner stood there, a charming figure that shook hands with everybody. Beautiful women lined up to kiss his cheeks and the uniformed maids added ever more gifts to the monstrous pile towering in the corner of the banqueting hall.

"A bell was rung and all the guests were ushered to their seats at the dining table. Waiters lined the walls discreetly as the string quartet plucked the first notes. Fastnner stood at the head of the table and nodded his appreciation to all. Yet the seat next to him remained dismally empty. His wife watched him with concern as again and again his eyes returned to the Banquo's chair. Eventually, Goral walked in, a slight and stooped figure, bearing what was obviously to all a small painting, the one corner already tearing through the thin wrapping paper as he maneuvered his way to greet his host and patron. The crowd grew still as the two old friends embraced and Fastnner seemed to be the happiest man alive. Goral sat down, and stared down at the tablecloth, nodding a silent affirmation at the offer of wine from his host. The guests muttered to each other behind their napkins, but soon Goral's legendary intransigence was forgotten and feast began in earnest. Speeches were made, wine was supped as the merry assembly devoured geese, plaice and roast venison in great mouthfuls, their faces red and lips shiny with the cavalcade of courses.

"Soon, it was time to for Fastnner to open his gifts. The lights were lowered, save for a small spotlight that shone on the opulent mountain of presents. The cigars were passed around, and glasses were charged with sherry and cognac as he approached the first parcel. With great care, and only with the occasional lurch did Fastnner remove the wrapping on each gift and in a stentorian voice, read out the kindly words from the cards attached. He held the present high above his head, and the audience laughed and clapped their hands with merriment. Goral sat quietly in a corner, smoking a cigarette. Fastnner seemed to be avoiding his gift. And sure enough, the very last present that Fastnner raised aloft, to the clamour of the giggling crowd was the poorly wrapped parcel, the paper torn and slightly stained with spots of oil. The happy drunken mass shouted encouragement and the host nodded his appreciation in the direction of the artist. Fastnner beamed while a wine steward replenished his crystal goblet with wine as dark as a mare's eye, which he held out to Goral. The crowd stood up out of their seats and cheered and raised their glasses, and Goral rose up smiling and raised his own in a toast to the patron.

"The jovial host silenced the noisy assembly with a deft lowering of his open hand. And slowly drank from the goblet, his eyes never leaving Goral's face. He drank of the heady wine greedily, the sounds of his pleasure audible right across the large room. His wife watched him with a thinly disguised concern. He finally lowered the goblet and picked up the last remaining gift. Goral and the crowd moved imperceptibly nearer to the patron as he tore away at the fragile wrapping. It was a painting of sweetly serene woodlands scene, full of dappled trees and a tranquil stream that coursed through the shadowy glade. A golden framed picture of joyous, natural twilight, quite befitting the sixty year birthday celebration. Another unexpected deviation for Goral, who was not known for idyllic impressionism.

"Fastnner raised the canvas to the light and mumbled something inaudible under his breath. His forehead creased in a deep frown. He cast a quick, searching look at Goral and returned to stare, to glare at the forest scene held in his fat hands. The artist looked nervous and confused and started to open his mouth, but changed his mind in mid-breath, and stood there silent and mildly forlorn. The guests started to whisper amongst themselves, and soon the soft sounds fused to become a constant hum which grew and grew in magnitude. Until Fastnner, carefully placing the painting on a chair for all to see, turned to Goral. With arms wide and a smile that dazzled, he embraced the artist. Goral's face was light with relief as he returned the embrace, and the two men stood there for quiet moment, locked in the warmth of their friendship. Fastnner placed his arm around the artist's waist and raised a glass of wine to the sea of faces massed around him.

"'Ladies and gentlemen, My Guest of Honour, and such a rare honour it is too, is my most cherished friend, the exceptional Goral.'

"He stood back and grasped both of Goral's hands in his own. 'My dear friend, my most astonishing and unique friend. You humble me with your gift, and once again astonish everyone here with an inimitably beautiful landscape, which is in a style that warms the very air around it with its vibrancy. Everyone, please, do come past and see the depth and joy of this truly wondrous scene, my great gift from my great Goral.'

"The crowd filled past the table, murmuring their praise. Fastnner stood there, proud and grinning. 'Champagne, champagne for all,' he called and the waiters appeared instantly with the finest bottles. 'Celebrate with me tonight this amazing man, my old friend and companion. Thirty years we have worked, fought off the press together. Thirty years of laughter, money and magnificent art.' he paused in mid rhapsody to wipe away a tear. 'Three decades of trust, faith and honesty have cemented us together; into a team that the art world admires and fears. And with good reason, ladies and gentlemen. But now tonight, on my birthday, spoilt as I am with all the magnificent gifts and the food and wine, I beg an indulgence. I know that it is inappropriate and perhaps selfish of me, but I ask for one more gift. One final gift that I have been aching for, so silently and discretely for the past decade or so, dear Goral. And you are free to refuse my plea, for you have your pride too, I of all people do know that.' He paused and now it was Goral's turn to frown deeply. The crowd grew still and only the crackle from a log on the fire dared to disturb the tension of the moment.

"'And what, my kind host, might that be?' Goral and Fastnner stood face to face, the room a tremble with expectation. Fastnner remembered his dream and smiled. 'I have always wanted you to do a portrait. Not a portrait of me nor of some stuffy admiral, nor a mayor, but one of my gentle and delicate daughter, Ibis. I know that you have sworn on your life never to demean yourself to portraiture, but as your oldest and dearest friend, I beseech you, before all these fine people gathered here tonight, to allow me that great joy before I grow old and cold, and break your iron vow. Ibis by Goral. May the world be shaken out of its dull sleep.' He clapped his hands enthusiastically and the crowd shuffled nearer, drinks in hand nodding their encouragement. The ideal host glowed with pleasure at the effect that his words were having upon the room. 'It's a simple thing that I ask of you. Here, let me help you in your decision by formally introducing you to the sweet Ibis, who has matured into a thing of rare beauty and is my pride and joy.' He looked around and beckoned to the small bright face that stood at the back of the crowd. 'Ibis, do come and introduce yourself to my old friend Goral, you met him many years ago, when you were but a butterfly come to us from the heavens.'

"The well dressed throng parted as the young girl nervously approached her father. Goral did not look at her, as she quietly took Fastnner's side. He eyed his friend with a mixture of fear and discomfort, searching his face for a clue to this public exhibition. His epiglottis bobbed erratically with visible consternation. Torn between rebellion and loyalty, Goral stood as a man at the crossroads, unable to move in either direction. The audience jostled against each other, toes were stepped upon and apologies mumbled as they strained to fully drink in this unusual event. The gift lay on the table, rendered small and insignificant by the scale of Fastnner's seemingly innocent request. Goral stared down at his feet. The waiters stood by in the shadows, trays of drinks held tightly in gloved hands.

"A tiny involuntary cough from the young woman at Fastnner's side made him look up. He studied her mildly flushed elegant face, and drew in his breath at the curvature of her neck, graceful as a wisp of a fragile cloud that slowly disintegrates in the sky above. A deer in the shade of her father's mountain frame, her small shape trembled in the firelight, yet she met his gaze with a smiling composure. Goral took a step back, captivated at the crossroads. His breath was shallow and laboured as he bowed to her gracefully. She curtsied impishly and her smile drew sighs from the audience. Fastnner smiled proudly. She moved towards Goral and offered him her delicate hand.

"'So good to meet you again, sir. After all these years. I do remember you from my childhood, when you came to visit us. Your painting has given us great pleasure.' She nodded at the impressive mural behind him. 'It helped me dream at night.'

"He took her hand fearfully. 'Those words are a gift to me, on this day of abundance. My greatest pleasure, madam, is to give others a means to dream. I am honoured to have contributed at least a spec to your inner world.'

"They stood there, hand in hand, oblivious to the crowd that held its breath. Until Fastnner asked: 'Well, what do you think, maestro? Is this pearl's beauty not worth preserving? Say yes, and make a father dance with joy. I shall enter my old age with a portrait of my love painted by my dearest friend. Ibis immortalized by Goral. The heavens know of no better union, I wager.'

"Ibis blushed and withdrew her hand, and in that moment Goral felt as though the world had slipped through his fingers.

"'I will do it. If Ibis agrees to a sitting for me, I will do it with the greatest of pleasure,' he announced quietly, his gaze fixed upon her face.

"'Well done, my friend. Excellent. Your generous spirit bring tears to my tired eyes. Give me a hug, you old

234

genius.' And sure enough, there were tears streaming down the father's face. The men hugged mightily and the throng cheered and the waiters became animated and champagne frothed from the glasses. Ibis traced the surface of the painting on the table with a small pink finger, her face alight with pleasure. The orchestra began to play a slow waltz and Fastnner called for his wife to take his hand. He led her to the centre of the room, freshly cleared of furniture, and the old couple began to dance, soon to be joined by the other guests. Goral stood in a dim corner, watching them with mild amusement. On the dance floor, Fastnner's wife moved as graceful as a swan on a lake, but her face was drawn and unsmiling.

"Goral's eyes strayed towards the lithe figure of Ibis, who oblivious to his gaze, laughed and whispered with her young friends at the dessert table. He sighed and quietly, without a word to anyone, took his leave."

o   o   o

Chapter Fifty Three

Vashti

"Dear Sabrina, summer has arrived with its angry heat and the days are getting longer. Father has grown an extravagant beard and calls himself a 'proud reclusive'. With one eye on Mother, he mopes around the house, humming the same repetitive tune to himself. I spend more time away from the home, walking in the nearby woods with our neighbour's dog, Sprokett or with Vashti and her family. I ache for greater physical intimacy with my pale girl, but of late she has grown frail and is often quite exhausted by the remorseless heat. We share ice creams under the ceiling fan of her bedroom. Her hair as soft as dandelion, dancing in the breeze, and we kiss away the stickiness from each other's lips. Her mother's face always lights up when she spies me walking up the garden path to their door. Sometimes the two of us sit together on the verandah with tea and biscuits, especially when Vashti is feeling poorly and is asleep in her room underneath her fan. The pale girl is getting paler and her mother's voice cracks with emotion when we discuss Vashti's health. I save up my pocket money to buy flowers, chocolates, books and games for my tender love. We watch each other in the cold light of the film at the local cinema, our story being more evocative and pleasurable than any celluloid offering. I often noticed that her hand became hot and clammy as she held mine so tightly that it hurt. A fever seemed to rage beneath that smooth skin, while her face pressed against my own was as cool as marble. I mentioned this worrisome discovery to her mother, in a quiet moment on the porch, but the pain that appeared to cross the gentle woman's visage silenced any further enquiry.

"I blame the accursed African climate for eroding the frail Vashti to a brittle version of the girl that kissed me on the river shore on that luminous day, so many months ago. I almost feel guilty about being light and lively next to my drained companion, Sabrina, and wish that you were here to apply some healing balm to calm her fevers. I am sure that some concoction of carp extract or a poppy seed brew would blow away the devils that seem to gnaw at her vitality. I hold her closely to me as we lie there in the swirling heat, watching the curtains billow and sigh in the tropical scented air. She often falls asleep in the cradle of my arms and I listen to her breathing, the sounds eventually lulling me into the twilight spaces."

Chapter Fifty Four

The Sitting

"My beloved boy, I am quite concerned about your Vashti's health, for, from what I am able to discern, she seems to be of an ethereal nature, where the veil that separates this world from the other can be painfully thin. I have enclosed a small tube of carp extract, it's very effective in alleviating fevers and symptoms of melancholia. I even used some on your mother, many years ago, when Otto died and she grew thin and hollow-eyed. A light dab of the ointment to the temples at night quickly restores the body's natural cycle. Carp are known for their longevity and for their virility and even Aldous Huxley wrote about these magical fish in "Those Barren Leaves", which is still on my shelf, mouldering away with a vengeance. Do send her my love and I will burn a candle to her tonight.

"The art world hummed with excitement, my dear Jaro, as the news of Goral's novel gift to Fastnner spread. Many of those that knew Goral did not believe the rumours. His agreement to the commission seemed to violate his own rigid code of beliefs. 'The freedom of expression is unassailable.' he would growl, and add 'Portraiture is the last bastion of dignity.' For the great man to suddenly drop his ideals and pick up an easel with a portrait in mind seemed to suggest an almost miraculous revolution in his philosophy. Fastnner moved quickly to stem the tide of speculation and called for a press conference, where he officially verified that Ibis would sit for a portrait by Goral. He answered the myriad of questions that ensued, with relish and a twinkle in the eye. The journalists had never met such a compliant and patient subject. Amidst the ceaseless popping of the camera flashes, he thanked them amicably for their time and everyone adjourned bewildered yet satisfied. The Miracle was happening.

"Ibis stood in the entrance of the great hall that served as Goral's studio. It was an old church that had stood ramshackle in a field for nearly a decade when Fastnner secured the purchase as a gift to the artist. The stained glass windows were repaired to their original state and inside the hall glowed with bounteous brilliance. The young woman squinted her eyes against the brightness, and called out his name softly. Above her, sitting on some rafter, an invisible bird flapped its wing, and a feather fell slowly through the illuminated space toward her. She was about to pick it up, when a movement beside her made her start. Goral stood up from his chair and wiped his hands on his paint flecked apron.

"'Ibis, the sacred bird, singing at my door. Come in, and, sit here by me, my girl.' He indicated a chair upon which a cat lazed. Goral hissed through his teeth and the hefty feline trotted away. 'Do you know that the Ibis was a bird revered by the ancient Egyptians, and one that would fight off winged serpents from infesting the land? A long legged graceful creature that was sometimes mummified along with the Pharaoh, in order to protect his soul from the ravages of hellish beasts. You carry your name well, my dear. Some sherry?' He lifted an ornate decanter and from a shelf and she nodded. He filled two glasses on a tray with gleaming brown liquid and she perched on the side of his chair.

"They raised the glasses to each other and sipped quietly for a moment, enjoying the tranquility of the huge space around them. Ibis stared down at his small creased hands, and hid her smile when she noted that each finger nail was smeared with a different colour, like a moving palate, she thought. The bird above them sneezed, and he frowned. 'Would you like take a refill and to see the sitting area, Ibis?'

"After a moments hesitation, she nodded. The sweet wine and his tenderness made her feel comfortable and light, and she followed his stooped gait to far side of the hall, where a high chair stood against a white sheeted wall. He placed a thick cushion onto the seat and she demurely sat down, still holding onto her glass while he walked around her, humming to himself. Goral stood behind her, and with a soft hand, brushed aside a strand of hair that had fallen across her eye. She looked up at him and for a moment they watched each other in the silence of the intimacy.

"He took a step back and walked around her, frowning pensively. 'Perfect. Most excellent, Ibis. Could you possibly tilt your head a fraction to the left, but keep your chin up. There, that's it, exactly.' He dragged another chair across the floor and seated himself before her. She took a tiny sip from her glass, her face open and serene. Dust particles danced in the still warm air between them. He sighed heavily and stood up. 'Let me bring the easel, my dear. And lets see what happens next.'

Chapter Fifty-five

Paradise Stands In the Shadow of Swords

"Dear Sabrina, I am reading the story slowly, in between my studies and frequent vists to Vashti's side. This final year at school is draining away at my time and the exams are looming large and ugly on the horizon. I received another annual official letter from the Army, gently reminding me of my duty to the country. Most of the boys in my class have received similar dark invitations and there is a great deal of talk around the quadrangle at break-time about serving in the army, navy or in the airforce. National conscription may sound quite innocent on paper, but here it means two sorry years in a drab brown uniform, and of being sent to borders where an undeclared war is turning boys into mostly willing puppets of a regime that has no remorse nor guilt about the dangerous slide into the abyss of a race war. The news of this conflict is heavily censored, and the nightly television teems with images of the president raging against the threat to our national security. Father is convinced that all will be well, and that with a strong hand at the controls, this country will weather the tide of ill will, but the stories told by my friends whose older brothers are serving 'somewhere north' leave me feeling frightened and helpless.

"I don't wish to disturb your serenity, my gentle aunt, but this White Man's Paradise stands in the Shadow of Swords. Some boys whose families have roots elsewhere are planning to take up and leave the country before the conscription trap closes upon their child. For me, sad to say there is no such choice. I hold the passport of a pariah nation that no civilized society respects. Out of the Eastern block frying pan into a racist warmongering fire. Father believes that we have nothing to fear, and that the armed might will preserve our place here in the sun, on our porch, watching the sweaty black back of the gardener as he toils to beautify our surroundings. I am under no such illusion, a fly caught in the web.

"But on a more cheerful note, your elixir seems to have given the sweet Vashti a new zest for life and colour has returned to her cheeks. Our days are spent outdoors, as the spring takes hold of this exquisite land. Flowers are exploding in the garden and the days tingle with their scents. I have taken some poor photographs of us in the park, and yes, I am not wearing my glasses in any of them. I am trying to wean myself off their dreary mystique, so please do forgive me squinting myopically at the camera in each of these. And we are still very much virginal, I feel that I must emphasize that to you, my worldly one, yet we do share trembling moments that sigh with promise. I started to read the Huxley that you previously mentioned in your letters, and find him a mischievous delight. Thank you for being my eternal guide. I am waiting most keenly for the next chapter of the Goral saga, although find it strangely disquieting reading, mainly because my heart is both open to love and cautious to pain."

o o o

Chapter Fifty Six

The Vision is Blurred

"Ibis would arrive in the early morning and the two sat together in the overgrown garden, sipping tea and feeding cake crumbs to the sparrows and starlings that jostled noisily for the morsels at their feet. The artist loved this precious time, when the light was as delicate as a murmur, full of promise of the day to come. At his request, Ibis wore her hair loose and free and the blond ringlets shone a hint of red in the rays of the new born sun. As the last of the tea was drained, they would rise as one and take up their positions for the sitting, he at the large canvas and she seated most prettily on her cushion.

"Goral painted like a man possessed, looking up at her intermittently, while taking swigs of water from the decanter at his side. A large brass alarm clock on a nearby mantelpiece watched over them, and at the stroke of every hour Goral would stand up, frown and walk away from his work and carefully place the canvas against the wall, out of sight of the curious Ibis. She was captivated by the ferocity of his labors.

"'Not yet, my dear. All in good time. I want to honour you with a gift that is as unique as the one that you have blessed me with. In fact, I do feel that my talent is a pale watery thing by comparison to the bounty with which the gods have bestowed upon you, gentle Ibis, sacred bird girl.' Ibis smiled at this unusual compliment, blushing sweetly.

"Lunch was usually a simple affair of bread and cheese washed down by a glass of fine red wine. The afternoons passed quickly and as the light grew grey and tired Goral would sigh and stand up, knees creaking with fatigue, and escort Ibis down the garden path to the main entrance. The chauffeur stood by as the dreamy-eyed girl planted a kiss on the old man's cheek before sliding into the rear seat of the large vehicle. As the tyres ground the pebbles on the driveway, Ibis always turned back, waved and waved at the hunched figure that stood smiling in the diminished light. She never saw him turn, nor did she see the consternation that so quickly replaced the mirth on his kindly haggard face. Goral walked back to his studio and stood gazing at the portrait until the gloom grew thick and heavy. This he did every night after each sitting. His meagre supper would often remain untouched as he sat there, studying the canvas, alone with a candle and a bottle of wine for company.

"The next day, he rose and prepared breakfast, placing fresh flowers in the vase and setting the table in preparation for her return.

"After a few weeks, Fastnner called upon his friend. Ibis was in the garden, playing with the kitten as the two men stood in the doorway, watching her teasing the animal with a piece of golden ribbon. The beast stalked and pounced at the adornment to the trill of her laughter.

"'How is it going, my friend?' asked the patron cautiously. 'She loves to come here, you know. Always on about you and the house and the garden. But she's quite cagey about the progress of the sitting, and people, ahem... important people, are asking me questions. You do realize that you and the portrait are quite the talk of the town? Could you let me have a tiny peek at the portrait? Just to satisfy my fatherly curiosity and to let the world know that Goral is close to unveiling his new, unprecedented masterpiece?'

"'I'm afraid that I have to disappoint you there, Fastnner. I had a recent inspiration that made my previous version quite pedestrian, so I tore it up and yes, I began another version yesterday. Different focus with an adjusted perspective. The first attempt was a banal test run for the next. I didn't tell Ibis of this, she still thinks that I'm still busy with the original.'

"There was a great pause, and an icy silence filled the void between the two friends. 'What do you mean by a Different Focus, Goral? It's a simple portrait. The girl's been sitting here, day after day for the past three weeks now, and you tell me that you are exactly where you began? I realise that to create something unique does take time, but what do I tell the journalists, hungry for an update ? And with Ibis so blissfully unaware of this new turn of events. How much time do you need?'

"'I don't know,' replied the artist pensively, 'it's not that simple.'

"Not that simple? You, who can accomplish anything, sculpture, metalwork, you who can create a devastating mural as big as a house, is having trouble with a painting of a young woman? Forgive me my ignorance, old friend, but what possibly could be simpler to a man of your talents?"

'It's not that simple, Fastnner. Give me some time. I can't be rushed through this. It's a completely new territory for me. You, of all people, should know and respect that.' Fastnner grunted with exasperation, yet held his tongue. They continued to watch Ibis in the garden. She stood up holding the cat to her chest, and smiled. Both men nodded at her, and looked away, each lost in his own thoughts.

"The patron left glumly, and Ibis, once again, arranged herself on the chair in the studio. Goral's face was a stony mask as he unscrewed the lid from his tube of pigment. She watched him with mild caution. He noticed her thinly veiled apprehension and placing his brush aside, walked across to where she sat, and quietly embraced her. She closed her eyes and let her head rest against his chest. She could hear the beating of his heart through the coarse material of his dust coat, and breathed in the clean and comforting oil paint essence that clung to him like a ghost. The only sound in the room was the pendulum of the clock on the mantelpiece, as it swung ceaselessly back and forth. He worked in silence for the remainder of the afternoon, pensive to the point of detachment.

"Ibis was quite relieved when he finally replaced his brush into the jar of solvent. The light in the studio had dimmed to a lowly murk, and deep shadows had appeared under his eyes. She waved to him frantically from the back of the vehicle that took her away. His hand felt heavy as he waved back to her. That night, neither of them slept. Ibis lay awake for many hours, watching the moonlight creep across the room. Goral's sleep was a shallow sweat drenched affair, the sheets forming a tourniquet around his restless feet, echoing the pressure that clenched at his heart.

"The next morning, Ibis arrived for breakfast as usual, but she seemed to have aged a little during the night. Goral too seemed wan and frail as he poured out the coffee. They looked up at each other, and laughed out loud, the absurdity of their exhaustion an unspoken punchline that broke over them. The day passed quite happily, yet there was a new urgency between them that was quite palpable.

"For the following five weeks, the work progressed at a frantic rate but with an odd twist. As soon as the portrait neared completion, Goral would grow enraged and petulant, shake his head with frustration and begin again. The work in different stages of completion, began to accumulate, at a ever quickening pace, lining the side of the studio like an army of forgotten soldiers. Ibis tried to steal a glance at one stack of these rejects but Goral's face darkened with disapproval, and she quickly returned to her cushion.

"The news of the strange phenomenon of the indefinite sitting soon reached Fastnner. The old crone that served as a housekeeper at the studio was quite explicit about the unfinished work piling up against the walls. She whispered of the artist's dark moods and of the devoted faith with which Ibis sat, hour upon hour before the frustrated Goral. The patron was not pleased. His own position as the driving force behind this much advertised venture was being compromised by what he deemed to be pure artistic pique. He arrived at the studio unannounced. Ibis was sitting dutifully before Goral, who had recently embarked upon the growing of a fullsome beard. The artist looked wild and unkempt as the door flew open and the scowling Fastnner bustled in, his fur coat veritably bristling with the static of his exertions as he made his way towards the startled couple.

"'I have been patient, Goral. In fact, I have been exhausted by my own patience. But at this point of exhaustion, I cannot afford to allow this non-event to continue. What have you been up to, all these months? My clients are starting to ridicule me, the press has long lost interest in this affair and Ibis remains as mute as a clam on the subject. It's quite obvious that you are either struggling with the medium, or have some perverse need to keep the girl at your side. I have always admired you, nay protected you, and our interests were never at odds with each other. I ask you as a father to this child and a generous patron of your work, what is going on with this commission? Show me some of the work, Goral. Apparently you have a sizable collection of rejects that I am keen to see."

"The artist took a step back, his jaw tightening. He looked old and worn as he motioned towards a pile of canvases, stacked against the wall. "Help yourself, Fastnner. They are yours, all of them. But useless. Pale and bland and useless." His voice was a dry crack of a twig. 'Meaningless,' he added, as the patron raised a portrait into the light.

"'Meaningless? I did not commission you to paint my daughter with meaning. She's a fresh beauty, not an abstract, Goral. God, this one is magnificent. And this one even better, look at the likeness. Astonishing. Incredible work.' He gesured to Ibis. 'Come here, my dove, and see what Goral has been hiding from the world.'

She made her way past Goral. A small pale girl that stood next to her red-aced father, who was almost shouting with joy. 'Masterful, Goral. A masterpiece upon a masterpiece. You should have stopped weeks ago, my eccentic artist. I can fill my entire house with these gems.'

'They are empty shells, Fastnner. Nowhere near in capturing her grace, her magnificence. Can't you see that? Shockingly hollow, I see more in her than I can ever honourably translate onto the canvas. What I feel is ricocheting through my soul, but it won't come out, it can't come out."

"'Poppycock. It's excellent work, all of it. Each and everyone is my Ibis, in a different light. Well done, Goral. You have truly made me anxious, but these,' he swirled around, standing ankle deep in portraits, 'were worth every agonizing moment, my dear friend.' Ibis nodded and blinked up at the artist. Goral turned his head away. 'Consider the commission successfully completed. I will hold an exhibition at my house soon. So many works, quite startling. A Triumph. Our great triumph, Goral.' The father and daughter departed. Ibis and Fastnner waving back from the rear seat of the vehicle.

"In the empty driveway, Goral looked up at early evening sky and his lip trembled. The wind clawed raw and cold at his frail frame. When the buffalo fight it is the grass that suffers, my gentle boy. The story continues, but now I must tend to the roosters, old and crotchety as they are becoming. I even grind the corn for them more finely these days, for they are not long for this earth. Look after that swan of yours, for she too seems a fragile beauty and has touched your life deeply, your letters are sonnets to her uniqueness."

o o o

Chapter Fifty-seven

The Assembly of Grass

"You boys are the Cream of this nation, the Engineers of the future, and it gives me great pleasure to see you assembled here today." The Army Major stood on the podium above us. Behind him, upon rows of plastic chairs, sat the Headmaster and the teacher body, solemly starting at the schoolboys assembled below. It was National Pride day at school, whereupon an important business person or a high ranking officer was invited to address the pupils, with special emphasis given to the senior boys, who were about to end their school careers and to enter society as young adults. The bulk of the students sat on the waxy polished wood of the assembly hall, while the final years were allowed to sit at the back of the gathering, on chairs similar to those enjoyed by the teachers. Flies flew in and out of the windows, and every now and then, a boy would twitch and slap at an offending insect casting an apologetic glance at the unsmiling rank of teachers. The plastic reeked of chlorine as I squirmed listlessly, while the Major cleared his throat.

"Today, it is my pleasure and duty in celebrating National Pride day with you. Our country has only the very best to offer its children and those that will leave this fine school in months to come will be received into a society which is as modern as it is just. I am envious of you, for you have a chance to make the transition from an exemplary secondary education into further study or into business that will enrich both yourselves and the country that has protected you and your families. There are many young men from this noteworthy school who have fought for Freedom in both of the Great Wars, and their names are eternally enshrined on the mighty bronze plaque that you have seen so often, there on the Wall of Honour at the entrance." We all turned dutifully, and admired the Wall of Honour in the far end of the hall. The names were many and none of us had really made any concerted effort over the years to truly study it closely. In most of our minds it was something that every school had, alongside a canteen or a playground. Behind me, I heard some of my more cynical friends grunt with derision. I kept my eye on the Major, who seemed to be hinting at something unpleasant. "Not only is it the Wall of Honour, boys, it is also the Wall of Sacrifice." he paused and behind him the headmaster puffed his out chest.

"Make up your mind," a pimply wag next to me whispered under his breath.

"Yes, sacrifice, the ultimate gift that a young man with a bright future can offer to his country."

"I don't like where this is going," I mumbled and those around me that overheard, sniggered loudly. The headmaster glared across the podium in our general direction.

"Many of those about to leave this hallowed establishment will enter into the Army. You may have brothers or relatives serving there now, and I am sure that you are proud of them. As I am, for it is my privilege to have seen countless boys enter the service of their country, and to excel at any task placed before them with dignity and joy."

"Two fucking years of excelling for the Major. Count me out," the wag grimaced quietly. I masked my laughter as a highly artificial cough. A few younger boys in front of my chair turned around to stare at me.

"Look ahead, you fools." I hissed through tight lips. They quickly complied, exchanging glances.

"There are some, however, that do not agree with conscription, and for those individuals I feel only pity and sadness. These selfish folk wish to live of the fat of the land, and to enjoy all the bounty that this magnificent land has to offer, without a glimmer of guilt. Without a notion of Sacrifice. They want to have their cake and to eat it. The country is facing a Communist onslaught on our borders. There are some rabble rousers within our borders, that wish to bring about chaos and fear to our peace loving community. These cannot be tolerated and just as external security must be maintained, so must internal law and national order be scrupulously enforced. Seeds of doubt sown by liberals and pseudo-intellectuals are toxic to this great nation. Their time will come. The greatest threat to the nation at this time is the dissent fostered by anarchists, Bolshevik rumour mongers who thrive on division and dread. They want you to believe that there is nothing worth fighting for here, that we live in a fools paradise, destined for the garbage pail of history. Our forefathers came to this savage land and turned it into a civilized country, which is the envy of many. Did they have any doubt about what they were doing, when they entered a barbaric continent, rife with danger? No, they suffered and toiled in silence and with honor, just like those boys did in Flander's Fields or in Normandy. To quote Churchill, 'We will never surrender.' And so beware of the agents of doubt, dear pupils, the journalists and the foreign press and their ilk. They know not what they preach. They are happy to twist reality and to contaminate innocent minds." A fly settled on his lapel and he brushed it away with a frown.

"Psst, aren't you planning to study journalism, Jaro? Are you going to blur reality like the rest of them?" Another witty aside from someone behind me, and with a poke in the ribs for emphasis.

"These swine seem to be doing a pretty good job of it themselves," I snarled over my shoulder. "Just listen to this clown." A distant irrate ruffle of the headmaster's coat made me sit up and I stared ahead, my face blank. Innocently I scanned the hall and eventually let my eye rest on his face. He glared back at me. Behind me, there was general tittering and amusement.

"So I would like to leave you today with a Message of Hope and of Joy. Enjoy your life beyond these school walls, go forth and conquer, and live out your destinies. But don't forget to honour the country that has allowed you these privileges.

There are many countries, in Africa and in Communist Europe where the freedom that you enjoy today and will delight in tomorrow is but a dream. Thank you." The Major stood solid and proud while first strains of the national anthem rang out from the speakers alongside the hall. The assembly stood up as one and we bellowed out the old refrain. The headmaster's eyes were on me as he sang, verse upon verse, and I shivered under his gaze. At the end of the rousing song, we filed into the bright African sun. Flies swarmed around the garbage pails as we milled around laughing and talking. A few of the older boys disappeared to have a cigarette.

A young lad nervously picked his way towards me through the noisy throng and after a moment's hesitation asked, "Is it true that you and your family are Communists, Jaro?"

"The older boys hooted with mirth and jostled him nearer to me. He quaked like a leaf. I groaned. "Yes, it's true. We left everything behind, the house, the family, the clothes and a granny just to be Communists in a country that hates Communism. We got on a midnight train, in the snow and ran away with nothing but two suitcases and daschund between us. We left the glorious East to be plumbers and conscripts in the West. God, we were such fools, to leave behind a regime that made you dread a midnight knock and where you stand in a queue twice around the block for a dram off butter. Are you mad?"

"Easy Jaro, he's just an idiot kid."

"Sorry, Jaro," whined the urchin, "someone said that you were One, and I have never seen One before."

"He wants to be a journalist, and we all know what they say about journalists," shouted a great oaf.

"Troublemakers, dissent mongers. The Major is watching you," cackled another and at that point we all laughed, the idiot kid grinning with incomprehension.

"Jesus," I ground my teeth, dramatically and stared up into the azure sky, "out of the Communist hell into the Ignorant Fire. Someone up there is truly messing with my life." We filed out of the gate, many of the seniors hastily removing their school ties before popping open the top button of their shirts and lighting up cigarettes. The younger boys ran by with their satchels on their backs bouncing cheerfully. A fly flew around my head into my ear and buzzed noisily, and I slapped it away, suddenly feeling quite foolish about berating the young naive fool with his barely comprehensible question. Another fly appeared and chased my tormentor, and the two disappeared into the hazy heat. I walked home, daydreaming about the silken Vashti and the lonely Goral and the seemingly immortal roosters.

Chapter Fifty-eight

The End of Light

"Goral returned to his studio. The tea tray stood untouched on the table in the half light of the cavernous room. He sat down and poured himself a cup of cold tea. The countless renditions of Ibis stared up at him from the floor. He averted his eyes, choosing rather to tilt his head backwards and to study the pattern of the high ceiling above him. The emptiness inside him grew deeper with the lengthening of the shadows. At the end of the week a truck arrived and a few men rapidly removed the work. Fastnner was keen to exhibit Ibis by Goral at his mansion. The artist watched the men wrapping up each piece and stood by quietly as they labeled and numbered every canvas. The foreman offered him an invoice to sign and the group withdrew. Goral gritted his teeth at the sound of the truck revving it's engine, the heavy wheels tearing up the gravel. At last, there was silence in the studio again, and he retired up the stairs to where his make shift bed was, in the attic. He stretched out and gazed at the final version of Ibis that looked down at him from above the fireplace.

"Goral was never seen again in public. He ignored the invitation to attend the unveiling of Fastnner's exhibition. The host made suitably sincere apologies for his absence. The journalists nodded sagely as the photographers crushed against each other to capture the best image. He grew thin, bird like and brittle, and slept very little. The old housemaid cooked him thin stews and dusted off the silent studio. His coughing at night made her hold a pillow over her head, so as to shut the sounds that racked her senses. He became surly and laconic when she implored him to see a doctor. Fastnner listened to her stories of his friend's ill health, but resisted the old urge to call and to offer assistance. He was busy with endless interviews and frequent travel made great inroads upon his time. Goral's last exhibition, unveiled a week before he died, was shown at an obscure gallery, located deep in the unfashionable part of the town. The people crowded around the work. Ibis stood there amongst them, holding onto her father's arm. Each painting described an almost identical scene, with minor variations. A small bee, with wings torn and broken, attempting to escape out of locked and grimy window, into the living sunlight outside. The exhibition was entitled "The Forsaken, Domesticated Insect." The crowd passed silently, like ghosts, from room to room, staring numbly at repetitive images."

Chapter Fifty-nine

Passages

"Dear Sabrina, it is with a heavy heart that I write this letter, surely the most soul searing gathering of words that I have yet penned. You have always been a consistent star in my often turbulent sky and have laughed and cried with me throughout my journeys, soothed me with stories of magic and wisdom that have given me sustenance across the years. I am more as a result off these wise tales, and always will be. I now have to share with you my most recent experience which has darkly eclipsed the sun of joy that shines in my chest, blotting out the signposts that ensure safe passage on these broken roads.

"If I ever needed a guide through this maze of a life, it is surely now. Mother and Father are like two angry deer, their horns locked in an eternal battle as they stomp and snort at each other, while on the sidelines I, unseen, grow older. The country is slowly slipping into a police state with army road blocks becoming an daily occurance, a place where handbags are screened under x rays on conveyer belts, before one enters a supermarket. Empires come and go as you once told me, and so be it, and the conscription papers that I laughingly threw into the waste bin, year after year, will pop through the mail again, like an annual malaise. And this time I have no antidote to their call. My schooldays are about to end, and the Major is waiting. But it is my tiny empire which is threatened with collapse, it is my heart that ticks like bomb at the station of my chest. It is my dreams that have experienced a Total Onslaught. And you warned me about this time, about the season of the flies which you saw in your hallucination, in your prophetic illumination.

"I walked down the dusty road, my well trodden path to Vashti's house, reveling the scent of jasmine and lavender that swirled around my head, in the heat of the day. Fat bumblebees hung pendulously in the warm afternoon air and their low steady hum tickled my ears most ravishingly. I was ecstatic, full of youth and spring and excited at the prospect of a dreamy day with my Pale Queen. The flies swarmed and wrestled in the dust at my feet. They followed me doggedly, my sweat no doubt offering them some scented allure. Another day in Africa, I thought. A group of black children ran past me, barefoot and giggling, and I was surprised when they greeted me as they scampered past. A gangly young white fellow, I imagined that I was to be viewed with suspicion and scorn. The army and police are forever in the townships these days, Sabrina, keeping the peace with their armoured vehicles and their bulldozers. Yet they smiled and waved as they ran by, the soles of their feet pink and healthy as they stirred up the dust, with their teeth so gloriously white and their eyes full of mirth and puppy joy. I smiled back and for a moment all was well with the world.

"Vashti's mother was lying in the hammock on the verandah reading a book, sipping an ice tea when I arrived. She was dressed in white, with a frilly blouse and slacks and she leapt up to give me a hug and to brush my hair back. We are truly fond of each other and I sat there with her while she swung gently on the hammock, prattling about the book that she was reading. I sipped some of the ice tea and the flower essences hung like a invisible tapestry over us. She swiped at the flies and laughed as one fell into her tea and swum around noisily, angry wings beating up a tiny froth of bubbles on the golden surface.

"'Vashti's upstairs in her room, resting underneath her fan. She was feeling a little frail again today, I'm afraid Jaro. I haven't seen the girl for hours so do send her my love. And take up some tea to my frail flower, she's been so very excited to see you. You two truly bring out the best in each other,' she purred and called for Gladys, the Housemaid to bring a tray with a fresh jug of iced tea, glasses and a plate of biscuits.

The African lady soon appeared and I took the tray from her, and delicately climbed up the stairs, taking great care to not to spill the sweet nectar. A bevy of flies followed me, darting around my face as I slowly approached her bedroom door. I walked lightly across the carpet in order to surprise her and I could almost taste her delightful lips upon mine as I gently tapped on the door. The yellow light shone in from the huge window at the end of the passage making the ice tea glow like amber and the silver tray shone with a lunar glow. There was already a fly swimming around in the tea and I cursed under my breath as I tapped on the door again, a little harder this time. There was still no response.

"'Vashti, it's me, with some tea, for two and a biscuit, for me and you,' I sang tunefully, in the golden light outside Vashti's bedroom door. I listened carefully, but again there was no sound, no voice biding me entrance, no snore of my gentle girl came wafting towards me. Nothing. Only the drone of the fly that determinedly swirled around my head like a noxious tiny satellite. The heat, no doubt, had lulled her into a fitful afternoon's sleep. I placed the tray on the carpet and quietly turned the handle of the door, hoping to catch a glimpse of her sweet face while she smiled in calm repose.

"The door swung open and sure enough, there on the bed, below the rotating fan on the ceiling that blew her finer hair in a blonde haze across her face, lay my darling Vashti. With her eyes closed and lips parted, her bare arms across her chest, she was the picture of a fairy tale princess in summery slumber. She was wearing a lively short blue nightdress of fine cotton. Her legs were bare and I stopped in my tracks to admire this forbidden sight, savoring the guilty pleasure of seeing her so innocent partially nakedness. The virginal soft skin and the blond hairs on her long thighs made me tremble.

"It was a vision that was planets away from the Father's fist pushed towards my nose, far away from the stolen sweaty sight of the whiskey woman from across the road. It was the answer to the burning ache of a country in racial conflict. It was the antidote to the Major on the stage. I drank it all in, careful not to make any sound that could disturb the sacred moment. The window was open and the fly screens were down. She always preferred to suffer the presence of the insects than to have her view of the garden and the blue sky obscured by the severity of the mesh. Flies flew around the room in arrogant spiral patterns as I approached the bed. I was almost at her side when a movement, a flurry caught my attention. A mass of flies had settled between her thighs, just out of sight, beneath the blue nightdress. As I bent down over her, my eyes blinking against the light, the swarm rose up, revealing a matted pool of blood that had soaked into the sheet. Her face was as white as marble, and she had no breath. They swarmed around me in great arcs, buzzing and swooping. The sound of the beating of their myriad of wings filled the room as they dived and darted and sang in an unholy unison. I stood there beside her body for a long while, transfixed by the insect din and the smell of fresh blood that grew ever more caustic to my nose threatening to penetrate to the very core of my being. I swatted at them uselessly and at once, overcome with grief and horror, I collapsed sobbing to the floor. The satanic tribe flew about me, and crawled into my hair. I lay there in a silken heap for what seemed like an eternity of agony. At last, billious and shaking I rose and steading myself against the bed, I gently touched the skin of her arm. It was cold and clammy. I sat beside her and I lifted her hand to my cheek. I closed my eyes and the rage of the disturbed flies faded as the roar of my own blood that throbbed in my ears, took centre stage. She had died in her sleep, her delicate virginal flow blessing the bed, a feast for the infernal insects. The Pale Queen surrounded by black coated minions.

"I opened my mouth and screamed an open mouthed keening shriek that obliterated everything else. My girl, Sabrina, my sickly swan, had flown from me. The rest happened very quickly in a tortured kaleidoscope of visions that will stay with me for the rest of my days. Vashti's mother lying on the bed, holding her dead child in her arms. The ambulance siren in the distance. Men rushing in with a stretcher. Her brother, a corpse that howled his soul out into the wall as he banged his head there repeatedly. Mother and Father in silent anguish as they helped me into my bed. The sedative injection needle in my flesh, the night of dreams. Of you, chasing roosters in the snow. I woke up, cold and empty to write this letter to you, my mystical aunt. Send me prayers and send me peace, Sabrina, I implore you. Someone has stolen them away."

Chapter Sixty

From Sabrina with Love

"It is with shaking hands that I read and re-read your letter. It is a tragedy, my joy, and I feel helpless in the distance and I have no story for you, in this moment, to soothe and to make it all better. Death is near to us with every breath. I have seen much in my confused path through this life, and yet am still such a child in the hugeness of creation and destruction that is the breath of this world, my boy. And through you too, I have lived a life far more exquisite and expansive than I could have ever imagined. All I know, in these creaky tired years that are left to me, is that everything is precious, yet nothing is ours to possess and to cage. We are only here for a day, this earth spins on and on and we hold on tight and hopefully, with reverence to the gifts that come our way, and that inevitably slip out of our hands. Lovers fade, seasons shift and young boys and girls become men and women.

"Rejoice in your Vashti and try to celebrate the glory of the magical time that was offered to you. The gift of love and joy which you both grabbed with open hearts and hands, running together down life's pathway for a short time. There is no shame in crying a pool of tears for what you love, and for what has drifted down into the great black sea into which all rivers lead. Into that same sea will slip Sabrina, the roosters and Communism. And so I now implore you, my delight, to grieve well and deeply, for that depth is where Vashti touched your soul. The lesson that Death can teach us is that it is vital to honour the living, and that all life is sacred because it is passing. Many people grieve for the love that they failed to show in the moment, second by second, year by year, to those around them. And then the sea calls and it's too late to say those magical words which could have made a such a difference. Never forget to to reach a hand out in quiet devotion. To love is to pray to the god of life that mischievously offers you a chance to be either in the moment, with heart and soul or to be a passive bystander watching it all float down to the roar of the black sea that can be heard in every molecule of all creatures on earth.

"Perhaps it is a time to open your heart to your family. I know that that relationship has grown sour, but time is passing, and the river is running. Even sorrow is a passion, dear Jaro, and passion is the very breath that the gods blew into our lungs when we were born. I will miss it all when I am gone, and though it has been a giddy ride, here on earth, for me and for you and for everyone in their own right, it's a carousel worth its weight in gold. I cannot begin to comprehend the pain of your loss, and perhaps my words are too airy to afford you any real substance in the depths of your pain to act as a bridge to the other side, where the light is warm and the flowers have not yet lost their bloom. But my heart burns for you, my child and all I can offer is the strength of my life: joy.

"Sometimes, Luck and Wisdom take a backseat, or go off fishing together, letting the world sway and spin on its rickety axis. But they soon come back to guide and to help in healing the lost and the confused. Take strength from the fact that no one and nothing can take away the time that you shared with that sweet pale ghost of a girl. It is yours to cherish, it is there for you to take with you, into that ocean. Like the Vikings of old, our duty is to fill our Death Ship full of the riches of magical experience, golden love and silver tears, treasures gathered to follow us into the afterlife. Only a fool will avoid drinking from the bitter sweet cup of life, and refrain from calling upon the generous bartender for more. Our letters will be on that boat with us, best boy. Strength and joy, Sabrina."

o o o

Chapter Sixty-one

Wisdom Finds Shelter in a Broken House

"Dear wise Sabrina, it has been a time of sleepwalking through the days and waking up damp with sweat and fright at night. The funeral was a simple affair with the two poles of my life finally meeting at the edge of the grave. Father placed his hand on my shoulder while Mother wiped away the tears that coursed down my cheeks, clucking gently. Her lips trembled and I could feel the hidden earthquakes of sobs shudder inside her, but she never said a word. Vashti's mother buried her face in the chest of her son. The African diggers, their smooth faces shiny with sweat, watched us with an almost childlike curiosity, for there was no singing nor dancing at the European funeral and certainly no feasting. Instead of sharing a bowl of goat stew and raising a glass of maize beer to our lips, our tribe trembled with silent grief. For a passing moment I felt the loneliness of a soul trapped in an overeducated body and I bit my lip.

"When the coffin was finally lowered into the blood red earth, I shook away the hand on my shoulder and moved closer to the grave's edge.

"Father reached out to me but Mother restrained him, while I removed the heart that I made from your rooster's feathers and threw it onto the box within which my Vashti lay. Everyone moved closer to stare at the dark red feather heart that lay upon the lunar white lid of the coffin. One by one we each threw a spade full of soil onto the coffin.

Father's pile dislodged the heart from the lid and it lay in the dust like a broken bird. I hissed at him through my clenched teeth. The diggers filled the hole, singing quietly in unison under their breath.

"I have one more exam before me and with that behind me my school career is officially over. The headmaster recommended that I should have an official stay from writing my final exams, due to the trauma that I have been through, but I refused the offer. My mind is clear yet my heart is made of cold mud. Hold me tightly, across the miles that separate us, gentle Aunt and I'll be fine. I am more than the pain that I feel, you've taught me that. The mud will thaw. And carp will flap their magic flippers again, like underwater roosters."

o o o

Chapter Sixty-two

War

I sat silently between Mother and Father on a bench at the station, my suitcase at my feet. Watching as the many young men huddled like myself in the temporary safe enclaves of their families, casting nervous glances at the strutting uniformed military policemen that swaggered amongst them. The train stood like a fearsome monument on gleaming rails. A whistle was blown and orders were barked and Father gave me gentle nudge with his knee.

"I think that they are calling the boys to line up, old Jaro. Time to join the ranks." I looked at him but his face was impassive. Mother gave my hand a warm squeeze and I stood up. The brass band started up a rousing rendition of the national anthem and cold fear threatened to strangle my words as I kissed them on the cheeks.

"Wish me luck. I'll call you when we get there," I croaked.

"Keep your head down, and don't answer back. Watch that sharp tongue of yours, dear boy. You wouldn't wish to provoke these people," whispered Mother, helpfully.

"No," I replied slowly, staring at the gathering of men. "I certainly would not." I walked towards the ever growing line of frightened faces and turned to wave at the two figures on the bench. A military policeman nodded a solemn greeting at me and I took my place in the line.

I coughed in the dust raised by the countless feet and looked up into the endlessly blue sky, wishing for wings to fly me away from the sound of that accursed band to the far away cellar that smelt of plum brandy and coal. A young man behind me tapped me lightly on the shoulder. "Umm," he mumbled nervously, "do you know that there is a bird wing sticking out of your bag?" I peered at the red tipped feather that had found its way out of my hastily packed luggage.

"Yes, it's an old friend come to watch over me," I replied blithely, and we both laughed.

End